Portrait in Murder
and Gay Colors

A Portrait in Murder and Gay Colors

H. Paul Jeffers

Knights Press

Stamford, Connecticut

Designed by Able Reproductions, copyright © 1985
Cover design by Harry H. Long, Aries Creative Design Concepts, Copyright © 1985

Published by Knights Press, P.O. Box 454, Pound Ridge, NY 10576

Library of Congress Cataloging in Publication Data

Jeffers, H. Paul (Harry Paul), 1934–
    A portrait in murder and gay colors.

    I. Title.
PS3560.E36P67   1985   813'.54   85-4275
ISBN 0-915175-09-6 (pbk.)

Printed in the United States of America

For Richard

"Yes, he was certainly wonderfully handsome, with his finely curved scarlet lips, his frank blue eyes, his crisp gold hair. There was something in his face that made one trust him at once. All the candour of youth was there, as well as youth's passionate purity. One felt that he had kept himself unspotted from the world."

The Picture of Dorian Gray, Oscar Wilde.

Contents

Prologue

The Partners

The Detective

The Tapes

The Bought Boy

The Break

Epilogue

Prologue

When he heard a noise, he sat very still in the water, listening. Leaning forward in the tub, he tried to see into the dark living room, but he had pushed the bathroom door almost shut because of a chilling draft. Hearing no other sound, he relaxed and began bathing again, deciding he had been mistaken about hearing something in the apartment.

Then he heard two voices. Distant, muffled, the voices were in the hallway. They ceased as he heard the door to the next apartment open and close. He assumed what he had heard earlier was the neighbors coming in.

Dipping his hands in the warm, soapy water, he relaxed, enjoying the bath. Usually he showered, but he was extremely tired and thought a soothing sit-down bath would be good for him. He hadn't sat in a bathtub since he was a kid. The water sloshed as he moved his legs, making waves dash against the sides of the tub. With a smile, he almost wished he had a little sailboat like one he'd had when he was a kid.

He heard the noise again. He was sure it was in the living room just outside the slightly-ajar door. "Hey! Is that you back already? I'm having a bath!"

When there was no answer, he stood up in the tub and stepped out onto the furry bath mat. He moved hesitantly to the door.

A slant of bathroom light shot diagonally across the living room. He'd left on a reading lamp in the bedroom but it was too dim and far away to provide any illumination into the darkened living room where the noise came from.

Opening the bathroom door all the way, he stepped cautiously into the doorway. He saw his elongated shadow in the center of the truncated pyramid of light spilling across the living room floor. "Hey!" he called into the darkness. "I thought you were going. . . ."

For a stunning instant he thought he had been hit in the face with a baseball, like the time when his brother had thrown a really wild pitch.

The impact flung his head back and he saw the light in the middle of the bathroom ceiling had turned bright red. He felt terribly dizzy and reached out in the blinding redness for something to hold on to. His mouth seemed to be filling with salty liquid which trickled into his throat and prevented him from crying out. Suddenly the red light went black. He fell forward and splashed headlong into the tub, unconscious.

Soapy water flooded his bloody mouth and seeped into his crushed nose. Water and blood, sucked by his labored breathing into his lungs, drowned him.

The Partners

1.

Lyman slept through the blizzard.

Technically, it was not a blizzard by meteorological standards because the winds were not strong enough and the temperatures were not cold enough, but the authoritative voice of newscaster Gary Alexander on all-news WCBS was calling it a blizzard as Lyman's clock radio woke him up. "Eighteen inches of snow fell in Manhattan while parts of Long Island and Westchester got as much as two feet. In New England, where it's still snowing, highways are blocked. Ski resorts say as soon as the roads open they're going to have the best skiing of the season."

"Shit!" Lyman turned off the radio and blinked bleary eyes at the digital time: 7:15 A.M. He'd slept almost twelve hours.

While Lyman was shaving, Terry Garraty phoned. The voice of his young, red-haired, exuberant, freckle-faced partner sounded disgustingly alert and bright to Lyman on a snowy morning. "Some storm, eh, Sheldon?"

Lyman answered, "The radio says it's bad but I haven't had the nerve to look out the window."

"My street appears to have been plowed, but I'll leave a little earlier just in case."

"The avenues should be okay," said Lyman.

"If I get there early we can have time for coffee in that restaurant across Second Avenue from your house."

"Buzz me from the lobby when you get here."

"Sure thing."

Normally they would set a time and Lyman would wait for Garraty in the lobby, but today, given the weather, Garraty would come and have the doorman buzz Lyman's apartment. Dressing slowly, Lyman picked an older suit and a pair of boots that the slush in the streets wouldn't harm. As always, he gave himself the once-over in the full-length mirror behind his bedroom door and came to the conclusion that he looked like a cop. The blue suit, conservatively patterned blue tie and white shirt were a combination a banker might wear, but on him they spelled *cop*. He knew people who said they could invariably spot a cop. A few boasted they could smell a cop. Lyman never doubted them. He could spot cops readily. It used to be he would say that all you had to do to recognize a cop was look at his feet. Now he looked for signs of fatigue, anxiety, resignation. He saw all of those signs in himself, in his blue-green eyes, thinning gray-streaked brown hair, slightly slouched posture. Like all cops, even the young ones, as Lyman looked at himself in the mirror he was mindful of eventual retirement. Six years!

The buzzer buzzed and the doorman announced Garraty's arrival. Lyman asked, "Is it still snowing?" The doorman replied it had stopped. Leaving his apartment, Lyman encountered a young man who had the apartment across the hall. His name was Jerry and he was a jogger. Jerry was going jogging this morning, even in the snow. "You can't let up," he explained to Lyman. Jerry's jogging had given him a lean, hard, health-radiating body which his red-white-and-blue jogging suit showed off: the powerful chest, the strong thighs. Lyman believed the jogging fad bloomed because jogging clothes drew attention to sexual parts: breasts bouncing, penises bulging in stretch pants.

The elevator had him at the lobby in a few seconds. Terry Garraty was in animated conversation with the doorman. Basketball, probably, Lyman decided, crossing the gleaming white marble floor. Joe, the brown-uniformed elderly doorman, had a smile for Lyman. Garraty gave a nod but kept talking. In his sheepskin-lined storm coat, tan corduroy suit and snow boots, Garraty looked like a college boy heading out for a ski weekend, not a homicide detective on his way to work.

When they went through the revolving door to an immaculately shoveled sidewalk, the snow seemed deeper and more formidable than it had sounded on the radio. "It turns out," explained Garraty as they single-filed through a narrow cut in a piled snowbank to cross Second Avenue where Twenty-seventh Street deadends, "the Mayor has banned all but essential traffic in the city, so getting around isn't difficult. I got downtown with no problem at all."

"Didn't even need the siren?" asked Lyman. It was a joke. Garraty was always keen to lean on the siren and the lights. Jokes were common between them, and personal—Jew-Irish jokes or gallows humor having to do with their work. They were a good team, as Lyman figured they would be when he picked Garraty to be his partner. Two years had flown by since. Two good years, for a good team, the best teaming Lyman had had in all his years with Homicide. There was something to be said for teaming an older veteran with an eager-beaver youngster, especially lately, with the grueling work schedules that had gone into effect.

"There's nothing I can do," shrugged Lieutenant Paul Parker as he had announced the need for longer shifts, fewer men on duty on each shift, stretched manpower. The shrug said it all: cutbacks, belt-tightening, the economic crunch, the word from downtown—Austerity! Garraty did not mind the pace, but Garraty was ten years younger, twenty pounds lighter, and still hungry for the decorations, citations, and chances at higher rank that would mean a bigger pension. Garraty had a wife and kids to think about. Lyman had been the same way at Garraty's age, but with his wife dead and their daughter grown and living on the west coast, a pension didn't mean much anymore.

"Hi, fellas," smiled a matronly waitress named Eve in the coffee shop as Lyman and Garraty came in. "The usual?" she asked Lyman. Lyman nodded. Garraty ordered ham and eggs and coffee with a large orange juice.

Eve knew about Lyman being a widower and was always a little like a wife to him when he came in for breakfast. Lyman always left a good tip. "She has eyes for you," Garraty suggested over the rim of his coffee cup.

"She's just friendly."

"It's beyond that, Shelly."

"She'd be wasting her time."

"It's been over a year since Betty died."

"I'm not getting married again."

"I was thinking of occasional companionship."

"I appreciate your concern, Terry."

"Okay. I'll mind my own business. It's just that I have a natural uneasiness about people being alone. That's what comes from being part of a big family. Also, it's part of being Irish. We're friendly folks. Togetherness and all that."

"I'm not Irish."

"Jewish people are big on togetherness."

"And on being alone. Don't forget, Moses spent a lot of time in the desert—and all those prophets off in the hills by themselves!"

"Well, you know what's best for yourself."

"I do, Terry. I do, indeed."

"So," Garraty said, lowering his cup, "maybe we'll have a slow day today on account of the storm and we can catch up on all the friggin' paperwork at the office."

The snow plows had gotten into Fifty-first Street between Third and Lexington Avenues, making a clean sweep right up to the curbs on both sides, not only because of the need for space to park the blue-and-white cars of the Seventeenth Precinct but also because there was a firehouse in the block. Garraty squeezed their plain gray sedan into a space and uncomfortably crowded a fire hydrant.

The desk officer looked up from his paperwork to wave at Lyman and Garraty as they pushed through the swinging door and into the lobby of the Precinct. The floor was slick with melted snow, and a long rubber runner had been put down. Wet, it gleamed like new and gave a rubbery smell to the lobby.

Upstairs, the desks of the Third Homicide Zone were almost unpeopled. Only two detectives, Brown and Hadley, were at work finishing reports on a shooting in a bar that previous afternoon. Like most murders, this one had involved people who knew each other. The motive for the shooting: an argument over a debt. Brown and Hadley had weary, bored, resigned looks. They mumbled hellos and kept on working.

Garraty began making fresh coffee.

Lyman sat at his desk to tackle the backlog of paper.

Outside the window, light snow was flurrying.

Like a sudden burst of a machinegun, Brown's typewriter rattled noisily for a moment. When the typing stopped, Brown called across the squad room. "Hey, Lyman. You know that bar on Fifty-third where we used to have a couple of drinks?"

"What about it?" asked Lyman, swinging around on his swivel chair.

"It's turned gay," said Brown, rolling a thick sheaf of report forms and carbon paper out of his typewriter. He made a face. "Too bad. It was a nice bar once."

"Is that where you had the homicide?" Lyman asked, leaning back in his chair.

"A couple of hustlers in a hassle over money owed," said Brown. "One of the dudes had a Derringer. Nifty little piece.

Wanna see?" Brown held up a plastic evidence bag with the tiny two-shot gun in it.

Lyman went over to have a look. It was a nice weapon, he agreed. One he wouldn't mind having himself. "Too bad it'll wind up at the bottom of the ocean," Lyman said, laying the bagged weapon back on Brown's desk.

Brown winked. "I figure I can flag it with one of my pals in the evidence section. Of course, if there's a trial it may be a long time before I get the piece back. With luck, the dude who used this little gem will plead guilty and the evidence will be released."

"Good luck." Lyman went back to his desk where Garraty had brought coffee.

"He's *really* a collector, huh?" whispered Garraty, with a nod toward Brown.

"Always has been," said Lyman. He sipped the hot coffee, made a face, and reached in a drawer for a packet of sugar. "Did you ever see his collection?"

"One or two pieces only."

"It's probably worth a lot of money by now," said Lyman, stirring the coffee. "Personally, I never had a taste for souvenirs of my cases. Maybe that's a mistake. Maybe I'll regret it if someone ever asks me to write my memoirs."

"You laugh, but you've got some great stories, Sheldon."

"A few," Lyman replied, opening the first of the folders in his backlogged paperwork.

"You and Brown were partners?" asked Garraty, sitting on the corner of Lyman's desk.

"A few years ago. We worked the Sex Crimes Squad."

"The Mansfield kidnapping?"

"Um. Brown got transferred out after that. I asked for a transfer a little later. Brown got carried away and beat up the suspect. Brown had a little boy of his own, about the same age as the kid that got killed. Ugly crime, as you remember. Brown let himself get too personal about it. Always a dangerous thing."

"Occupational hazard," shrugged Garraty, pushing off Lyman's desk and going to his own, just behind his partner's.

Garraty dawdled over the stack of paperwork for a moment and stared at his partner's back. Lyman's old suit, shiny at the elbows and in the seat of the pants, was loose on him. Lyman had lost a lot of weight since his wife died. The weight loss came from not caring much about what he ate unless he was in a restaurant with his partner or the boss, Lt. Paul Parker. Cut from the same block of granite, those two. Parker, a cop right out of Central Casting, was Lyman's rabbi in the Department but even Parker had given up trying to cajole Lyman into going for higher rank. Why Lyman never went for a lieutenancy, no one who worked with him ever found out. Unless it was true, what he said: "I'm good at my job and have no desire to rise above my level of competency. Parker's got the proper iron butt for all the meetings and paper shuffling. I'd rather get out on the street." There was no better street man. Never had been, Garraty had been told when Lyman chose him to be his partner two years before. He had hoped Lyman would pick him, but he thought his chances were slim. There was no better teacher in Homicide than Sheldon Lyman, he had been told again and again, and in two years, he'd seen the truth of it.

The lessons started on their first day together, and, not surprisingly, they began with a lecture. It was, Garraty recalled with amusement and fondness, like being back in the Academy. They'd met for breakfast in the same coffee shop across the street from Lyman's apartment house. Eve had brought them their food, making the same flirtatious remarks. Garraty had expected some opening words, some thoughts about how Lyman expected them to work together, what the confines of their relationship would be. Instead, Lyman sipped his coffee and munched his toast, smiling, gesturing, slapping the table with his big palm, drawing little circles in a dusting of spilled sugar, being philosophical about police work, about the detection of crime, about being a cop with homicide as his specialty.

"Do you read much in the literature of crime?" he asked his new partner; then without waiting for an answer, went on, "I don't mean the text books and the law or any of the books of regulations. I mean the real literature of crime. The mystery books. The novels. The detective yarns. You should read them. To learn what it is we don't do as cops, and some of the things we ought to do. I guess every guy who wants to become a cop, a detective, thinks of himself as a kind of Sherlock Holmes. But it isn't like that, as you've doubtless learned by now. We don't go one-on-one with the bad guys like Holmes or Hercule Poirot or Father Brown—or even Columbo. It's a very one-sided deal, this business of crime detection. We've got all the power and the advantages. The poor, hapless bad guy! It's him against us. We've got all this stuff, the forensics, the crime labs, the files, the computers, armies of men to put in the field to run down leads and interview witnesses, to sift the wheat from the chaff. And if by chance some poor crook gets holed up somewhere and wants to make a stand, we've got TAC teams and tear gas and all the time in the world to wait him out. It's all rather unfair, isn't it? All so impersonal.

"Not that we can ever totally divorce ourselves from what we do. There's always one case that comes along when you can't keep yourself out of it. That's when we can get into trouble, on thin ice. Like Brown when he beat the crap out of that kidnapper in the Mansfield case. Sure, the people who read about it thought Brown was justified in beating him up. After all, the guy had grabbed a little boy—a beautiful little boy—and violated him, then brutally murdered him. Any decent man would have wanted to tear the killer limb from limb. Only, you see, the killer was a mental deficient. Retarded. His mental age wasn't much more than the kid he raped and killed. It didn't take long for the public to turn against poor Brown, and for a time there was a very real chance the killer would be turned loose because of 'police brutality.' Fortunately, the family of the man and the lawyers on both sides figured it would be better to have the fellow committed. Never came to trial. Had it, that personal involvement by Brown might have wrecked the case. So, Mr. Terrance Garraty, my new partner and one of the bright new faces in Homicide, don't take it personally, what we do. And if you see me taking something personally, you kick me in the ass and let me know about it. Is that a deal?"

"It is," smiled Garraty, offering his hand across the table.

"Good. That leaves only one other matter to get straight between us before we begin this partnership in crime."

"And that is?"

"You do the driving."

Garraty's phone rang.

"Third Homicide! Garraty!"

Lyman looked over his shoulder at Garraty making notes on a pad. When Garraty hung up, he asked, "Anything?"

"Suspicious death. Second Avenue and Fifty-sixth. The uniformed officers have already called for the M.E. and the lab teams."

"What else?"

"The victim is a male caucasian; age, early twenties; found in the bathtub; face bashed in. Could have been a fall. But for now it's listed 'suspicious.'"

"Did the officer say why he thinks it's suspicious?"

"Nope. I didn't ask. I have a way of trusting the first impressions of the patrol car guys."

"Me, too," nodded Lyman, heading toward the door.

2.

Lonnie Harris, a slender youth who dreamed of being a dancer on Broadway, had been out in the street because of economic necessity. On a day of deep snow he desperately needed money to pay the rent. Walking across snow-clogged Fifty-sixth Street, Lonnie hoped to borrow some of the money from his friend Larry Apperson and to get the rest from a man whom Lonnie had been seeing once a week for several months. Head down against the wind, Lonnie took little pleasure in the whiteness of the city, in its crisp, fairyland look, as he walked in the very center of abandoned, snowy Fifty-sixth Street.

Larry Apperson lived two doors from the corner of Fifty-sixth and Second Avenue in a third-floor walkup. Snow was drifted against the stoop and made a big pile against the front door of the apartment house. The outer door was never locked because the inside door was supposedly controlled by tenants who could buzz in those who identified themselves on the intercom. But the whole system hadn't worked for weeks, so Lonnie simply pushed open the inside door and went up the three flights to Larry's floor. He never doubted that Larry would be home. Everyone in New York was at home because of the blizzard except poor beggars like himself trying to raise the rent money. Lonnie knocked loudly and confidently on Larry's door.

He knocked several times with no answer. Once upon a

time he would not have had to knock. He'd had a key to Larry's apartment until Larry asked for it back. "It's not that I don't trust you," Larry had assured Lonnie, "but my, uh, friend needs one and it's a hassle trying to get one made." Lonnie said he understood, although he was hurt by Larry asking for the key back.

As he was turning to leave, the door of the only other apartment on Larry's floor opened and the man who lived there came out, a pleasant but aloof fellow who claimed to be a writer (although neither Larry nor Lonnie had ever heard any noises even approaching the sounds a typewriter makes). He nodded recognition at Lonnie. "I haven't seen your friend for a few days."

"Thank you," replied Lonnie, moving toward the stairway.

"You smell something?" asked the neighbor, sniffing at the air. "Smells really bad."

Lonnie sniffed. "I don't smell anything." In fact, his nose was stuffy from having walked crosstown in the cold.

"Smells like a dead rat, only more so," said the neighbor. "You don't smell anything?"

"My nose is stopped up," shrugged Lonnie, starting down the stairs.

The neighbor made a face as he leaned close to Larry's apartment. "It's in there, whatever it is. Does Larry have a pet or anything? Maybe his dog died while he's been away, or something."

"Larry doesn't have a dog," Lonnie replied, pausing on the stairs. Unless, he thought a new roommate brought one. He came back to the door. He could, with effort, smell something awful, faintly, through his runny nose.

"I think I'd better get the super," announced the neighbor, striding purposefully to the stairs and hurrying down.

The superintendent of the building lived in the basement, and Lonnie had never liked him very much. He was, to his credit, an efficient super, always somewhere in the building doing something, fixing this or that, checking to be sure all the things that had to work actually worked. A short, muscular, hairy man in his early thirties, Tony Da Capo dressed in black and wore sneakers and could be heard when he approached only because of the jangle of the huge knot of keys he clipped to his belt. The jangling grew louder in the stairwell as Tony Da Capo hurried to the third floor in the company of the worried neighbor with the sensitive nostrils. Tony Da Capo gave a curt nod of greeting to Lonnie, then pounded on Larry's door.

"I tried. Nobody answers," Lonnie patiently told him.

"Smells bad, doesn't it?" observed the neighbor.

Tony Da Capo said nothing as he fanned through his keys to find one that would open the door to Larry Apperson's apartment.

Like a huge ocean wave, the stench of death poured through the opened door. Lonnie did not go inside. He could see through the living room to the open door of the bathroom, and there, draped over the side of the tub, his head out of view, his naked buttocks toward the door, was Larry. From the smell, he had to have been dead for quite a few days.

"Jesus, Mary and Joseph," groaned the neighbor.

Tony Da Capo put a handerchief over his mouth and told Mr. Weinstein, "Go to your apartment and call the police."

Mr. Weinstein did so, promptly.

Lonnie Harris sat down on the stairway with his back to the open door of his friend's apartment. He was still sitting there when Detectives Lyman and Garraty arrived.

3.

"What makes you think it wasn't just an accident?"

Lyman waited, leaning against the door jamb outside the crime scene. Police officer Edward Casey of the Seventeenth Precinct thought for a moment about his answer before giving it. "I've seen quite a few people who've had accidents in their homes. Some who fell in bathtubs. I never saw anyone who went in like that kid did and got all the damage he got. I think he was assaulted."

Lyman nodded. "Okay." He turned away from handsome young Casey to be confronted by the ashen, drawn, forlorn figure of Lonnie Harris sitting numb and morose, possibly in shock, on the stairs. "Is that the guy who found the body?" Lyman asked Casey.

"Him and a neighbor and the super," Casey said. "This guy is a friend of the deceased."

"I'll want to talk with him, but he doesn't look so good. Ask him if he needs a doctor or something."

"Yes, sir."

Lyman turned away and began thinking in terms of what he'd find inside the apartment whose door was plastered with a warning: CRIME SCENE: DO NOT ENTER. The sign would stay there until the investigation was completed, however long that took. Lyman supposed it was a crime of felony homicide. Murder in the course of burglary, in this instance. A draft coming through the open door of the apartment carried with it the lingering, sweet, stomach-turning smell of rotting flesh.

Stepping over the threshhold of the apartment, Lyman reached into his overcoat pocket and took out a miniature tape recorder.

Nearly everyone had scoffed when he picked up an idea from a television program he had seen and adapted it to his technique as an investigator. It was simple, really; he never understood why no one tried it before. He could not recall which TV show he had been watching. He remembered only that the people on the show wore tiny microphones clipped to their clothing. The little mikes solved a perplexing problem for him. For a long time he had considered using a small, battery-operated tape recorder instead of a notebook for jotting down his notes during an investigation, but he had discarded the idea because holding the tape machine limited the use of his hands. With one of those clip-on mikes and a voice-activator attachment on a tape machine that would slip into a jacket pocket, he would be free to roam, to use his hands, to freely associate in his thought process, and to record detailed impressions and intuitions and observations, something rarely possible if he relied on scrawled notes on a pad. Later, he could transcribe accurately on paper those things he might be called upon to testify about in court—where he could refer to notes but not, obviously, play back from a tape machine. The first day he used the little mike and the small tape recorder, he took quite a ribbing. It was not long before others in Third Homicide were following his example.

He began, always, by describing the scene of the crime when he first arrived, following all the rules he had learned in the Police Academy years ago, in classes he had taken since, in all the cases he had investigated over the years. It was all very systematic, very neat and orderly, very efficient: murder investigation by the numbers. He always gave each tape a number. The average homicide case, when solved, needed half a dozen tapes.

Clipping on his tiny lapel mike, which looked like a flat-nosed bullet, and flicking the RECORD button on the compact pocket tape recorder, he stepped into the scene of the suspicious death of Lawrence Apperson. When he spoke, the voice-activator switched on the tape machine.

Standing in the doorway, I see the living room of a third-floor rear apartment in a walk-up building. It is an L-shaped room, the major stem of which is a living room, the bend of the L being a dining area. Three doors lead off this room. One goes to the kitchen from the dining area, one leads to, apparently, the bedroom. The third, whose door is open, is to the bathroom, where I see the corpse lying partially in the bathtub, partially without. The living room has two windows in the wall to the left. Between the windows the wall is decorated with framed theatrical posters. The furniture is Danish-style modern, not very expensive looking. All of the furnishings appear to be in place. Along the wall to the right, flanking the door to what is apparently the bedroom, shelves have been installed to hold numerous books, a stereo set, records, a small TV set, and various decorative objects including numerous statuettes which are reproductions of museum pieces. The dining area is furnished with a table, four chairs and a sideboard. The table is cleared.

Entering the room and crossing it, I am now standing by the open door and looking into the bathroom where the body lies. The lights in the bathroom are on.

Casey? Come here.

Yes, sir?

Were the lights on in the bathroom when you arrived?

Yes.

What about the rest of the apartment?

All off.

Thanks.

As I stand at the door, to my left is a rack of weightlifting equipment—barbells, extra weights, one ten pound dumbbell. On the wall is a mirror, which I assume was used when whoever worked out with the weights worked out, a common practice among weightlifters.

I am now entering the bathroom.

Garraty was kneeling, chatting with the Medical Examiner, a short, balding young man wearing Ben Franklin glasses and a white lab coat. The M.E. had draped a large towel over the corpse, leaving only the feet visible. They reminded Lyman of a day at the beach two years before and seeing a boy lying on the sand with only his feet sticking out from under a towel. Lyman had been shocked at the sight because the boy looked like a covered corpse. Now, here was a corpse reminding him of that young boy on the beach.

Garraty stopped talking and looked up at Lyman. He let his partner take over.

The M.E. was a familiar face at death scenes. His name was Murdock Flemming. Everyone called him Doc Dock. "In a word, Sheldon," he said, anticipating Lyman, "it is a probable homicide."

"That's two words, Doc."

"Um."

"I'm gonna check the bedroom, Terry," Lyman said. "Talk to you when you've had a little more time, Doc."

The first thing Lyman noticed in the bedroom was a portrait above the bed. A large full-length oil painting, it caught a golden time of summer skies and soft beach sand framing a sun-bronzed youth with straw-yellow hair, blue eyes, and a quizzical smile. The boy in the painting was nude. The penis was erect.

The bed below the portrait had been turned down but not slept in. On the night table lay a novel, closed but with a bookmark halfway through it. A pair of eyeglasses lay folded by the book. A lamp on the table was off. Lyman checked the switch and discovered the bulb had burned out. The other furniture in the room consisted of a dresser, a bureau and a desk on top of which were an open portable typewriter, two boxes labeled bond typing paper, a phone, and an address book. Lyman riffled through it. Plenty of names, he noted, written in careful block letters. He put the address book into his pocket.

Three items in the bedroom were exceptional, he noted on his tape: the address book, the burned out bulb, and the portrait.

Garraty came in, stopped in the doorway, and gaped at the painting. "Well, that is quite a picture!"

"Is it the kid in the tub?"

"Looks like him. Can't be sure. The-kid-in-the-tub's face is smashed in, and lying in all that water a couple of days . . ."

"Same build though?"

"Yeah," nodded Garraty, stepping into the room. "How do you suppose that guy could keep a hard-on going long enough for someone to paint a goddamned picture of it?"

"Garraty, you are obscene."

"So is that picture."

"The artist probably did that part from memory."

"Well, that sure makes this look like a fag killing, doesn't it?"

"Why?"

"Hell, the kid must have been a homo. I mean, to pose for a picture like that and then hang it on the wall?"

"Why not simple burglary?"

"Windows are locked. Door was locked. Place doesn't seem to have been ransacked."

"Have you found the kid's wallet?"

"No."

"Burglary for money?"

"How much money could a kid like him have?"

"How would a burglar know? He could have come in, thinking the apartment was unoccupied, surprised the kid taking the bath, then panicked after the kid was killed, and grabbed what he could easily take. A wallet."

"*Or* this kid picked someone up, or vice versa, and they came up here for sex and the kid wound up dead with the wallet taken by his lover. There's a hustling area just down the street, you know."

"I know."

"And three gay bars that I know of."

Lyman went back to the bathroom. "Doc, we'll want to know if the kid had had sex around the time he died."

"Did he ingest semen?" added Garraty.

"Are you figuring a homosexual killing?" asked the M.E. without looking up.

"Maybe," said Lyman.

"Is that what you were thinking, Doc?" asked Garraty.

"I don't think until I've finished making all my observations. And then I try to avoid making assumptions not based on the facts. Just give me the facts."

"We'd appreciate the facts about whether the kid had sex around the time of death," said Lyman, turning away.

Garraty asked, "Do you want to talk to the kid who found the body?"

"What's his name?"

"Lonnie Harris."

Lyman found Lonnie on the stairs. He had been crying judging by the look of his eyes.

THE LONNIE HARRIS TAPE

Lonnie, I'm going to ask you some questions, and I want you to know that I will be making a tape of our conversation. This tape is just a convenience for me. It's a lot easier than me trying to write down notes. Okay?

Yes.

You identified the body?

Yes. As best I could. I mean, after all this time and the way Larry's face was smashed, I mean. . . .

But it looked like your friend Larry—hair color, build, and the like.

Oh, yes.

You knew Larry very well.

Yes. We roomed together for a time.

I understand. You and he were roommates.

Yes.

Were you more than friends and rommates?

We were lovers. Yes. I'm not ashamed of that.

How long did you live here?

A few months.

Can you tell me about that?

We were lovers. What more is there to tell?

Why did you leave?

We broke up. Lovers break up, you know.

But you remained friends.

Certainly.

Why did you come here today, Lonnie?

To borrow some money. My rent is due today. God, I'll bet I've been locked out. My landlord is a son of a bitch about prompt payment. All my things are probably out on the street! Officer, may I please go?

In a few minutes. I'll send you home with one of the officers, who can speak to your landlord, if you wish, and tell him you've been tied up today helping us with an investigation.

That's all I'd need. To come home with a cop escort. No, thanks.

When you came here and got no answer, that made you suspicious?

Not really. It was the neighbor who got suspicious because of the smell.

The smell didn't make you suspicious?

I had a stuffed-up nose. Being out in the cold, and all?

How long has it been since you lived here?

A few months.

Is this the first time you've come back?

No. I was at a party here last week.

So you and Larry patched things up and you were still friends so he invited you to a party?

Yes. And I wanted to see his new friend.

Who would that be?

Ellis Marsh.

Had Ellis Marsh moved in with Larry?

I don't believe so. At least, he hadn't when I was here last week. Ellis lives in the East Village and attends N.Y.U. I don't know if he since moved in or not.

Would you look around the apartment for me, now, and tell me if you notice anything missing?

You think a burglar did this?

Right now I'd like to know from someone who's been in this apartment recently if anything is obviously missing.

No, it looks okay to me. I mean, the TV and the stereo are still here. Those are the things a burglar would take, right?

Yes.

Larry had some cameras, fairly expensive ones. He kept them in that cabinet. Is it all right to open it?

Yes.

His Pentax is not here. That was his favorite. But the others are here.

Anything else?

He has a portable typewriter. Larry was always talking about writing a book. He kept a typewriter on his desk in the bedroom. Shall I look in there?

The typewriter is there. I saw it when I was in the room. Anything else in this room?

No, not that I can see. His TV, his stereo, his records,

his cameras—except that one. His exercise gear. But one of the weights is missing! One of those little ones you use for building up biceps. The other one of these.

One of the dumbbells is missing?

If that's what you call this, then one is missing.

You are sure he had two of them?

Oh, yes. I used to watch him using them. He worked out in front of the mirror. He was always nude when he worked out and I liked to watch him.

What did Larry do for a living, Lonnie?

I'm not going to lie to you, Mr. Lyman, because you'll find out all about Larry anyway, won't you?

Yes.

For years, since he first came to New York when he was a teenager, he hustled. Not on the streets, except for a few months at first. Larry was too fine a boy to have to stay on the streets.

He worked as a call-boy?

For the last five or six years. Lately, he decided he should think about the future. I used to tease him when he'd get very serious and talk about how he wasn't going to be young and beautiful all his life. He was going to be an actor. Oh, I know what you're thinking. 'I've heard that story before!' But in Larry's case it was working out. He was very good in an off-off-Broadway production last year and he was taking lessons and was up for a movie. So, Larry was getting out of the hustling thing. He really was.

But he still did some hustling?

There were a few people he saw from time to time.

Can you give me some names?

They're all in a little address book Larry kept in his desk.

Did he have relatives? We should notify someone.

A younger brother, Peter, lives somewhere in Pennsylvania. He should be in Larry's book if you can find it.

That's very helpful, Lonnie. Thank you.

Does that mean I can leave?
Yes. The officer has your address?
He does.
I'll send you home in car, if you wish.
No, thank you.
Very well.
Larry is . . . was . . . a wonderful person. Everybody loved him.
Thank you, Lonnie.
I mean, please don't think badly of him just because he was a homosexual.
I won't, Lonnie.
I'm going now.
One other thing, Lonnie. The portrait in the bedroom. It is of Larry?
Yes.
A good likeness?
As good as any photograph.
Sometimes painters exaggerate and flatter.
Not in this case. That is . . . *was* . . . Larry. Beautiful, wasn't he?
Yes. Thank you, Lonnie. You may go now.

Crossing the living room, Lyman examined the exercise gear by the door to the bathroom, bending down and studying the single dumbbell. Where, he wondered, had the other one gone? Rising, he stepped into the bathroom again and waited silently, watching intently, as Doc Dock dragged the corpse from the tub and spread it on the floor on the same towel that had shrouded the victim. The corpse plopped, its watery, bloated condition making it as soft as a rag doll. The face was a mess, both crushed and inflated, a raw mash of torn and pinkish flesh. The arms, the belly, the abdomen and, the genitals were grotesquely swollen, yet even in the awful disfiguration of four- or five-day old death Lyman could recognize that the boy had been as handsome, trim, muscular and attractive as the boy in the painting in the bedroom. "Doc?"

"Your basic homicide for sure!" said the M.E. without looking up.

"He didn't just slip on a bar of soap?"

"Nope."

"I didn't think so."

Doc Dock looked up. "Still doing my job for me, Sheldon?" It was teasingly intended. The two men had been on too many cases together for anything but good relations, affection even.

"I've got to have learned something by now," smiled Lyman.

"What makes you think homicide, not accidental?" asked Garraty.

"He was outside the tub when he fell, standing on that bathmat. There are traces of dry soap on his feet and legs. His footprints are still in the pile of the mat, pointing away from the tub. He was standing with his back to the tub. If he had slipped—and the soap is in the dish, by the way—he would have gone in backwards. Is that the way you see it, Doc?"

"Then how did he happen to go into the tub the way he did?" asked Garraty as Doc Dock smiled and nodded agreement with Lyman.

"The kid was having a bath—I always thought kids today only took showers. Anyway, he was bathing, got up, stepped out of the tub, crossed to the door. Something happened, and he wound up as we see him now, dead."

"Not immediately, Sheldon, although your scenario is right on target. When this boy got to the door, the blow that messed up his face was struck, a very heavy blunt instrument."

"Could it have been a ten pound weightlifter's dumbbell?"

"Easily."

"Someone hit him with something heavy, and then?"

"He stumbled backward, toward the tub, finally collapsing into it, face down in the water."

"Where he. . . ."

"Drowned."

"The poor sonofabitch."

"Do you want all the medical terminology now on your little tape or will you wait and read it?"

"Tell me when, Doc. When did he die?"

"Four, maybe five days ago. Putrefaction begins at about 48 hours, so. . . ."

"I'll read the report, Doc, and you won't forget—I want to know about the sex thing."

"Sheldon, I will certainly tell you all that I can possibly determine as to whether the deceased had sexual relations prior to his death and I will to the best of my ability tell you whether it was oral, anal, homo- or heterosexual, or what used to be called the solitary vice."

"Does this look like a fag murder to you now, Doc?" asked Garraty.

The M.E. shrugged. "I won't draw that kind of conclusion. That's your job."

"The neighbor who also found the body told me the traffic through this place was steady," added Garraty. "He figured this kid was either selling dope or himself. Or both."

"Some neighbor," grunted Lyman. "Where is he?"

"In his apartment. Next door."

"Name?"

"William Weinstein."

"I'll talk to him," nodded Lyman. "Check the rest of the neighbors, see if they heard or saw anything, and what about the super?"

"Tony Da Capo. Want me to talk to him, too?"

"You or I, doesn't matter."

All of the witness statements would go into reports. Crime was a generator of paper. Police experts would ponder their discoveries, their hunches, their assumptions, the results of their tests and measurements and photography and analysis and comparisons, and it would all be reduced to words, to exhibits, to charts, sketches, and photos in black and white and vivid color. And it would all come into his hands—his and Garraty's—but he was the senior partner, and he would be the top man in the investigation.

This homicide, like all the others, would become a team project that would involve dozens of detectives, scores of men in uniforms, all feeding the bits and pieces back to him, dropping their reports on his desk, funneling their findings to him via interdepartmental mail, forcing him to make another file, to add another dossier to his open cases.

He knew all the routines. The only thing he never knew was how it would turn out. That was the part that kept it interesting.

Murders often went unsolved.

'Gay' murders, especially, tended to remain open.

Militants of the gay movement suspected the worst of that statistic. One gay leader once complained to him, "The fucking cops don't give a shit about the killing of a gay. Gay murders get lower priority than murders of straight folks. Just as cops don't give a shit about who killed somebody black or Puerto Rican. They are corpses without a constituency. Make a show, create a little flurry of activity, and then let it all slide in favor of solving the murders of white folks, straight folks— that's the way you cops work."

The truth was, he explained, murders of gays *were* harder to investigate. He cited the case of the murder of a "John" in a Times Square hotel. A Scarsdale businessman with a wife and kids and an impeccable reputation had checked into the hotel with a young man, said the newspapers—always a giveaway, the little journalistic hint that this was a "fag murder." The man was found in the morning, nude, robbed, butchered. There was no arrest and no likelihood of one. "Because you don't care!" shouted the gay leader, his anger hot in his face.

Lyman let the accusation pass without a response.

The murder had never been solved, but Lyman knew how it happened. It was a textbook 'gay murder.' He and his partner had been able to put it all together, all but the arrest. The victim had been to a hustlers' bar on Eighth Avenue where he was seen by a dozen people leaving late in the evening with a young man dressed as if he were a cowboy, complete with hat, boots, jeans, leather vest and work shirt. The hustler had been around the bar for a couple of weeks, scoring easily because he was a new face and because there was about him a hint of latent violence, a powerful enticement to some men who bought boys. More over, the cowboy— there had been no consensus as to his name: Kelly, Dallas, Cowboy, Eddie—boasted that he had the biggest, baddest, most beautiful equipment in the city, maybe the whole East coast. The cowboy claimed he had prospered, and few hustlers doubted him. He worked out of a bar steadily, from afternoon to early morning, and he even had repeat business from two of the men who picked him up. Finally, he left with the man from Scarsdale and never came back. He had, Lyman supposed, caught the first bus or train or plane out of town while the mutilated corpse of the Scarsdale man waited to be found by a maid the next day.

Then, as in every murder he had investigated in his career, all the apparatus of modern crime detection had gone to work—forensics, pathology, photography, fingerprints, skilled interviewing, leg-work, questions-and-answers—until all the elements were sifted out. All but the big answer. Who was the cowboy killer and where had he gone?

Now, here he was on the scene of a murder again, and the apparatus was humming, starting the processes that would generate stacks of paper filled with answers to questions. If he were lucky and sharp enough, the stack of paper might provide the answer to who killed Larry Apperson and why.

Lyman paused at the door to the apartment and looked back at the activity. A sprinkling of powder covered objects that might contain fingerprints. Tape was already on the floor and the tub where the body was, outlining it. A photographic team was popping bulbs and flashing lights everywhere for a photo record of the death scene. On Lyman's word, everything in the apartment, except the body, would remain, locked up and sealed, until he was satisfied that all the physical evidence that could be gathered had been. Even the portrait would remain on the wall above the bed, although the photographers had asked to take it to the lab to photograph it properly. The portrait was the only available likeness of the victim, and Lyman wanted hundreds of prints made of its photograph for possible use in the canvassing of bars, baths and streets that would have to be done to pursue this investigation to the limit. Before long, all the detectives and uniformed officers of the Seventeenth Precinct and Third Homicide would carry little snapshots of Larry Apperson in the hope that someone somewhere would look at one of the pictures and exclaim, "Hey, I saw that dude! I saw him on the night he was killed and he was with a guy. . . ."

Ah, to have a witness! Lyman wished.

There was a chance, although the odds against it were great. The probable route to learning who murdered Larry Apperson was in the tangled skein of his life, his friends, his acquaintances, his haunts. In all likelihood, the name of the killer was spelled out in the painstaking block printing on the pages of Larry Apperson's address book. "Murder is an intimacy among friends." Lt. Parker liked to point out. Lyman shook his head in wonder at the truth of it.

He left the apartment and crossed the hall to the apartment of William Weinstein. A slight, balding, worried-looking man, he sat on a small couch by the window, which was open despite the brutal cold outside. "I got sick from the smell and seeing that body," he said, puffing hard and looking as if he might throw up at any moment. When asked, he declined medical attention. "I'll be okay when I get some more fresh air."

THE WILLIAM WEINSTEIN TAPE

You told my partner that you thought Apperson was dealing in dope or was perhaps a male prostitute?

There was a lot of traffic in and out of that apartment. Men and young men. I'm as liberal as the next guy, so I don't get involved. None of my business. I think it was probably sex he was dealing in, though, rather than dope. I used to hear them as I went past the door. Excuse me for being blunt, but I know the sound of fucking when I hear it, and I never saw women go in there.

But the super didn't do anything about having the kid evicted?

Why should he? Larry was quiet and very nice. He never bothered anybody.

The murder. . . .

Murder! I thought it was an accident?

We believe not.

Oh, Jesus.

It may have happened about four days ago. Do you remember anything unusual at that time?

No.

Larry Apperson was just his usual quiet self? Nothing out of the ordinary?

Oh, there was an argument he had in the hallway with a black man.

What kind of argument?

I think Larry didn't want to see the man. I got the impression he was brushing him off.

Do you know the man?

Afraid not. Just one of those visitors Larry had.

When did this argument take place?

Oh, Thursday, I think. Four, five days ago?

Four.

Yes.

Did you get along well with your neighbor?

Very well.

Thanks, Mr. Weinstein. Are you sure you don't want me to get you some medical attention?

I'm fine.

Good.

Mr. Lyman? That boy who came here when we found the body?

Lonnie Harris.

Yes. You don't suspect him of anything do you?

Why do you ask?

Well, he and Larry had been, well, you know. . . .

Roommates.

. . . lovers.

And?

They had a big fight before Lonnie moved out. Woke me up in the middle of the night.

What kind of fight?

Nothing physical as far as I know. But a real battle of words. Lonnie moved out next day.

I'll check into that. Thanks.

You are certainly the expert when it comes to this kind of thing; murder, I mean. But isn't it possible that Lonnie could have killed Larry, waited a couple of days, then come back ostensibly for a visit so he would be the one who found the body and then be above suspicion?

'S possible. Anything's possible.

It's all so awful!

One final question, Mr. Weinstein. It is possible that this murder may have occurred during a burglary. Has there ever been any trouble with burglaries in this building?

This is New York City. Name me a building that hasn't had burglaries.

Have there been recent ones in this building? I notice that the lock system on the front door doesn't work.

That's a recent thing. There have been burglaries. Nothing big. Money. Pieces of jewelry. Things that could go into a pocket. I, for one, always leave a five dollar bill in plain sight, no matter where I live, in the hope that if I'm hit by a burglar the money will be enough and he'll leave without getting the good stuff.

The five dollar idea works?

It worked once here about six months ago.

Thank you, Mr. Weinstein.

4.

Lyman went back to the bedroom and sat in a chair at the desk. Turning, he faced the wall dominated by the nearly life-size portrait of the late Lawrence Apperson and ran down a list of motives for murder: for profit, for the elimination of a person who had become a threat, for revenge, for reasons of jealousy, for political reasons, for sadistic pleasure, for sexual reasons. These, Lyman had been told in his days as a recruit at the Police Academy, were the seven definite groups into which murder could be classified.

"Each of us," the lecturer had said, "has a threshold to murder, the point at which our reaction to a situation may result in the taking of another human life." The lecturer, a Deputy Inspector who had been the senior member of the committee that rewrote the New York City Police Department's *Manual of Procedure* told the class that a Southerner would be more inclined to resort to arms to even a score. Residents of backward rural areas would be more ready to kill. The threshold to murder was very low in slums, in the jungle atmosphere of big cities. A murderer, Lyman had been told, was likely to be a male, a Negro, low on the economic ladder, a drinker. Yet in the years since that lecture, Lyman had worked on homicides that broke every one of the tenets laid out in the academy. Now, here was the killing of young Lawrence Apperson, done, surely, for one of those seven motives, possibly the one which Garraty had already embraced—sex. The painting on the wall—the portrait of that handsome, smiling, voluptuous, sexually aroused youth—spelled sex if it spelled anything.

There is even a little black book, he reminded himself, reaching into his pocket and taking out Larry Apperson's telephone book. Leafing through its small, lined, alphabetized pages, he read dozens of names and numbers, most with addresses, almost all of them the names of men, written in neat, artistic, block-printing.

This is where we begin, he said to himself, looking up again at the portrait of Larry Apperson. Somewhere in the book, he expected, was the name of the person who had killed for one of those seven motives.

"The super's outside. Wants to talk to the man in charge," announced Garraty, leaning in the doorway.

"Haven't you interviewed him?"

"Yep. He says he doesn't know a damned thing about what happened here. As far as he knows, he says, Apperson was away for the weekend. He never suspected anything wrong until the neighbor came to get him."

"What's he want to talk to me for?"

He wants to know how soon he can rent the apartment."

"Jesus Christ!"

"He's out in the hallway."

"What's the guy's name?"

"Antonio Da Capo."

The superintendent frowned and got to the point. "Sure as hell the owner of this building is going to want to rent out the apartment. In these days you can't let a good apartment like this sit around unoccupied."

Lyman bridled. "There's been a murder here, Mr. Da Capo."

The super blinked. "I know that."

"Don't you think that finding out who killed this kid is a

little more important right now than renting out his apartment?"

"Sure, but you don't know the owner. People are going to be calling up to rent this place. A building I ran once had a suicide in it and the day that story was in the papers there were seventy-five people banging on the door wanting to rent the apartment. This is going to be in the papers, am I right?"

"I wouldn't know, Mr. Da Capo. I'm just a cop."

"I guess this was a robbery, hunh?"

"Why do you assume that?"

"Well, that's the way it looks to me."

"Have there been a lot of robberies in this building?"

"This is a secure building. No matter what you may hear. I run a secure building. The front door lock has been broken only a few days so. . . ."

"When's the last time you say Larry Apperson?"

"Oh, I don't know. Tenants come and go all the time. I don't keep track. I guess it's been a couple of days. He's been dead a while. God, the smell."

"You didn't notice the smell yourself?"

"No I didn't. Nobody did until today."

"How well did you know Larry Apperson?"

"He was a tenant."

"It's possible this was done by someone he knew. Did you ever meet any of his friends?"

"I seen people come and go. Never met them."

"When you didn't see Apperson for a few days, that didn't make you wonder if something might be wrong?"

"I'm the super. It's not my job to keep tabs on the tenants. Maybe he was away. Who knows?"

"If I'm going to be away I let the doorman in my apartment know."

"This isn't a doorman apartment house. People have keys. They come and go. If someone wants to let me know he's gonna be away that's up to him. And up to him if he doesn't want to let me know. Apperson minded his own business and I minded mine. Say, are you thinking that I had something to do with this killing?"

"I'm just trying to get a handle on the case, Mr. Da Capo. It's natural that a cop would wonder about a guy who has a key to the apartment where someone's been murdered. You have a passkey. You also keep an eye on your building. You know who comes and goes. Who's at home, who isn't. What kind of cop would I be if I didn't wonder if the building super figured he could rip off someone's apartment, thinking the tenant was away, and then got caught and resorted to murder?"

"I didn't kill anybody."

"Tell your boss we'll release the apartment as soon as possible. And you, I may want to talk to again."

Disgusting, Lyman thought as he turned away, that all the murder of a young man meant was an apartment to be put on the market.

In the bathroom, the M.E. was finishing up. Next he would supervise the putting of the body into a plastic bag. Doc Dock wagged a finger. "I know, Shel, you want a report right away. Yesterday isn't soon enough."

Garraty, leaning against the bathroom sink, chuckled.

Lyman said to him, "Run a check on the super of the building. See if he's got any kind of record."

"You think he . . . ?"

"I think he could have killed the kid if he blundered into him during a burglary attempt. Who knows? Right now the whole wide world is brimming with suspects. All we have to do is eliminate the ones who couldn't have done it and the one left is the killer. Process of elimination. Probably the kid's killer's name is in the little black book."

"A big roster of suspects?"

The body lay on the floor neatly wrapped, awaiting Doc Dock's return with men to haul it away in a plastic bag. Lyman turned away. "It's a pretty good list. A to Z, about two dozen or so. Some of the entries look a bit old. It's hard to say how many current names might be prospects worth talking to. What about the neighbors?"

Garraty shrugged. "They know from nothing. Typical New Yorkers. Mind their business. I go along with you in thinking that the murderer's name is in the book."

"And If that fails, we hit all the bars and the baths and the streets."

"And hope that we'll get lucky and find someone whose conscience can't bear the strain anymore, and he walks in and signs a confession."

"I gave up believing in Santa Claus long ago, Shelly. Long ago."

"There's a *mob* of newsmen out front," announced Doc Dock, coming in with the Emergency Service men and the plastic bag for Lawrence Apperson's corpse. "They've already talked to the friendly next-door neighbor."

"Shit, Weinstein's been giving interviews?"

"Lurid," said the M.E., bending over to watch the placing of the corpse into the green bag. "He has told the New York press corps that the late Mr. Apperson was a flaming fag."

"Sonofabitch," said Lyman, jamming Larry Apperson's little black book into his pocket.

"Who's out there?" asked Garraty.

"Are you asking me if Richard Donnelly is out there?" asked the M.E.

"Yes."

"He is."

"I knew that fucker'd be there," Garraty groaned. "Well, now we know how the New York press is going to play this one, huh?"

"Big and dirty," said the M.E., watching Larry Apperson's bare feet go into the green bag.

"Well, there's no avoiding it," shrugged Lyman. "Let's go out and talk to the sonsofbitches."

And try to keep from blowing the case before it's even begun, he thought.

5.

Garraty backed their car onto Second Avenue and headed it south. "What do you suppose makes a man like Donnelly tick?" he asked, looking out the window at the newspaper reporter as he climbed into his own car.

"Dunno," said Lyman, slumped in the seat and facing the other way, where a sanitation truck fitted with a plow was moving a huge pile of snow back off the street.

"You know what Donnelly's story is going to look like in the next edition of the *Post?* Huge black headline:

CALLBOY SLAIN

COPS PUZZLED"

"Prob'ly."

"I don't know how you managed to keep your cool with him, Shelly. I really don't."

"He has his job, we have ours."

"That was no news conference. It was a grand jury. He's going to blow this up out of all proportion, and then you know what happens next. The Gay Rights Crowd gets into the act."

"Maybe not."

"Ha. Bet your ass on it."

"Nothin' we can do about that, I guess."

"Where are we going? Back to the office?"

"Yeah, but first, let's check to see if this fellow Ellis Marsh is at home."

"Where's that?"

"In the East Village," Lyman said, digging out Larry Apperson's address book from his inside pocket. "East Tenth Street. That's across First Avenue, other side of St. Mark's Place, near the Polish church."

"I know it. Used to be Hippieland. Man, I walked that beat a lot back in the Sixties. Riot duty. God, glad that's over with. You were working homicides even then?"

"Even then. Seems like I've always been working homicides."

Garraty surveyed the empty, snowy avenue and shook his head. "Man, wouldn't it be great to have the streets this empty all the time?" Fifteen minutes later, he cursed the snow when he found East Tenth Street unplowed. "Where the hell's the Sanitation Department?"

Pushing open his door and plunging into the deep snow, Lyman replied, "These poor bastards'll be lucky if they get plowed out at all. This is not one of the better neighborhoods. Not much clout with City Hall around here."

"Where's this Ellis character live?"

"Middle of the block," said Lyman with a nod.

"What are we supposed to be down here, fuckin' Nanook of the North?"

Lyman was glad about his decision to wear older clothes and shoes. The snow in the street came up to their knees and none of the pavements in the block had been shoveled. The snow was so deep on the steps at the address of Ellis Marsh's home that the policemen could not tell where the steps were.

Garraty pressed the button on the mailbox next to Ellis's name. There was no answer. Garraty buzzed the name next to Apartment One, assuming the building's super would live in Apartment One. "Who is it?" came a voice on the intercom.

"Police," replied Garraty. "Are you the superintendent?"

"Yes."

"Let us in please."

"How do I know you're cops?"

"Come out and we'll show you our badges," Garraty snapped. To Lyman he said, "Who the fuck would be out in this street on a day like this one except cops?"

The super was an elderly man, bald except for a few strands of gray above his ears. He wore a tattered black sweater and gray flannel pants. He carried a heavy cane. For protection, Garraty decided, because the man did not limp as he came down the narrow corridor to the window of the locked door. Garraty showed his gold badge. "You can't be too careful," said the super, opening the door.

"We've come to see one of your tenants. Mr. Marsh?"

The old man nodded. "He's away for the weekend. Was going skiing, he told me. Skiing! Could do that right out in the street!"

"When did he leave?" asked Lyman.

"Four, five days ago. I didn't keep track."

"May we see his apartment?" asked Garraty.

"Is that legal?"

"Would the police do anything illegal, sir?"

"Wait here until I get my keys."

"May we wait in the hallway? Kind of cold out here."

"Yes. Sorry. Come in."

Lyman had been in a thousand apartment row houses like this one: narrow hallways, steep stairs, creaking wooden floors, architecturally shaped like hourglasses to make room for air and light shafts. They marched in endless rows along the streets of Manhattan but were gradually disappearing, replaced by highrise luxury apartments. Ellis Marsh's apartment was at the rear of the fifth floor.

They entered a small hallway with the kitchen to their right, its small window looking out onto the air and light shaft, so close to the kitchen window opposite that a friendly neighbor could have easily handed a bottle of milk across the gap. The hallway opened onto the middle room, a living room, also with a window onto the air shaft. The living room connected to the bedroom with a small walkway and a bathroom. The bedroom had two windows. Like similar apartments all over the city, the cramped space could have been dark and grim, but Ellis Marsh had a flair for decorating with light colors and brightly textured upholstry. It was, Lyman decided, a nice apartment. The super hovered behind them as they walked through it. "Thank you," Lyman smiled. "We'll let you know when we're finished."

While Garraty went over the living room, Lyman went into the bedroom looking for anything, everything, and nothing in particular.

In a drawer in the nighttable by the double bed he found a Polaroid snapshot.

"Terry, come in and have a look at this," he called out.

Garraty took the photo and studied it in the light at the window. "How about that?"

The Polaroid showed Larry Apperson standing beside the portrait of him that hung in his bedroom. He posed in the photo exactly as he had posed in the portrait. There was no doubt, now, that the boy in the painting was Larry Apperson. On the back of the photo, he had written: "To Ellis, Love, Always, Larry." Garraty handed Lyman the photo.

Tucking the picture into his pocket, Lyman asked, "Anything of interest in the living room?"

"Nothing."

"Well, we'll have to come back when Mr. Ellis Marsh is at home."

"*If* he comes home," replied Garraty.

In the car, plowing uptown, Lyman asked, "You think Marsh is a prime suspect?"

"Don't you?"

"Um."

"Damned coincidental that Marsh leaves town at about the time Apperson buys it."

"The super says the kid went skiing. Makes sense in this weather."

"Fags don't go skiing," said Garraty.

"*What?*" Lyman turned, grinning, amazed. "What the hell do you mean, fags don't go skiing?"

"They go south in the winter."

"Since when are you the big expert on the vacation habits of fags?"

"There's one who lives in my building. Nice enough fellow. My wife likes him a lot because he's very polite and gentlemanly and helps her out with the laundry and stuff like that."

"Sounds like he might be making a play for your wife, Terry. You sure this guy is gay?"

Garraty let the jibe pass. "Anyway, Benjamin—that's the fag's name—always goes south for his vacations in the winter. He times them to college vacations because of all the boys who go to Florida. Benjamin also goes to Fort Lauderdale around Easter, when all the boys are there. Summers he goes to Europe. I have never heard of Benjamin going skiing."

"On the basis of knowing one gay who doesn't go skiing, you are telling me that no gays go skiing. Jesus. What kind of logic is that?"

"It's damned peculiar that Ellis Marsh takes off for parts unknown and his lover-boy is lying dead in the bathtub. Mr. Ellis Marsh has to be Suspecto Numero Uno."

"Yes, on that you make a lot of sense, Terry. We'll give it a couple of days, to see if Marsh comes back of if he has in fact flown the coop."

"Meantime, what do we do?"

"The usual legwork, partner."

"Yeah."

"We dig into the life, times, friends, follies, and death of Lawrence Apperson, and while we have a Suspecto Numero Uno, maybe somebody else out there in this snowy town did it and is just waiting for us to come and slap on the handcuffs. There is also an unhappy task to be done. One of us has got to call the brother of this kid and tell him what happened. The number's in Apperson's phone book." Lyman fished out the little book and found the name of Peter Apperson in it, next to a 215 area code number. "I never got used to telling a next of kin the bad news," he said, pushing the book back into his jacket.

"Want me to call the brother?"

"Nah. I found the phone book."

The number, he found out shortly, when he called from the squad room, was a fraternity house at the University of Pennsylvania. "Pete took off a few days ago," explained one of the residents, surprisingly unfazed by finding himself talking to a New York City policeman.

"Do you know where he went?" Lyman asked.

"Nope. I think he's got a girl friend somewhere."

"Well, when he returns, it is urgent that he call me in New York City. Have him call collect. The operator should call Detective Lyman at the Seventeenth Precinct."

"Got it," said the boy in Philadelphia.

"I can't stress how urgent it is, son."

"Yes, urgent."

"The brother's not there," he told Garraty. "Shacked up somewhere, his frat brother says. I left a message for him to call me at the Seventeenth rather than our number. It wouldn't be too good to have a kid come back from getting his ashes hauled and be told to call a homicide number."

Lyman stared across the noisy, bustling squad room.

Bad enough, what that kid's got to find out, he thought.

"Maybe I can ease the blow when he calls up," he said, to no one in particular.

Terry Garraty had seen it countless times: the humanity of his partner, the little extra word, the soliticitous concern for the comfort of people caught up in tragedies, the conviction that he owed it to victims to be more than the avenging arm of the law. It showed, too, in his relations with the men of the squad. He had gotten into trouble by rushing to defend Mike Brown when he beat up a murder suspect, but no one who knew Lyman was surprised that Lyman would forget about his own hide while defending a partner. More, there was not a man in Third Homicide whose wife or kids didn't get a card or a gift or phone call on birthdays or anniversaries or graduation days from Sheldon Lyman. Certainly none of the men in the squad reaped as much attention as Terry Garraty. Lyman was almost a member of his family. All tried to return Lyman's kindnesses in the difficult period when his wife died and in the long, dismal days that followed when it seemed as if Lyman might not rouse from his depression.

Garraty knew that the last years of Lyman's marriage had been miserable and that the collapse of the marriage was not wholly Lyman's fault, although Lyman seemed to believe he had been the main culprit when he talked about the final days of his wife's life. When Garraty argued with him, Lyman became lost in his own world of inner doubts and fears and recriminations. Only lately had he begun to snap out of it, but Garraty knew that Lyman's long dark night of self-doubt, recrimination and soul-searching was not over. He noticed it in Lyman's occasional inattention when small talk was going on. He saw it in wandering glances, in spells of reverie, in a tendency to look back at his life, as far back as his adolescence when, he said, he had never been happier.

Garraty believed his partner was a survivor, and he expected that sooner or later Lyman would come out of his off-duty solitude to seek new companionship. In the meantime, Garraty tried to be understanding of the great cop who daily sat beside him in the squadroom and in their car. Garraty tried not to notice the loneliness evident in Lyman's eyes, a loneliness broken only by an occasional call or letter from his daughter in Seattle, an occasional Sunday dinner with the

Garratys and the constantly supportive comradeship of the men of Third Homicide.

"What the hell are you dreaming about, Garraty?"

Lyman was beside Garraty's desk, frowning down. "I was thinking about you, actually."

"What about me?"

"I was thinking what a nice guy you are."

"Bull."

"I was, really."

"Well, forget about me and let's get some of the paperwork done on this case, hm?"

"Sure thing, partner!"

Garraty smiled and reached for forms and carbon paper.

Later, Lyman bent over his desk, typing, and thinking about the mass of papers that went into a case. As a routine matter, he would send copies of his initial report on the Apperson case to the Sex Crimes Squad in case the M.E. found evidence of this as a sex crime. A report would go to the Burglary Squad, listing the possibility that the crime took place during a burglary. In view of Weinstein's statement that there had been burglaries, in view of the faulty locking mechanism on the apartment house door, and in view of three items missing: the dumbbell, the camera, and the wallet, there were strong indications that it was a simple burglary which brought Larry Apperson's killer to his apartment.

The disappearance of Ellis Marsh perplexed Lyman as he typed his report. If Marsh killed his lover, he might have taken the wallet and the camera to create the appearance of a burglary. The weight was taken, it seemed to Lyman, because it had been the weapon.

It all went down onto paper: the fact, the theories, the little they knew.

Garraty was using two fingers on his typewriter to list the

names, phone numbers and addresses from the victim's address book. Once he did some verifying by phone to see if the names addressess and numbers were current, the two of them would take the list and start paying visits to the people whom Larry Apperson considered important enough to put into his little black book.

6.

When Lt. Paul Parker, boss of Third Homicide came in, Lyman and Garraty went into his office to brief him. Parker was an old hand at homicides. He listened well, and when Lyman and Garraty had summed up what they knew of the death of the victim, Parker concluded, "It looks like two possibilities. The kid was wasted by one of his friends or lovers or you have a felony homicide during the commission of a burglary. Right?"

"One of the two," Lyman nodded. "Garraty favors the lover-did-it theory."

"Why?" asked the boss.

"It just has all the earmarks of a homosexual killing, and the items taken, I believe, were taken to make it appear like a burglary."

"Sheldon?" asked Parker, steepling his fingers and rocking slightly in his chair, a familiar Parker habit.

"My first instinct told me burglary, but I've been wrong before."

"Too bad the news media latched onto this," sighed Parker. "Are we going to have a *cause célèbre?*"

"Only time will tell," said Lyman.

Parker had had plenty of scrapes with the news media and gotten a few lumps. "Keep me up to date," Parker said, ending the meeting. "I'll do my best to keep the Fourth Estate off your asses."

That was Parker's signal to them that they would be free to direct all inquiries from the news media to the boss. He'd take the heat and he was welcome to it. Parker was good that way, although the media relations experts in the Deputy Commissioner's office considered him a public relations menace.

The publicity surrounding a murder case, especially a sensational one, was not new to Lyman, but having been burned once, he preferred to leave the handling of the press to others. When reporters had gotten wind of how Brown had beaten up the suspect in the kidnap-murder of the little Mansfield boy, Lyman had said to a reporter that it seemed a natural reaction of any man, especially the father of a little boy, to be enraged at what the kidnapper had done before killing the boy. "Partner Defends Cop Who Beat Suspect in Mansfield Case," one of the newspapers headlined. Since then, unless he had no choice but to meet the gentlemen and ladies of the press, Lyman let someone else do the press conferencing.

Fortunately, Lt. Parker was willing.

Half an hour after their meeting with the boss, Lyman and Garraty received the report from Doc Dock. "It appears," said Lyman, laying aside the report and turning to Garraty, who was still reading it, "that the victim had been chaste for at least twenty-four hours before he died. That rules out your sex motive."

"Unless he was killed for resisting having sex," replied Garraty.

Lyman sighed. "It would have been convenient to have a little semen present, some very helpful pathological evidence to connect somebody to the kid at the time he died. Nothing like an incriminating blood test result to help make a case."

"Think of it as a challenge," smiled Garraty.

A little later, a second report came in: fingerprints. There were, said the report, lots of fingerprints, many of them matching the victim's prints, taken from the corpse. Most of the others remained unidentified. There was no fingerprint file on the victim in the F.B.I. files. "Never fingerprinted," muttered Lyman. "That's the trouble now that we don't have a military draft. Kids don't get fingerprinted the way they used to. Apparently, the late Larry Apperson never was arrested, either."

"So, we hit the streets," said Garraty.

"I don't fancy trudging all over this snow-covered town checking out all the names in that little book of his."

"No choice," sighed Garraty, picking up the typed list.

"What we need is a confession from a remorse-stricken perpetrator," said Lyman, putting on his coat and following Garraty out of the squad room. "God, just once, why can't it be easy?"

The Detective

In a plastic cube frame on his desk, Lyman kept snapshots of his wife and daughter, all of them taken in happy times at the beach.

Summers, he used to manage to get away for a little while to a house only two blocks from the water in a little coastal town in New Jersey. They could not have afforded the house on his pay as a cop, but his wife had come into a small inheritance that covered the whole cost of the bungalow. They had talked about renting it out except for the couple of weeks when he had his own vacation, but he preferred to give his little girl as much time outside the city as possible. Betty, too, benefitted from the sun and the sea air, returning each fall when their daughter had to go back to school, both of them blooming with health and refreshed spirits. He called them on the phone every night, to be linked with them, to hear what had happened to them that day, and then he was alone in the apartment, rattling around.

When he went to the beach he was able to let all concerns about his work, his pending cases, slip from his attention. He always had good partners, so his work was always in good hands. Like his girls, he blossomed at the beach, but he tired of it sooner than they and was always glad to be back at work.

After his daughter got married and moved away, he and his wife didn't go to the beach, and they sold the house, using most of the money to help their girl get on her feet. The rest had been tucked away for their retirement in Florida. Most of the nestegg went for his wife's funeral. His friends said he was being foolishly extravagant, but he didn't listen. Only Garraty figured out that Lyman spent all that money on the funeral because he felt guilty that the final years with his wife had not been happy ones.

It was his fault, Lyman feared.

He had spent too much time working.

They didn't have fights toward the end. Mostly, they were silent in each other's presence.

When he looked at the pictures in the plastic cube on his desk, he tried to remember only the good times.

A stack of paper almost obscured the cube frame as Lyman dropped heavily into his chair at his desk. He took his tape recorder from his pocket and changed the cassette, labeling the one which had recorded all his impressions, his interviews of witnesses in the apartment on Fifty-sixth Street. He pulled open a drawer and dropped the cassette in, until he could get to it to make out his report.

The squad room was filled with detectives. Phones were ringing, typewriters chattering, laughter bursting out now and then among little knots of policemen going about their office work. Brown and Hadley were not at their desks. They'd gone to court on a case they'd handled nearly a year ago, so their latest murder was taking a slide for a few hours.

Lyman looked at his watch. 11:30 A.M.

The watch had been off his wrist for only one long period of time—for repairs after it got doused with water in the Marines—since his father gave it to him as a graduation gift. "I wish I was giving a watch to a future district attorney," his father said, clasping his son's hands in his, "but I'll be happy to know that it's on the arm of the best damned policeman in the City of New York."

Later, as Lyman took courses in criminal law at John Jay College, his father's hopeful anticipation that he might still turn to law as a profession blossomed once more, never to flicker again as the young man slowly made a career for himself on the police force.

Untold seconds had ticked off on the watch, seconds that marked dreary hours on a beat, endless circulations in a prescribed territory in a patrol car, breathless hours in dangerous stakeouts in pursuit of dangerous men, boring days in courtrooms waiting for cases to be called.

But the watch had also clocked pleasant moments— summers at the beach, his daughter's birth and childhood, her maturing into a lovely young woman, the frantic hours before her wedding. Too, it ticked away the raucous, comradely afternoons at the end of duty tours with buddies in blue uniforms and, later, in mufti. Between high school and the police force, the watch marked the years when Sheldon Lyman was a United States Marine.

And hours had dragged during dark nights when he realized all the civility had gone from his marriage until, at last, the watch marked the countdown to his wife's last breath.

Looking at it telling him it was 11:30 A.M. and two hours since the first report of the suspicious death of Larry Apperson, Lyman had a thought about what an antique the watch was, a precision instrument made decades ago. "They don't make 'em like that anymore," Garraty had remarked when admiring the timepiece. An antique watch on an antique cop, Lyman thought, frowning at the thought.

Sometimes in the morning when he was getting dressed and eyeing himself in the mirror, seeing a cop no matter what he wore, he frowned at the paunch he had developed and wondered if he had ever been the slender, narrow-hipped, flat-bellied boy whom the Marine Corps assigned to be a guard at the U.S. Embassy in the eternal city of Rome. Sharp, spit-and-polish, and a credit to his country, his commander said of him then.

Nonetheless, he still was in pretty good shape. The doctors at his annual physical always told him he was in good condition for a man in his job and at his age. He would accept the news graciously but never without telling the examining doctor that he'd been *something* when he was a kid. "You know," he laughed, "there is nothing more beautiful than a beautiful Jewish boy at his prime, and I *was* beautiful. Hard as a rock and smooth as a whistle." To which the doctors replied with sage advice about staying in shape and watching out for the rich food, the cigarettes, the booze.

He wasn't eating as well since Betty died. Cigarettes were never a big thing with him. A couple a day when he was on a hard case or tense. At home, he liked a pipe. The booze was not an occupational disease with him the way it was with a lot of fellow cops.

The thought of food made him realize he was hungry. "Hey, Garraty. Want to get some lunch?"

"Great," smiled his ruddy-faced partner, rubbing his flat belly.

"We can stop on the way downtown."

Garraty knew what "we can stop" meant. A cheeseburger and coffee around the corner on Third Avenue. "How about we finally go to that health food place?" Garraty asked, reaching for his coat, knowing what Lyman would say.

"I ain't no rabbit!"

In the lobby on the way out, they glanced at a pair of uniformed officers booking a black dude. Pursesnatching. Lyman thought, even in the goddamned snow, the bastards are grabbing purses!

Garraty had a salad, and Lyman teased him about it. "You should get food that sticks to the ribs, boy!"

"Gotta watch my waistline," said Garraty, munching green leaves.

"Hell, you are so skinny you don't even have a waistline!"

Lyman smiled, enjoying watching Garraty bask in the compliment to his physical condition. Tough and hard and sleek. That was Terry Garraty. Big-boned and raw, like the Irishman he was. No one to tangle with in a fight. But just the guy to have backing you up in rough places. Important in a team whose senior partner wasn't as fast as he used to be.

It was Garraty's physical condition that swung the decision in his favor as Lyman weighed all the potential candidates when he had to pick a new partner. Lt. Parker had a list of suggestions from which he wanted Lyman to make the choice. "These are the comers in the Department," he had said, passing a bundle of file folders across his cluttered desk. "They're all bright, of course; all hot to be in Homicide. They all want to be partner to the legendary Shelly Lyman, but don't let that go to your head, Shelly." Parker's eyes twinkled and his rubbery face stretched into a grin.

"They've got quite a pair of shoes to fill," replied Lyman, referring to his most recent partner. "Eddie Brooks was something. A cop and a half."

"Which is why he's downtown now, up to his keester in the ebb and flow of headquarters politics. He's made for it. A few years and he'll be Chief of Detectives. A job a certain fellow could have gone for, you know."

"I never had the political ambition, Paul. You know that. I'm a case man."

"Take your time and let me know which of these fellows you think might be to your liking. Unless you have a candidate of your own?"

"Nope."

On paper, Garraty was almost unbelievable. Firearms, scores in physical tests, I.Q., psychological scores, performance evaluations—tops. And brave without being foolhardy. Citations. An award for valor in a tenement fire when he'd been the beat cop. Combat veteran in the Army, although, as a former Marine, Lyman might have preferred another ex-Leatherneck.

Before he spoke to Garraty at a police gym, he watched him at a punching bag, marveling at the grace, the quickness, the sureness, and seeing a bit of how *he'd* been just starting out. He remembered himself at summer camp, where all good New York Jewish boys went, and wondered if Garraty had been to summer camps, if Irish kids got sent away in summers like Jewish kids. His favorite camp had been in Pennsylvania's Pocono Mountains. Handsome, athletic, muscular, he had been a fine swimmer in the muddy brown stream that flowed through the camp. He and the boys swam naked, unashamed, uninhibited, lithe and sunwashed amid the flow of the brown water, the smell of high green grass. He swam when he could in the Marines, but when he came out of the service and into the Police Department in the heart of a city he turned to workouts in gyms, steam baths, and runs in Central park to keep him in shape.

Although he had been fit, he probably never had the keen edge that he saw in Garraty.

When Garraty finished his workout, Lyman crossed the gym floor, introduced himself, and asked to talk. They sat on a wooden bench in the sweaty, clammy closeness of the locker room, a smell that always took Lyman back to his high school days and camp, to the bruising, roughhousing, towel-snapping, kibbitzing-about-sex comraderie of those days. "How do you think we'd work out as a partnership?" he asked the red-haired Irishman whose face was dripping with sweat.

"Seems to me you're the guy to answer that question," Garraty replied, dabbing at beaded sweat on his chin.

"You handle yourself very well, Garraty."

"I work at it."

"I know. That's what gives you the edge. I like to know I've got a guy beside me who has a keen edge."

The paperwork took two weeks to make them a team.

Leaving the coffee shop after lunch, still being bombarded by surprising flashes of remembrance, aware of Garraty striding beside him, heading for their car and their afternoon's work on their new case, Lyman asked, "Terry, have you ever regretted switching from a uniform to plainclothes?"

Garraty stopped short, amazed. "Hell no!"

They walked on. "It's funny to me, and always was, to know that a lot of what attracts us to coming into the Department is that damned blue uniform with its silver badge. I mean, the authority it represents! The way it says that we're on the side of right, the side of the angels. Yet before long we're wanting to put aside the blues and get into street clothes, to hide our identity. It's funny, isn't it?"

"I never thought about it that way."

"I have. Lots," Lyman said, opening the door on his side of their car and sliding in.

He remembered his pride in being a Marine, in finally having the right after the hell of boot camp to wear the most impressive of all American military uniforms. He remembered—felt again, down his back—the chill that surged along his spine the day he stepped off in dress uniform to march in a final review at Parris Island while the band played "Halls of Montezuma." Later, he was thrilled to wear a dress uniform on sentry duty at the gates of the Embassy in Rome and to wear it in the streets of Rome, proudly, affectionately at a time when it was something to be proud of if you were seen in an

American uniform. "I wouldn't wear a uniform out on the street," one of his buddies complained, "'cause when these Italians see you, especially the kids, they're after you all the time for money." Lyman didn't mind at all about that, and the first time it happened, he was even a little proud.

Scalinata di Trinita del Monti.

The Spanish Steps were banked with flowers. The air was freshly scrubbed by a spring shower and the plaza which had been abandoned during the rain was bustling with people again. Lyman, who had ducked under an awning, emerged into the sun, his dress uniform resplendent in the brightness. He paused by the still-wet low wall edging the eliptical Barcaccia Fountain in the center of the street at the bottom of the Spanish Steps and looked up the famous stairway at the riotous flowers flowing like waterfalls down the steps. Tourists wanting to go up to the church at the top of the hillside had to step around young Romans who had left only a narrow pathway up from the *Piazza di Spagna* to the twin-towered church above it.

A boy who could not have been more than twelve had been standing under a vendor's umbrella during the rain, at the bottom of the steps, and Lyman knew the boy had been watching him, admiring the uniform. Black hair tumbled over the boy's forehead. Dark eyes peered from under the shadow of the forelock, and the sun cast a shadow of the boy's wide straight nose across full lips, which stretched in a smile when Lyman looked his way. The boy wore a pale-blue short-sleeved shirt open at the neck and darker blue short pants. He followed Lyman as Lyman went up the steps, pausing half-way at the landing to look back on the scene below. Finally, the boy came up beside him to look up at him, smiling.

"*Ciao*," Lyman smiled.

"*Ciao*," the boy replied. "American?"

"Yes. *Si*."

"Soldier?"

"Marine."

"I speak English. We learn in school."

"You speak very well."

"You want to come with me? I show you sights."

"No. *Grazie.*"

"I very good boy for you."

"*Grazie.* No."

The boy turned and ran.

Surprised, Lyman wondered why the boy didn't ask for a handout, as he'd expected.

"The boy thought you wanted him."

Turning, Lyman looked into the broad, bearded face of a man. "I beg your pardon?"

"The boy thought you were looking for a boy. For, uh, a little fun."

Shocked, Lyman turned away and ran up the stairs to the famous church.

Months later, passing by the Spanish Steps on his way toward the Embassy, he spotted the boy again, at a distance, chatting amiably with a man and then walking jauntily away with him, disappearing into the crowds.

Lyman had been eighteen years old at the time and had been around, but it was the first time he ever knew about young boys selling themselves to men for sex.

"Have you ever been to Rome, Terry?" Lyman asked as Garraty edged the car from the curb toward the middle of Fifty-first Street.

"Once on a tour." Garraty eyed the traffic and waited to let a Hertz rental truck slide past before he took their car all the way out of the parking space. Safely maneuvered out but waiting in the backed-up traffic, he looked sideways at Lyman. "You certainly are in a reflective mood all of a sudden."

"Am I?"

"You haven't been yourself, Shel. You know it. you ought to take some leave time. Get a good rest. I know cops who've had breakdowns."

In the silence as they waited for the traffic to move, Lyman wondered why he was thinking so much about the past. He decided it was the death of this kid—this Larry Apperson—which made him remember. Death was more and more a reason for looking back the closer one got to one's own end. Since Betty died he was more inclined to ponder his own mortality.

Hell, he thought as the car hopped forward a bit, under the right circumstances Sheldon Lyman could have wound up dead while just a kid. Survival was largely a matter of lucky breaks.

While the traffic light stopped them at the corner of Fifty-first and Lexington, Lyman jumped out of the car to buy a newspaper. The headline on the front page of the *Post* consisted of one word:

SNOW!

"Well we're not the main story in town after all," he smiled, showing Garraty the headline. The story of the murder was on page three:

'GAY' CLUBBED
TO DEATH: COPS

by
Richard Donnelly

The nude and battered body of a young man was found in the bathtub of his upper eastside apartment, apparently clubbed to death in a savage murder with gruesome homosexual overtones. The victim, Lawrence Apperson, age about 23, was found by a friend and a next door neighbor, William Weinstein.

Disgustedly, Lyman tossed aside the paper. "I can imagine the rest of it."

"Is your name in the article?"

Garraty was being cute, trying to apologize for the remark about breakdowns. Lyman wrinkled his nose in disgust over the newspaper. "The son of a bitch would probably get the spelling wrong. You know what's going to happen now? Because of that headline all the gay groups from Harlem to Bowling Green are going to be yelling, demanding to know what we're doing to solve the murder of one of their own." He stared out the window at men working to clean the snow from the pavements in front of the Lexington Avenue entrance to the Waldorf Astoria hotel. "Once the protests get going, then Donnelly and his kind will make it into a bigger story, one they can blow up beyond all proportion. God, anything to sell a newspaper!"

"Maybe publicity will help. Somebody might read about the murder and come froward."

Lyman turned with a look of utter disbelief.

Garraty shrugged. "It's happened before."

"Be serious, Terry."

"Okay, if I can't cheer you up by looking on the positive side, how's this? Right after we get back from where we're going—where are we going?"

"To talk to a creep by the name of Neal Davis. From Lawrence Apperson's little address book."

"Well, right after we interview Mr. Davis, we'll drive down to South Street, to the offices of *The New York Post*, and I will personally kick Richard Donnelly in the balls. How about that?"

"Love it! I just love it!" Lyman laughed.

Garraty felt good, getting a laugh from his partner. The trouble with Lyman was, lately, he didn't laugh enough.

Lyman studied the streets, squinting into the glare as the sun broke through the clouds. "Maybe we should take Forty-second over to Broadway and go downtown that way. Broadway should be plowed pretty well."

"Where's this dude live?"

"Greenwich, in the Village, near Seventh Avenue."

"The heart of 'gay city,'" sneered Garraty, turning into Forty-second Street and heading west. "Why did you say this Davis fellow is a creep? You know him?"

"He's a pimp. I know him. From 'way back."

"Listen, Lyman, do you know *everyone* in this city?"

"Of course. The pimps, the hookers, the dopers, the dealers, the bandits, the muggers, the ripoff artists, the rapers and the rapacious, the godfathers, the capos, the soldiers, *and* the porno purveyors, the strippers, the con men, the bunkos, the burglars, and the bad guys with the white collars and ties who get away with a hell of a lot more than the common crooks. You name 'em, I know 'em. You might even say they're family." He looked at Garraty and grinned.

"You love it, don't you?"

"I surely do, Terry. I surely, surely do."

You had to love it. It had to mean more to you than anything in the world—more than family, more than money, more than comfort. You had to want to carry a shield the way a Catholic boy with the call wanted to be a priest or the way a Jewish boy felt the tugging of the study of the Torah and became a rabbi. You had to have a zeal for it. You had to have a fervor for the feel of crime the way Brown had a fervor for the cold-blue-oiled feel of handguns; the feel of the fit of a uniform, the feel of a .38 calibre Special holstered on the hip or draped across the shoulder, the hug of a bullet-proof vest under the uniform, the burning of the sidewalks under your feet or the sagging of the seat of a patrol car beneath your butt. You had to want it all—the sensations, the thrills, the boredom, the closeness of working with a trusted partner. You had to feel a deep sense of outrage over the bad things that happened and that only a cop could try to do something about. You had to have a capacity for the anger that Mike Brown had shown when he beat up a child molester, but you had to temper it with a joy in, a trust of, and a dedication to the law, to justice, to doing the right thing. You had to believe, with all your heart, in good over evil, in the good guys besting the bad ones. You had to want to be an arm of the law and to love being it. You had to have a deep-seated, burning, passionate commitment, at your core, to finding out who it was who picked up a ten pound dumbbell and smashed it into the face of a beautiful young man and then left him to rot without even looking back.

Sheldon Irving Lyman wanted it, needed it, worked for it since he was a kid, long before he fully understood that upholding and protecting the law was a policeman's prime duty, long before he learned about Miranda decisions and the rights of the accused, long before he realized that hard policework could go down the tubes through plea bargaining, long before he understood that maybe it was okay to put a bad guy away for a lesser crime simply because it was the easiest and surest way of getting him off the streets.

His father had been disappointed, having hoped that his son would be a professional man. "If the law appeals to you, then why not think about law school, Sheldon?" His son's appreciation for and apparent dedication to the rule of law was an admirable thing, but being a policeman, at the very bottom of the legal apparatus, seemed a low road for a smart boy who could, if he applied himself, be a district attorney. The boy couldn't explain it—the difference between being a district attorney and a cop—except that, maybe, it was like wanting to be the farmer instead of the grocer. To the day his father died, Sheldon had not been able to explain it to his father. His mother, rest her immortal soul, was easier. She had wanted whatever her son wanted. His wife and daughter had accepted what he was. It was a given factor, and they accepted the worry, the absences, the weariness. It was what their man did, and that was that, and if they had ever asked him to choose, they knew what choice he would have made.

Going was slow down Broadway as Garraty swung their car into a single line of traffic at Times Square. Parked and stalled cars on both sides of the streets had made it impossible for the Sanitation Department to get their plows up to the curbs. Trucks heading for the garment district, buses going south, taxis, and a handful of private cars with spinning tires and racing engines trying to find traction in the ice and snow, clogged Broadway.

Lyman dug into his pocket and brought out the Polaroid snapshot of Lawrence Apperson naked beside his erotic portrait. The photo was intended to be lewd, pornographic, an erotic souvenir for Lawrence Apperson's new lover, Ellis Marsh, yet as Lyman studied the photo he discovered a quality of innocence, which the camera had caught in both the boy and the painting. Lyman wondered at how that quality in both photo and painting had dulled the edge of lasciviousness. He would not have said that boy and portrait embodied purity but, surely, each revealed a sense of not being spoiled.

Possibly, Lyman thought, it was the fact that the boy had

been the victim of a brutal crime that made him seem in photo and portrait so vulnerable, innocent, touchable and fragile, despite the shockingly impudent and daring nature of his pose—the hard nakedness of his sexual arousal. Curiously, it was not the explicit sexuality which finally held one's attention to photo and portrait, but the boy's face, the impish smile, a clear-eyed amusement, the shock of unruly yellow hair, the All-American-Boy quality of the kid next door. All over America there were thousands of kids just like him in looks and appeal. That this handsome youngster had died a lonely and brutal death in life's midstream was the obscenity, not the boy's nakedness. More than a crime, his death was a sin. It was a sin to take away a life that young. Despite what he knew about the boy's past, despite that he knew the boy had traded on his youth, Lyman felt terribly angry and overflowing with a need to discover who did this to Lawrence Apperson. Not just because it was his job. Not just because being a cop was what he had wanted to do, needed to do, for all the compelling motivations which he had never been able to explain to his father, but because someone had to do something to even the score.

Simple as that.

Somebody had to even the score for Larry Apperson.

Which is what he should have said to his father, something Old Testament in its simplicity. "Pop, I want to be a policeman because I believe with all my heart in evening the score. An eye for an eye. That's what your son is all about, Pop."

"My son, the hero!"

Samuel Lyman did not live to see his son a hero, standing up there while the Mayor of the City of New York and the Police Commissioner gave out certificates and hung medals with ribbons around the necks of the cops who had, the previous year, shown conspicuous valor in the line of duty, above and beyond the call. In a commanding and proud voice, the Commissioner read Lyman's citation while Lyman looked down from the platform at his wife and child in the front row, beaming with pride and shunting aside their memories of the fear they had felt on the day he earned his citation. "Police Officer Sheldon Lyman," intoned the Commissioner. "in a demonstration of the highest traditions of the Department and the highest purposes of mankind, risked his own life to save that of another Officer . . ."

Another Officer? Lyman thought. My *partner*! Lying there in the street, shot, and the man who shot him holding out in a store across the street, still firing his weapon! I did what my partner would have done for me!

It had been a botched robbery of a grocery store on One-hundred-tenth Street in Harlem. Lyman and his partner, Barney Emery, had been a block away in their car. Passing the store, Emery had looked in the window and seen the man with the gun. "Stop!" he shouted. "That dude's stickin' the place up." A moment later Barney Emery was dashing from the car and across the street. The robber came out, froze when he saw Emery running toward him, and fired. Emery dropped in the street. "Ten-thirteen!" Lyman called over the radio. "All cars stay off this frequency!" responded the voice in communications. "We have a ten-thirteen." Lyman sent the call: "Officer shot. Need assistance." And the address. Seconds later the help came, cars screeching to a halt and cops pouring out of them, as Lyman stretched out on the street, his body shielding his wounded, groaning partner. Two minutes later it was over as the perpetrator surrendered. "Hey," grinned Emery later in the hospital. "That was a nice thing you did for me. Why'd you do that?" Lyman shrugged. "Seemed the right thing. Besides, you horse's ass, didn't you know that I love you?"

Which was meant as a joke, but it wasn't a joke. They both knew what Lyman was saying. They were bonded, as all policemen are bonded to their partners, to their squad, their division, to their whole Department.

"Male bonding," said the psychologists in studying the habits of men; "The drawing together of males in our modern society is an echo of the hunting-bonding of primaeval men. The clubs, the fraternities, the military, the police—all-male societies are founded on that ancient bonding. Male-to-male. The pair. The team. The partnership."

Barney Emery came to the funeral of Sheldon Lyman's wife, throwing his arms around his former partner and crying like a baby over his partner's loss.

Love. Cop for cop. Partner for partner. Man for man. Marine for Marine. Boy-at-camp for boy-at-camp.

He considered Larry Apperson, a boy available for men to love and a boy who could and did love other boys, and he wondered why Larry Apperson had locked in on that kind of love, apparently, to the exclusion of the love of women. What had happened to fix him in that choice? Had he had a choice? Or was his homosexuality something ordained?

Could Sheldon Lyman at any point in his life have become a Larry Apperson?

Staring out the car window, he wondered, and as he wondered he recalled the boys and men of his life with whom he had been close; pals and partners and buddies with whom he might have crossed that invisible line between straight and gay, if those terms meant anything. What if he had followed that boy on the Spanish Steps in Rome? He had a friend in junior high school named Jim, a fair-haired, happy kid who loved gymnastics and who had the sleek, finely-chiseled physique of a superb athlete. In high school, it was his closest friend, Henry, with whom he was always trading punches on the arm of slaps on the ass. In the Marines he'd gone out drinking with dozens of guys, but his best buddy was a funny, drawling kid from Atlanta with whom he had shared a pup tent on bivouac and a double bed sleeping-off an all-night toot on pass from Camp Lejeune.

Of all, the closest he could recall coming to crossing the line with had been Jim. They were thirteen and he was staying the night at Jim's house because Jim had invited him. They'd sat in the kitchen of the house, bullshitting, talking about school, and when time came to go to bed they had glasses of milk before trudging upstairs. He undressed to his shorts but Jim went all the way, telling him he liked to sleep in the nude, if that was okay. Sure, he said to Jim, not knowing what else to say because he was Jim's guest after all. Naked, Jim was a symphony of grace, golden brown except for a narrow band of white around his hips. At the center of the white was a thicket of blond hair around Jim's heavy sex. Jim sat on the bed, turned and stretched out, pulling the covers up to his chest. Much later, when Jim thought his friend was asleep, although he was only lying there with his eyes closed and pretending, Jim eased the covers down. Then Jim turned onto his side, and he felt Jim near him, knew Jim was looking at him, and although he wished it would not happen, he felt himself getting hard in his shorts. Still not opening his eyes, he was hardly able to breathe, not sure of what might happen next, not knowing exactly what could happen. Then he felt a movement—a steady, easy movement, and in the darkness behind his closed eyes he knew that Jim was masturbating, all the while looking at the boy beside him.

They were stuck in traffic. At Herald Square, Garraty hung a right off Broadway by Macy's to get over to Seventh Avenue, but Thirty-fourth Street was as big a mess as Broadway. Frustrated, he drummed his fingers on the steering wheel and gave Lyman a sideways look as if daring his partner to make a joke about his driving, but Lyman was lost in thought, his chin pinched between his thumb and finger, his eyes looking toward but not seeing the people in front of Macy's determined to go shopping even in the aftermath of eighteen inches of snow.

Garraty concentrated on the clogged street and inched their car forward, content to leave Lyman with whatever it was he was thinking about. In due course, if Lyman wanted to talk about something, he did it, whether it was something about a case that was bothering him or something personal. It did no good to try to pry something out of him. Garraty had learned that lesson fast enough in the period when Lyman's marriage was falling apart, then later when his wife's life was ebbing. In both instances, eventually, Lyman opened up.

Whatever held his attention—the new case or something personal—Garraty was content to leave his partner to his thoughts.

A red light stopped them at Seventh Avenue and Greenwich, and Lyman looked across the intersection. Halfway down the block was Neal Davis's address. That Davis would choose to live on Greenwich was hardly a surprise. David would want to be close to the action, the very center of much of the life style from which he made a living.

Lyman gazed down Greenwich, a cruising street. His hands were jammed into his overcoat pockets, his eyes sweeping the long stretch of the street running at an angle between Sixth and Seventh Avenues. Where it met Sixth it also converged with Eighth Street, forming the closest thing the Village had to uptown's Times Square. At the busy crossroads were a subway and a conglomeration of newsstands, cafes, a Kentucky Fried Chicken, a produce store, flower stalls, banks, a Nathan's Famous hot dog place, shops, and a drug store. "Drive down there," Lyman said to Garraty, touching him at the elbow and nodding toward Greenwich. Deserted in the snow, in spring and summer and on crisp autumn days the sidewalks would be crowded with ambling youth—gay youth, strolling, meeting, laughing, gossiping, cruising, looking. At the corner of Greenwich and Christopher Street, they parked. "Up there," Lyman said, nodding to their right into narrow Christopher Street, "is where the gays had their famous Stonewall riot. Remember it?" Lyman got out and Garraty followed.

Garraty nodded. "Yeah, but I was in the Bronx then. Just a rookie."

"I was detailed to Sex Crimes then. It was at the time of the Mansfield case. So I wasn't personally involved in the riot either, but I had some close friends in the Intelligence Division, and they were really red-faced about it. 'Who would have thought,' my friends in Intelligence asked, 'that a bunch of homosexuals would actually turn on the police and set off an honest-to-God riot?' It started routinely. A raid on the Stonewall. The joint's not there anymore, but it's an historic spot to the gays, as historic to them as the bridge in Selma, Alabama, is to the blacks. The Gay Lib movement was born there."

They walked into Christopher Street's snows, following a path made by trampling feet. "All the way at the end of this street, over by the Hudson, are the trucks and docks and waterfront gay bars. Between here and there is a big part of New York's gay scene. Pickups and one-night stands, long-lasting relationships that are just like straight marriages. And, of course, brutality and murder. In short, along this street and others that chiefly belong to gays, you'll find every human emotion, every human failing, every human tragedy. I never cease to be amazed, Terry, what people will do to each other, gay or straight. I imagine Larry Apperson walked this street a lot." They stopped again, at the place where the Stonewall had been. "Not exactly Concord Bridge, eh?" he asked, smiling. They turned back to their car and drove away, circling through Village streets again until they were at a red light once more at Greenwich and Seventh.

Homicides brought him into the gay world from time to time, but not as much as his work in the Sex Crimes Unit had brought him into contact with New York's homosexuals. In Vice, he had spent a lot of hours among homosexuals, but the atmosphere had changed considerably in ensuing years. Then, homosexuals had been largely hidden, except for flagrant, attention-seeking freaks. There had been no gay movie theatres, gay strip joints, blatant hardcore gay sex books and magazines openly sold when Lyman first worked Vice. There had been only a handful of gay bars.

Since the Stonewall riot, the tide had been running away from the old ways of fear and secrecy and intimidation. The homosexuals began referring to the Stonewall event as the "Stonewall Rebellion," which was marked each year on June 28, the date of the 1969 riot, by marches, each one growing larger, until the police could count on paraders in the tens of thousands moving out of the Village, up Fifth of Sixth Avenues to Central Park for a vast celebration of the event, of their changed lives, of being gay. Public personalities constantly admitted to their natures—even one man in the New York City government.

Lyman found a change in attitudes in his work when he had moved to the detective squads attached to the Seventeenth Precinct, an area that encompassed Manhattan's so-called Silk Stocking District—rich, white, liberal—in the east Sixties and Seventies, an area which had sent John Lindsay and Edward Koch to Congress.

Lyman knew the tide was turning when he handled the case of Steven John Edwards, a young punk who'd been arrested dozens of times on petty charges, including male prostitution. Edwards had attempted extortion against a man named Vincent Doyle, a businessman who happened to be homosexual and who happened to have picked up Edwards a year earlier. When Edwards surfaced on the telephone demanding money, Doyle called the police. "We'll meet him," Lyman assured Doyle.

The arrest was made by Lyman and his partner, Dennis

Conlon, at the corner of Seventy-eighth and First. "That faggot's the one you should be busting!" Edwards screamed as Conlon snapped handcuffs on him.

"Just because a guy likes to suck a cock now and then is no excuse for what you tried to do, creep. Shut up!" Conlon replied, pushing Edwards into the back of their car.

Turning to Doyle, Lyman pleaded, "Mr. Doyle, we've got a good case here. Please don't drop the charges."

Doyle registered a look of utter surprise at the question. "Drop the charges? Why?"

Lyman smiled. "A lot of men would never have had the guts to come to us about a case like this, and some who have, eventually thought about it and backed out."

Doyle shook his head. "Not me! Nobody blackmails me, and if putting that sonofabitch in jail means I get known as a homosexual, well, then I won't have to lie anymore."

Edwards got five years. No one cared about a case of simple attempted extortion, least of all reporters, and Vincent Doyle never had his private sexual orientation made public beyond a courtroom.

As the light changed, Lyman was smiling. "Private joke or may I share in it?" Garraty asked as he nursed their car toward a corner parking spot.

"No joke," said Lyman. "I was just thinking about an old case. A gutsy man who wouldn't let himself be pushed around."

The Tapes

1.

Lyman selected Neal Davis from the list of names in Larry Apperson's address book because Lyman knew about Neal Davis. He had not been surprised to find Davis's name in the book, but he was disappointed. Despite the word of neighbor Weinstein that Larry Apperson had been suspected of being a male prostitute, Lyman had hoped—yes, he thought, *hoped*; that was the word—that the speculation about the dead boy's being a hustler had been wrong. Neal Davis's name went a long way to shatter the hope.

Lyman had first encountered Neal Davis when Lyman had been partnered with Mike Brown in Sex Crimes and when they had been assigned to special duty with what was then called the Vice Squad, captained by Elliot Morgan, a big Welshman who had organized and run the Department's world-famous Men's Welsh Choir. Morgan had the look and zeal of a preacher, and he approached his command of Vice with a fire-and-brimstone dedication that Brown admired but Lyman worried about. Morgan had been the commander of the special task force of detectives put together by the Major Case Division to handle the Mansfield kidanpping. Later, Neal Davis had figured in Vice's penetration of and crack-down on a child prostitution ring operating in midtown. At that time, long before the sensational hearings into child prostitution by a Senate Subcommittee to Investigate Juvenile Delinquency, chaired by Senator Birch Bayh of Indiana, child prostitution was almost unheard of by most Americans. Neal Davis had been suspected of running a "child pros" operation for the benefit of rich New York men but no one had ever been able to get any evidence to convict him. That Neal Davis trafficked in adult male prostitutes was no secret. He had been arrested for it, although he served only one light jail term. In the investigation of the Davis case, impulsive Mike Brown had flown off the handle during the questioning of Davis in the booth at the back of a Times square coffee shop. "You are really scum," Brown growled, clutching Davis's collar and shaking him so hard that his head wagged back and forth violently. Then, Brown slugged Davis, sending him sprawling to the floor. Getting up and rubbing his cracked and bleeding lip, Davis managed a smile. "Will that be all, gentlemen?" Ten years later, Davis was still pandering, and here was Lyman with a different partner heading for another conversation with Davis. The difference was, this one would take place in Neal Davis's penthouse apartment.

Garraty pulled the car as close to the curb as possible near the corner of Seventh Avenue and Greenwich. They had to walk around a pile of snow left by the plows. Much of the pavement had been shoveled and salted.

The lobby of the apartment house was massive, grand in the style of the highrise luxury apartment boom of the Sixties. The doorman was startled by the appearance of detectives' shields in his lobby. As far as he knew, he said, Mr. Davis was at home and no, he would not be foolish enough to buzz Mr. Davis to tell him a couple of cops were on the way up.

Whether the doorman lied about his intentions and warned Davis that the police were on their way up or Davis was just naturally controlled and cool in any possibly-threatening circumstance, Lyman couldn't know, but the Neal Davis who opened the door for him and Garraty acted like a man who had been expecting this visit from the cops. "Long time, no see," he said to Lyman with a smile.

"This is my partner, Detective Garraty," Lyman said, stepping into the elegant apartment. "I suppose you've seen the paper and know why we're here."

"I don't know anything about Larry's death, and I'm not sure I should talk about it or him without my lawyer present."

"We're just checking out the names in Larry's address book," Lyman said, sinking into a wonderfully soft chair. "You can surely have a lawyer but then we'd have to have this little chat uptown, and that would be a hassle for all of us, hm?"

"I'm always happy to cooperate with the police," Neal Davis shrugged.

He was a ruin of his former self, Lyman noted, although he was obviously working hard to keep his looks, which once had been good enough for the movies or magazine covers. Those young years and young looks had worked for Neal Davis, who never had qualms about selling his favors. Later, when his bloom was fading, he got into the business of selling others' favors. Lyman studied what looked like a hairpiece, although a good one. The tan was leathery, but it set off his pale blue eyes which were still vibrantly piercing. Those eyes were assessing the police officers with the skill of a man who has been fencing with police all his life. "Larry worked for me, if that is what you've come to ask."

"Recently?" asked Lyman.

"Yes."

"How recently?"

"Last week, as a matter of fact, although that was the first time in over a year. A special customer from the Coast had come to town. He'd known Larry previously, and he was keen on seeing Larry again."

"I'll need the name," said Lyman.

Neal Davis winced. "Must you have it? This is a very important name on the Coast."

"I must."

"Nelson Royce."

Garraty whistled faintly through his teeth. Lyman shot a disapproving look. "When did Royce and Larry see each other?"

"Last Wednesday, I believe."

"Where did they meet? Here?"

"No one meets here."

"Where, then?"

"At the Plaza."

"Is Royce still in town?"

"Yes. He's making a film here, but if you think Royce would have had anything to do with Larry's death, why, that is preposterous."

"Why?"

"They were very fond of each other."

"Royce is the only one of your customers whom Larry has seen lately?"

"As far as I know."

"How did Larry get along with your clients when he worked for you?"

"Larry was probably the most popular and successful boy who ever was on my rolls."

"Why was that?"

"First of all, he was the most beautiful young man I had ever known, not just physically, although certainly in that category. But Larry had a quality of character. Style. *Élan.* Know what I mean?"

"I guess so."

"A gentleman. No rough edges. He fit in places like the Plaza or the Pierre. He was absolutely dazzling in a tux, and believe me, eyes turned to look at him when he came down the aisle on a Broadway opening night. I can't imagine why anyone would want to kill him. All the people who knew Larry adored him and wanted to love him."

"Well, somebody killed him."

"Not one of my clients. Trust me."

"How did you get along with him?"

"Famously. He was my star."

"And when he left you?"

"I was crushed."

"Bitter? Resentful?"

"Oh, you do have a policeman's mind."

"You said he was your star."

"Mr. Lyman, I have been in the business a long time. I've had stars come and go. True, Larry was the most extraordinary boy I'd ever encountered in this business, but I fully understood and supported him when he came and told me that he had a chance to build a future. Not many of the boys who work for me ever think about the future. That is their greatest flaw and their ultimate tragedy. But Larry had his eye on the future. He knew that beauty was transient, that one day the Royces and the others who were mad for him would discover someone younger and drop him. Larry was determined to head that eventuality off. He'd been hustling nearly ten years. That's a long time and he knew it couldn't go on much longer.

"He was getting into acting, and I must tell you, because you are probably a very cynical policeman, that he had real talent for the stage. He did a show last year. Wonderful in it. It was extraordinary, too, because he kept his clothes on. I don't know how much you know about the theater, but many directors find it impossible to resist the urge to have a stunningly handsome boy such as Larry step on stage without showing off his muscles. Larry was a hit in that play on the basis of his acting, not his physique."

"Did you encourage him in his plan to give up the business, as you call it, and go. . . ."

"Straight," said Neal Davis, smiling and arching his brows.

"Legitimate, let's say."

"Oh, I can't lie to you. The day Larry said he was going

to give up working for me I was upset, but we had a long talk and I saw how earnest he was, how serious, how committed, so I couldn't stand in his way. Quite a few very prominent men in this town were very disappointed, however."

"The only time you called him up and asked him to work for you again was last week when Mr. Royce came to town."

"Yes."

"And Larry agreed, readily?"

"I confess that it took some persuading, but I have a feeling that Larry was a little hard up for cash. Necessity was probably more persuasive than I."

"How much did Larry earn that night?"

"I didn't ask."

"You mean you didn't get a cut?"

"I simply brought the two of them together for old time's sake."

"That's very generous of you, Mr. Davis," said Garraty.

"Money isn't everything, you know."

"It would seem to me that boys who work for you, meeting prominent men who wish to be very discreet, have an opportunity for. . . ."

"Blackmail?"

"Yes."

"It has never happened with one of my boys."

"Never?" asked Garraty, leaning forward in his chair.

"Never."

"How would you know?" Garraty asked.

"I assure you, gentlemen, if one of my boys tried to put the squeeze on one of my clients, I would hear about it immediately."

"Pardon me if I have some doubts about that," replied Garraty, leaning back again.

"In any event, if your investigation assumes that Larry Apperson was a blackmailer, you are off base completely."

"Why?" asked Lyman.

"It would be out of character. I am a great believer in character, gentlemen, and Larry was not the type to resort to something as loathsome as blackmail. Larry was making a very handsome living and had no need to threaten people for money. There were armies of men who were standing in line to give him money."

"That was a year ago. He hasn't worked for you since, except last week with Mr. Royce."

"Yes."

"A year's a long time to be out of work."

"You are wrong if you think of Larry as a blackmailer."

"What was he, then?" asked Lyman.

"He was," said Neal Davis, his eyes drifting toward the windows, "the most wonderful boy I ever knew."

"What was Larry's opinion of you?" asked Garraty.

"Favorable, I believe."

"Larry got along with you pretty well?" Garraty asked.

"Larry got along with everyone."

"A plus in his business," Lyman said.

"Not all boys have the knack for being nice. It did not have to be an act for Larry."

"Do you happen to know how he got started hustling?" Garraty asked.

"He was a runaway. You've heard hundreds of stories like his. He came to New York from Pennsylvania when he was thirteen. He met—was met by, is a better way to put it— Donny Wills. You know him, Lyman."

" 'Chicken' Wills," Lyman nodded.

"Wills spotted Larry as soon as he got off the bus, made friends with him, got his confidence, and turned Larry on to the business, although from a few things Larry said I have an inkling that Larry had known about hustling before he came to New York. I suspect that's why he came here. I believe that back in that little town in Pennsylvania Larry had a couple of men on the string. Larry was always wise beyond his years. If he was not getting blown and banged regularly before he hit New York I'd be surprised."

"How long did Larry work for Wills?" Garraty asked.

"I have no idea, but I suspect, not long. Larry would have been shrewd enough to get something going on his own with the better clients that Wills introduced him to."

"Did he do that to you?" Lyman asked.

"He did, yes, but that would be no reason for me to want to get even by killing the boy. Really, Lyman! Give me a break." He flashed a smile, just to keep the interview civil. He knew some cops who got physical, and he had qualms about Garraty. Lyman, he knew, would never hit an uncooperative interviewee.

"Where were you Thursday night?" Garraty asked.

"Here," smiled Neal Davis. "I was making a number of long distance calls, all of which you can verify, of course."

"Did he ever mention to you that he was writing a book about his life?" asked Lyman.

"No!" gasped Neal Davis, his eyes alight, a hand pressed to his lips. "Was he writing one? A scandalous 'Kiss-and-tell' book?"

"His friend Lonnie said he was, although we haven't found any manuscript."

"Oh, I would love to read that little tome!"

"Why?"

"Well, first of all to see what he said about me! Then to see what he said about everyone else. Oh, Mr. Lyman, Mr. Garraty, that book would be a best-seller. Believe me."

"You don't know if he was actually working on one?"

"No, I don't, but *there* would be a motive for murder, eh?"

"Possibly," nodded Lyman.

"Why, it's just like one of those TV movies!" sighed Neal Davis, his hands dropping to his lap.

"In your professional relationship with Larry, would he have confided in you about his clients?" asked Lyman.

"Oh, yes. It was absolutely necessary. I had to know what a man liked, what he did for sex. It is vital for me to know so that I can be sure that I make the proper connections between my clients and my escorts."

"So you had to know your boys pretty well."

"Certainly. I conducted lengthy interviews before I put a boy to work."

"Tell us about Larry."

"His life story?"

"Whatever you can tell us about him."

THE NEAL DAVIS TAPE

We met at a restaurant and bar called 'Charlie's Aunt,' on Third Avenue. Larry came in late on a Tuesday evening, which was always a busy time at 'Charlie's Aunt,' and it was as if a movie star had come in. All eyes turned, and there was a silence in the place such as has never been heard since. It was summer, and a very warm night, and he was wearing a pale blue golf shirt with short sleeves and a V at the neck. The blue accented his suntan. He wore faded jeans and his feet were bare in a pair of jogging shoes. The clothes were ordinary and worn, but you would have thought he had just come from modeling them for Yves St. Laurent or Calvin Klein. The boy could have worn anything and made the clothes beautiful just by being on him. I watched him from the bar, expecting this vision to be immediately surrounded, but no one approached him, and he drifted over to the bar, near me, alone. I suppose everyone was just too stunned, too awed by the sight of him, to even think about speaking to him. He ordered a plain soda water from the bartender. Finally overcoming my own astonishment, I spoke. 'You certainly won't get very high on soda.'

'Don't care much for whiskey and beer makes me pee.'

I laughed, and he smiled, and the ice was broken.

'You're new in town?' I asked.

'I've been around.'

'I've never seen you here before.'

'I guess we were just here at different times.'

'My name is Neal Davis.'

'Larry Apperson.'

'What do you do, Larry?'

'Well, you certainly are direct.'

'I don't mean what do you do in bed. What do you do?'

'I just get by.'

'Tell me to mind my own business, if you like, but do you have a special friend who . . . ?'

'Keeps me?'

'You're the direct one, Larry.'

'Not at the moment. Once, I had a special friend. And what do you do?'

'I run a business. An escort service.'

'Ah!'

'I wish I knew what that 'Ah!' meant.'

'Just 'Ah!''

'Not a disapproving 'Ah!'?'

'Not at all.'

'I probably, in the interest of good business, should ask you if you'd like to come to work for me, but what I really want to ask you is if you'll just come home with me.'

'Sure.'

The envy in that bar was tangible as Larry and I walked out. If looks were daggers I'd have been a dead a thousand times. Larry was aware of the stares, there was nothing unusual about that. I had never known a boy or man—straight or gay—who did not know it when he was admired for his beauty. Oh, I suppose out in the vast framlands of the middle west there are thousands of boys who are Adonis personified and don't know it, but in the big cities, especially in New York, when a boy knows he's goodlooking, he cultivates it. My God, Bloomingdale's would be out of business if it weren't for the boys of New York who know they are beauties. Larry Apperson was breathtakingly handsome and he was conscious of it. He started hustling when he was thirteen. He knew then he was special and had what men would pay for.

When we went to my apartment and he stretched out on my bed, he seemed supremely cognizant of the fact that he was young, beautiful, wanted and needed. He was splendid! Clear, smooth, taut skin. Unblemished. As Abraham's son must have been. As Jesus must have been in his youth. I almost wept as I laid down beside him to make love to him.

Of course, I fell madly in love with him.

I never knew anyone who knew Larry who did not fall in love with him.

My love for him presented an immediate dilemma because he told me the next morning that if I thought he could make some money by joining my escort service he would like to, very much. 'No, no,' I wanted to cry out. 'Don't do that to yourself, Larry. Just be free and untainted and loved.' But love alone will not sustain anyone in New York City. That takes money. You see, above all, I wanted to protect Larry, to see that he met the right people, to do all that I could—even while selling the boy and his beauty—to see that the boy and the beauty would be protected.

'If you really want to do it, Larry,' I said, 'I will set you up with a date with a very lovely, wonderful, talented man. His name is Frederick Sloan.'

'The concert pianist?'

Delighted, I smiled, 'You know of him?'

'Who doesn't know about Frederick Sloan? I had no idea he was gay.'

'The world is gay, Larry.'

'It would be a privilege to meet Mr. Sloan, even if it wasn't, you know, business.'

'Do you have a tuxedo?'

'No.'

'Then come. We'll go to the man who fits all my boys.'

'I don't have any money to rent a tux.'

'You charming, wonderful boy. First of all, we are not going to

rent one, we're going to buy it. And I'll pay for it. An expense of doing business. You can't go out with Frederick Sloan unless you have a tuxedo.'

The day after their first date, there was a picture of the two of them on Page Six of "The Post," at a gala party after an extraordinary performance at Lincoln Center by some visiting Russian pianist. That photo and the praise for Larry's charm and beauty and graciousness voiced around his circles by Frederick Sloan launched Larry Apperson in the rarified atmosphere of the very rich, very chic, very discriminating upper crust of New York City's homosexual community.

I fully expected Larry to leave me, but he told me that he wanted to remain in my escort book, and I was delighted to hear it. He became, immediately, my star attraction, and although I could easily have called him up every hour of every day with an appointment, I cherished him, protected him, and kept him for the very best of my clients—businessmen, artists, motion picture stars, politicians. Larry was caviar, and I directed him to clients who appreciated caviar.

Through it all, in spite of the adoration, the lavishing of gifts and money upon him, despite all the chances he had to fly to Europe, to live in the Bahamas, to take up residence in his own penthouse, he steered his own course, being his own self, being true to whatever it was he saw himself being. It was an amazing exhibition.

In a word, how would I describe Larry?

Class!

It was as if he were a kind of angel who suddenly appeared among us.

Class?

No. There is a more suitable word.

Divine!

Tears sparkled in Neal Davis's eyes, but he forced a smile as he looked across the room at the two detectives. "How we gay people do go on about each other, eh?"

"We appreciate your being frank with us," replied Lyman.

Neal Davis cleared his throat and nervously touched his lips again. "Do you happen to know what arrangements have been made about Larry?"

"You mean funeral arrangements?" asked Lyman.

"Yes."

"We are trying to contact his brother, apparently his only kin."

"That would be Pete. I believe he attends a college somewhere in Pennsylvania."

"Yes. He is away, so we haven't been able to reach him."

"Their parents are dead. A car accident or something awful like that. The insurance money and social security payments have been putting Pete through school. When you talk to Pete, if he has any problem with the, uh, arrangements for Larry, will you tell him that he can count on me if he needs help?"

"That's very generous, Mr. Davis."

"I always feel very inadequate in the face of death. I deal with life, and young life at that, so when I come up against death, I always feel a little—what? Embarrassed."

"I know," nodded Lyman. "Thanks for your help."

In the elevator, the two detectives were silent until they reached the lobby. "So, what do you think about him?" asked Garraty as the door slid open.

"I've known Neal Davis a long time. He's a very smooth character. An actor of the first order."

"Was he lying? All that remorse and mourning?"

"Could be," said Lyman, pushing through the revolving door into the chilling, dusky afternoon. "Terry, check with Telco about the calls. Get numbers, names of people called, times. I'm sure it'll all check out. Davis wouldn't have told us about the calls if they wouldn't check out. Call up the people he called and get statements to the effect that they spoke with Davis personally and at what times."

2.

They were back at Third Homicide in time to see the six o'clock news.

The snowstorm dominated the newscast. The murder of Lawrence Apperson did not come on until nearly forty minutes into the program. A young woman reporter who looked nearly frostbitten stood in the snowy street in front of the Apperson address to relate details of the bludgeoning-death of the young man. "He may have been a male prostitute," she pointed out. Next she turned to William Weinstein for an account of how the body had been discovered. Next came pictures of the corpse being removed in its green body bag. "Was this a homosexual murder?" asked the reporter, turning with microphone in hand in expectation that Detective Sheldon Lyman of Manhattan's Third Homicide Zone would have an answer to the question.

"Murder is sexless, miss," Lyman answered grimly.

A cheer went up in the squad room.

"We've only just begun our investigation," Lyman said on TV.

"Hey, Shelly, you'll never get to be a big celebrity with answers like that!" Mike Brown was speaking, making everyone laugh.

Lyman disappeared from the TV screen.

Short and sweet, he said to himself, watching. Just the way I like it.

The news story concluded with the reporter standing in snow, looking very serious and authoritative. "It's believed the murder took place a few days ago, before the big snowstorm. Whether this was a crime of passion, only time will tell!" Lyman barked a laugh. "That's for sure, baby," he said, turning away from the TV as the reporter told the audience who she was and handed the show back to the anchorman in the studio.

Garraty picked up the phone to start checking out the names and phone numbers in Apperson's address book to see how many of the entries were current.

Lyman rolled a report form into his typewriter and began putting into words what they knew, so far, about Larry Apperson's homicide. As best they knew: the who, what, where, when, how and why of it. "Resumé of Homicide" the form said at the top. Like a damned job application, Lyman thought, wishing someone would change the words at the top of the damned form.

There were a lot of blanks filled in with the word "unknown" as Lyman worked on the report.

They were idling, waiting for gay bars around town to get into full swing. Gay bars rarely came to life before eleven o'clock. Meanwhile, Lyman and Garraty would do the phone work, the paper, the nitty-gritty of their jobs. The apparatus of murder investigation was running efficiently. In a package before Lyman on his desk were hundreds of photos of the likeness of Larry Apperson, sent over by the photo unit, their work as excellent as always—pocket-size as well as eight-by-ten glossies of the face of the victim photographed from his portrait-from-life.

Later, they would show the pictures to the customers of all the gay bars they could visit through the night. In the morning, at precinct musters and detective squad meetings all over Manhattan, the closeup of Larry Apperson's oil-painted face would be handed out. In an ordinary murder where the victim's face was intact, pictures of the corpse's face would have been distributed.

Lyman was also planning. After their night in the gay bars—and maybe the baths if they had time—they would face a day of interviews, starting with Nelson Royce, movie star. Others would be contacted, depending on Garraty's success in confirming the names, numbers and addresses in the book, in the hope that one might provide the break. He hoped. He wished for someone to provide a confession. "Yes! I did it! I killed him! Take me away! I confess!" Even better: a confession that would not be repudiated and retracted once the killer had a chat with a sharp lawyer. And, if it ever got to trial, happiness for a detective would be to see a good case go to the jury with no plea bargaining. But the homicide of Larry Apperson was a long, long way from a jury.

The trial, if one developed, might be lurid.

A fag murder!

The press would have a field day.

All that opportunity to be flamboyant, exploitive.

There wasn't much that New Yorkers loved more than a hot homosexual murder with their morning newspaper and dinnertime TV news.

3.

The bars were a long shot, but they were clearing houses for the gossip of the New York gay scene. They also were gay human-commodity exchanges where, like their counterparts in the straight world, lonely people could meet for one-night stands or, as sometimes happened, for longer relationships, possibly even ultimate marriage. There was little evidence that Larry Apperson used the bars for his contacts, either social or business, but he had met Neal Davis in a bar and all the people Larry Apperson knew in his chic gay circle visited bars. The hope was that in the bars Lyman and Garraty would pick up some information, some bit of fact, some chance observation to help break the logjam that their case was experiencing. If Larry Apperson had been a secret hustler, if he had not moved in the rarified atmosphere of moneyed gays, the detectives might have had an almost impossible task of scouring the gay bars. Had he been a street hustler they would have had to search for information in the hustler bars of the east and west sides of town, the leather bars of the waterfronts, the rough-trade places in the Village and around Times Square where no one would have trusted a cop who came in with a picture of a dead hustler. A cop in one of those bars would simply clear the place by his presence. Larry Apperson would have frequented better bars, and that made their job easier.

They decided to split the work. Garraty took all the

likely bars north of Larry Apperson's address east of Fifth
Avenue. Lyman got those south and east. The west side bars
where Larry Apperson might have been a customer would be
saved for another night.

Lyman started with the one bar which they knew he had
been in at least once.

"Charlie's Aunt" occupied a corner of Third Avenue in the
Murray Hill section of brownstones, luxury highrises, health
food restaurants, and little shops and boutiques where lived
the affluent young New Yorkers who liked the area's proxim-
ity to work and play in midtown. The bar was discreet
outside, the kind of neighborhood gay bar that the neighborhood knew was gay only if the neighbors were gay. The sign
said: "Charlie's Aunt. Restaurant. Bar." Most of the business
came from the bar. The establishment's reputation for its
restaurant-offerings was modest. Beside the main door of the
brown-brick front hung a large photo of Ray Bolger in the
outlandish woman's costume he had worn in the film "Charlie's Aunt." The sly portrayal of a man in drag did not mean
that "Charlie's Aunt" welcomed drag-queens as customers.
The female-dressing gays of the city were welcome elsewhere.
Stepping inside, Lyman might have been entering any straight
bar. The customers were neatly, if casually, dressed. White,
clean-cut, soft-spoken, obviously moneyed, the customers
were predominately young. The older men inside were with
younger men. Unlike many gay bars Lyman had known, this
one was a bar where most of the customers knew each other.
In other bars which were strictly for pick-ups, customers
remained aloof, alone, eyeing each other with that expression
Lyman had seen so often in his days with Vice—the wondering, cool, carefully-examining gaze that was prelude to self-
introduction. "Nice night!" "You come here often?" "Buy you
a drink?" The studied opening moves of the gay-bar-human-

chess-games which were the reason for most gay bars' existence.

Even though "Charlie's Aunt" was not a hard-core pick-up bar for strangers, when Lyman came in, most of the eyes in the place turned in his direction. When he first started working Vice, he had been told the tell-tale sign of a gay bar was the way everybody in it turned to look at each person to come in. For the most part, Lyman had found the generalization to be true, especially in the pick-up places where the sole purpose was to meet someone to go home with, whether for the sexual connection itself or for the money the sexual connection would produce. "These queers are as promiscuous as Havana whores," his partner, Mike Brown, had commented with disgust.

Lyman gave the bar a quick study as he stepped inside. He had learned how to size up any bar in a few seconds, spotting the customers who might be hostile—even danger-ous—and those who might be approachable, who might talk to him without any inkling that he was a cop, and those who would continue to talk even after they learned who he was. Of the few customers at "Charlie's Aunt" who were obviously alone, he picked out a slender young man at the far end of the bar. Of medium height and slim build with brown hair and the pallor of New Yorkers who spent winters in New York, the boy had on a leather jacket with a fake-fur collar, an imitation of World War II flight jackets, a plaid shirt with no necktie, the inevitable jeans, and boots. He was drinking Heineken's beer straight from the green bottle. Lyman edged into a narrow space beside him and told the bartender, "I'll have what this fellow's having." With a sidelong glance and a flicker of a smile he said to the boy, "Best beer on the market, I think." The boy nodded agreement but said nothing. The bartender brought the beer. Lyman poured it himself, then lifted his glass in a gesture of a toast to the boy. "Cheers." The boy replied, "Cheers," as he turned away and gazed across the thickly peopled room. Lyman decided the boy was not a likely prospect for easy conversation. He wondered if the boy was waiting for someone. A few minutes later the boy put down his empty bottle and moved away, pushing through the thickening crowd, and left.

Lyman waited, nursing his beer. Finally he decided that this bar was going to be a hard case. Breaking the ice of idle conversation was proving difficult as the space beside him filled up, then emptied, with a string of handsome young men who exhibited none of the easy approachability that Lyman would have encountered in a hustlers' bar or a pick-up joint. Probably, he figured, he had the mark of a cop on him. He was new to the bar, knew no one, and clearly no one was making any effort to get to know him. In all likelihood, he concluded, the whole place had spotted him for a cop the moment he came in.

Watching the men from the bar, he noticed the easy conviviality which enveloped them. Although it had not reached out to embrace him, the friendship and outwardly demonstrated affection fascinated Lyman for a few moments. He watched, without being obvious, two young men in a booth in a dim corner of the establishment, their eyes fixed on each other, their voices low and intimate, their hands reaching out and touching an arm or a hand. Nearer, an older man and his friend were laughing as they talked about a show they had seen, a Broadway musical which had closed after only a few performances. The man was probably old enough to be the boy's father, but the two exhibited a rapport, an easy association which Lyman had rarely seen in fathers and sons.

All of the men and young men, it seemed to him, were at ease and comfortable, accepting the fact that they were homosexuals and knowing that in this place they could be themselves. Relaxed, content, confident of themselves, they were hardly the lonely, sad-eyed, sex-hungry homosexuals whom literature so often described. He knew many gay bars—hustling bars—where the eyes were always roving, where there was an almost tangible sense of being looked at, where picking up someone was the intent. Here, in "Charlie's Aunt," the atmosphere was low-key. No one whom Lyman saw looked frantic with loneliness.

Unless, he said to himself, it was Sheldon Lyman.

He was the loner in the place.

He wondered if it was loneliness, obvious loneliness, which made him a stand-out and, therefore, made him unlikely to be drawn into the comraderie of the place. Or, had he merely been spotted and marked for what he was—a cop? Sure of it, he threw aside his hopes for passing himself off as just another gay man spending some time in a gay bar in the expectation of meeting someone new, and signalled the bartender as if he wanted another beer. When the bartender came over, Lyman showed him one of the little police-photo-lab-mass-produced pictures of Larry Apperson. "Do you know this fellow?" The young bartender wiped his hands on his apron and picked up the photo. He studied it for a moment, then shook his head and handed back the picture.

"Sorry, I don't. Nice looking kid, though. What are you, his father?"

Lyman chuckled. "No. I'm a police officer and the boy in this picture was the victim of a crime."

The bartender's face lit up with recognition. "Oh, that's the boy who was murdered. In all the papers and on TV."

Lyman nodded. "You don't remember him being a customer here?"

The bartender shook his head, saying, "I don't recall him, but some of the regulars here tonight might recall him if he came here a lot, only I don't think the owners would think it was very cool to have a policeman bothering the customers."

Lyman said he understood. "But I have no choice. I have to ask around. You see, it appears that this young man was killed *because* he was *gay*." It was possibly a lie, Lyman thought, but the lie worked.

The young bartender who had seemed eager to move away from him now reached for the picture again and studied it sympathetically. Lyman pursued the opening. "My interest in this is as a homicide detective. I don't give a damn about hassling anybody in this bar or any other bar because he happens to be gay. My interest is in finding out who killed this young man and getting that killer off the streets *and* out of bars like this one." Lyman paused, choosing another lie for effect: "You see, we are sure that this boy met his killer in a gay bar. That's why I'm here tonight and why my partner is doing the same thing in other gay bars on the east side. You're sure you don't know the boy in that picture?"

The bartender chewed his lip and shook his head. "Sorry." He tapped a finger against the edge of the photo. "I could," he said, thoughtfully, hesitantly, "show it to the people standing here at the bar. If I did it and didn't let on that you're a cop, maybe that would help?"

Lyman smiled. "That would help a lot." He added. "Could you pass it around at the tables, too?" The bartender nodded and moved away, working his way along the bar, showing the picture. A few heads turned, and Lyman supposed that the bartender had explained that the picture belonged to the man at the bar. The scene was repeated at tables, but in the end, no one in "Charlie's Aunt" was able—or willing—to admit that they knew the boy in the photo.

"Sorry," said the bartender, passing back the picture.

"Appreciate the help," Lyman smiled.

"Excuse me," said the young bartender, "but you really care about this, don't you?" Lyman was startled. The bartender went on, "I'm pretty good when it comes to being able to read people's faces. Maybe that's why I'm pretty good at being a bartender. I just thought that you looked to me like you really care about this kid and what happened to him. More than it being just your job, I mean."

Lyman looked at the photo of Larry Apperson and slowly nodded his head. "Yes. I guess I do care a little more about this case than most others."

The bartender said, "I'm sorry no one here was able to help."

All the eyes in the bar followed Lyman as he made his way to the door on his way out.

He had never hoped for much success by combing the bars. At best he expected to spread the word among the gay community that the police were looking for the killer of Larry Apperson, that they were sympathetic, that they were not going to fill out all their pink and blue report forms and file them away as just another fag murder. Maybe, then—just maybe—someone would come forward.

So, dutifully but not with any expectation of breaking the case, he worked other bars. When they closed, he wended his way home. The phone was ringing as he came in. Garraty said, "I don't know about you, Shel, but I had so much beer in all those goddamned bars I'm gonna be pissing for a week. Not a ripple from anybody, and I hit half a dozen places. I am bushed. When you weren't here at the squad I figured you decided to hang it up for some shuteye, which is what I'm gonna do. What time shall I pick you up?"

Lyman thought. The next event would be to talk to Nelson Royce. The Mayor's Office for Motion Pictures and Television, whose job it was to encourage film production in New York, had told him in answer to a query that the filming on Nelson Royce's picture was going on all week at Madison Square Park.

The park was four blocks from Lyman's house. "Pick me up at ten," he told Garraty.

"You got it, partner!"

4.

Lyman picked up an anthology of crime stories he'd bought at the Barnes and Noble Sales Annex, settled into bed, and ran a finger down the Table of Contents for a story he might want to read. He chose "The Game of Murder" by Gerd Gaiser on page 272.

He always picked the murder stories.

> "Presumably you all know the game, which may well acquire a ticklish, somewhat dubious character when adults take it up. Pieces of paper are thrown together, each person draws one, sees what is on it for him and puts it away. Somebody will have picked the murderer's part, somebody else the detective's, all the other pieces of paper are empty, anyone can be the victim. Nobody may know who the murderer is. . . ."

He let the book sag in his hands and fall flat on his belly as he lifted his eyes from the page and looked up at his ceiling. Closing the book, he laid it on the nighttable and remembered the book on the table beside Larry Apperson's bed. He tried to remember the title. It was a novel, half-read. A pair of glasses lay folded beside it. He could not remember the title.

What happened to Larry Apperson was this, he imagined: He had gotten ready for bed, laying the book and the glasses on the table to be waiting there for him after he'd had a hot bath. He went naked into the bathroom, leaving the lamp turned on by the bed—the lamp whose bulb would burn out sometime after death got Larry in the bathroom. He'd been sitting in the tub, relaxed, enjoying the warmth of the water, when he heard a noise in the other room. He got out of the tub to see what had made the noise and his killer struck him as he came through the door.

What happened to Larry Apperson was this: He had been out to a bar, and in the bar he met another young man, and they came back to Larry's apartment. They talked, they touched, they kissed, they made love—unrestrained, impetuous love that unfolded in the living room, because no one had lain on the bed. Afterward, Larry wanted to bathe. His lover lingered and for a reason known only to the murderer decided to lure Larry from the bathroom, bludgeoning him as he stepped through the door.

What happened to Larry was this: He had been bathing. Someone came to his door, letting himself in. Or Larry went to the door and admitted his visitor. As Larry returned to his bath, he turned back to say something to the visitor, only to be struck savagely in the face.

What happened to Larry was. . . .

Lyman got out of bed and put on a robe. What happened to Larry was the open question. He walked into his darkened living room. Pausing in the center of the room, he tried to guess what had been on Larry's mind as he stepped from his bath onto the furry mat and moved to the threshold between light and dark. Something compelled him untoweled from the water, to the doorway. Something, someone.

Lyman sat in his favorite easy chair without turning on a

light. He hugged his robe against his bare skin and folded one leg beneath him. The dark blank face of the TV set stared back at him. With a flick of a button he could bring the laughter and color of The Late, Late Show into the dark room. He could bring life into his thoughts of death, but he sat in the dark, rubbing a hand over his chilly foot tucked against him, noting how cold his toes were.

When his wife was alive and he was sitting like this in the dark, a case weighing against him, she would call out to him from the bedroom, "Sheldon, come to bed! You'll catch a cold!"

As if she had called him again, he got up from his chair and went back to the bedroom. In the soft yellow light from the lamp by the bed, he visualized Larry Apperson's bedroom, not his—the table, the book, the glasses, the turned-down blanket and sheets. Above the bed, made softer and more charming by the soft light from the lamp, the portrait of Larry kept silent watch on all that happened beneath it.

He saw the portrait as clearly as if it hung above his own bed.

Who killed Larry Apperson and why?

"*Nobody may know who the murderer is. . . .*"

That was the eternal hope of those who did murder. That nobody would know they'd done it. That was the hope burning in the heart of someone who had come into Larry Apperson's apartment when Larry was alive, the someone who had taken a heavy object into his hands and smashed it into Larry's face for what had to have been a compelling, fearful, awful reason.

"*Nobody may know. . . .*"

"*I'll* know, Larry," Lyman said out loud in the loneliness of his bedroom. "*I'll* know who murdered you."

Going back to bed and turning out the light, Lyman rested his head on his pillow, then tilted his head back to look up at the wall above the headboard as if the portrait of Larry were there.

I will know who murdered you, Larry, Lyman said to himself.

He slept soundly, except for a few minutes before waking at his usual hour, when he dreamed about Larry posing for the portrait.

5.

The City of New York and its Police Department made it as easy as possible for motion picture producers to work in the city and to use its streets, houses, offices, waterfronts, parks and people as if New York were nothing more than a giant movie sound stage.

Lyman and Garraty found Nelson Royce in his trailer parked in what was usually a bus stop on the Fifth Avenue side of Madison Square Park. Looking at Royce, it was easy to see why he was a movie star. His eyes were blue, and Lyman had long-since noticed that most movie stars had blue eyes. The hair, which had been golden in the years of Nelson Royce's early films, was now platinum. There was no gray, but Lyman decided Royce did not color his hair. Aging had turned it platinum rather than gold. The face was lightly made up, but the skin beneath the makeup had a California tan. Although he had been making movies for a quarter of a century, Nelson Royce did not look much different from his first films, although he was no longer playing roles that called for callow, yearning, fumbling, lovable, vulnerable youths. He was, now, a leading man and his romances were in fancy cars and elegant nightclubs instead of sandy surf-washed beaches.

As finely honed as his acting skills were, Nelson Royce was incapable of masking his nervousness as he sat in his spacious and comfortable trailer to talk to two police officers about a side of his life which so far had not become public.

THE NELSON ROYCE TAPE

There is very little I can tell you that might be of any assistance to you, gentlemen. Yes, I knew Lawrence Apperson. I am sure you know the circumstances of how I came to know him. I am sure you will also understand the very sensitive position which your coming here puts me in. I will be glad to tell you all I know, but it is very little, I'm afraid.

When was the last time you saw Apperson?

One evening last week.

What were the circumstances?

I asked to see him.

Why?

I knew him previously, he was a trustworthy young man, very discreet, and I cared a great deal about him, Mr. Lyman.

Did you love him?

You mean did I love him or did he and I make love?

Both.

The answer to each is yes, but the romance was over. I loved him the way anyone loves a former lover.

But you still wanted to have sex with him.

As I said, I knew Lawrence was discreet.

Where did you meet him this time?

He came to my suite at the Plaza.

When was that?

Early last week. Monday or Tuesday. Before the snowstorm.

Where were you on Thursday night, Mr. Royce?

Working. We were shooting night exteriors at Lincoln Center. There are scenes in the film that take place at the opera. We were shooting some of those scenes. Anticipating your next question, Detective, we were working until dawn. It was difficult work because we were plagued with some equipment problems in the sound system. It took a long time to find out what was wrong. But I was on the set the whole time.

You've emphasized a couple of times the importance of Larry's discretion about his relationship with you. It seems to me that today a movie star's personal life doesn't amount to a hill of beans.

That is true, but I have a family, a mother and father who have no idea that I am a homosexual, and although they say they pay no attention to gossip columns or fan magazines, they are very sensitive when it comes to what they read about me. They would be deeply hurt by any stories that their son likes boys. My publicity image has always been very straight, very butch.

Is that why you deal through Neal Davis?

Mr. Davis has always been most reliable in providing his unique services.

How did you start dealing with Davis?

Another actor told me about him. He's dead now. He was one of the legendary names of motion picture history.

You never had a problem with any of the young men Davis introduced you to?

Do you mean blackmail threats and so forth? Never.

What would you do if you were the victim of an extortion attempt, Mr. Royce?

I don't know. I'd talk with a lawyer, I suppose. Possibly, I'd pay. I don't know. It has never happened.

Might you ask Neal Davis to help you out?

Possibly, but I am a man with means. I could probably handle something like that on my own.

You've been very good to let us have your time, Mr. Royce. Good luck with your picture.

I'll see that you're invited to a screening, if you'd like.

I would. Thank you.

They stayed awhile, watching the filming. Royce came out of his trailer in an overcoat and scarf and crossed in front of the forest of motion picture equipment arranged around a snow-cleared wooden bench just inside Madison Square Park. He sat on the bench for a moment and chatted with a man Lyman assumed to be the film's director. Lights went on. A silence descended and Royce spoke one line. "Okay, muggers, come and get me!"

Someone said, "Cut," and the scene was over.

Lyman chuckled. "The Mayor's office isn't going to like that line."

A few minutes later, another scene unfolded in which Royce and a young woman had a terrible argument. Royce was cruel in his lines and left the young woman in tears.

"He can be nasty, hm?" remarked Garraty, glancing at Lyman.

"Acting," said Lyman.

Lyman would run a check on Royce's story of having spent the night in front of movie cameras when Larry Apperson was murdered, but he knew the story would be confirmed. "That," Garraty rightly pointed out, "doesn't mean Royce couldn't have had anything to do with the murder. A guy with money, with his 'means' as he put it, could have someone do his dirty work for him."

"You're thinking that Apperson might have been a threat to Royce?"

"Could be. Or maybe it was just a way out of a love affair that Royce wanted out of."

"That's kind of drastic, Terry."

"For ordinary mortals, maybe, but not necessarily for a superstar."

"I doubt if there's any way we could prove anything like that, even if it was the only explanation for Apperson's death."

"You still think it was something very simple, don't you, Shelly, like felony homicide during a burglary?"

"It's too muddled for me to think very clearly about any of this, but we can't overlook the fact that certain things were missing from that apartment. A camera. The kid's wallet. Things a burglar would take."

"Why not the rest of the cameras?"

"Maybe the Pentax was just lying out in the open, like the wallet. Here we have a possible burglary. The burglar discovers there's somebody home. He hits him with something, probably the other dumbbell. He intended to stun his victim, not kill him. He panics when he's seen what he's done, but he's not so scared that he'd leave without something rewarding for his efforts. He grabs what's in sight. A wallet. A camera."

"What about the book this kid was writing? Pretty good motive."

"*If* he was writing one."

"Well, I have to tell you that this whole thing has a very bad smell to it, Shel, and if it turns out to be a felony homicide committed during a common burglary, I am going to owe you a steak dinner.."

"To you, it's a fag murder, nothing else?"

"You got it, partner."

"We'll see. If we solve the damned puzzle at all."

"Where now?"

"A chat with one of the world's greatest concert pianists. We go uptown, an address on Central Park West."

When they crossed Forty-ninth Street at Madison, the radio called them. Answering, Lyman listened to the message and wondered what the hell was up. "Call your Division commander on a land-line immediately!" said the police dispatcher.

On the phone, Lt. Parker was himself mystified about the reason behind his urgent message. "All I know is, Deputy

Mayor Heywood Johnson has asked to have a meeting with you."

"When?" Lyman responded, a knot of uneasiness tightening in his belly.

"Now, if you can do it."

"What the hell's the fucking City Hall got to do with me?"

"I don't know, Sheldon. Just go and find out, okay?"

"Hey, Paul, if someone is going to mess around with this case I'm on. . . ."

"If anyone messes around, you let me know, okay?"

"You bet your ass I'll let you know. Everybody'll know."

6.

"What the hell am I doing going to City Hall?"

Lyman sat with his chin resting on his fist and his arm propped against the arm rest of the car door, a scowl on his face, his eyes on the facade of New York City's graceful nineteenth century City Hall, its sandstone gleaming in the sunlight reflected off the deep snow in City Hall Park. The U.S. and New York City flags snapped on the crisp cold wind. Uniformed police guards ambled back and forth in the parking lot in the plaza directly in front of the Hall's steps. Serious-faced men and women visitors tramped up and down the stairs, going in and out of the building for whatever urgent business brought them there. Terry Garraty drummed his fingers against the steering wheel. "The way to find out what the hell we are doing here is to go and see the Deputy Mayor and ask him."

Lyman grunted. "I don't like the smell of this. It's got politics all over it. Somebody is trying to put the arm on this investigation, Terry."

"That is a so far an unwarranted assumption."

"Then what the hell is Deputy Major Heywood Johnson wanting to see me about? This guy is the Mayor's right hand hatchet man. C'mon. Let's see what the hell is going on."

"You're the man he wants to see."

"Yeah? Well, I want a witness at this meeting. You come along. That's an order, partner."

In the anteroom outside the door to the office of Deputy Mayor Heywood Johnson, a pretty secretary announced the arrival of Detectives Lyman and Garraty. Putting down her intercom phone, she smiled at Lyman. "Mr. Johnson will see you now Mr. Lyman."

"C'mon, partner," Lyman said, tugging Garraty's sleeve.

"Just you, Mr. Lyman, please," smiled the secretary.

Lyman shook his head. "You tell the Deputy Mayor that if he wishes to see me he will also see my partner, and if you don't care to tell the Deputy Mayor, *I* will."

The unnerved secretary used her phone to repeat Lyman's words. Laying aside the phone again, smiling, she said, "Go in. Both of you."

Deputy Mayor Heywood Johnson was a familiar face, not only to Lyman and Garraty, but to anyone familiar with the recent history of New York City. A handsome young black man, Johnson had been one of the leaders of campus anti-war activities at Columbia University and had been arrested in the takeover of the office of Columbia's President. He had been associated with Dr. Martin Luther King, Jr, in coordinating fund raising activities in New York. Later he worked for the energetic young man who won not only two campaigns for the House of Representatives, but a hard-fought campaign for Mayor of New York. Heywood Johnson had done much to deliver important black community support to the Mayor in the campaign and since. Like many radicals who found themselves with power they wanted to protect, Heywood Johnson had taken a conservative turn, muting the incendiary rhetoric that had made him a leading anti-establishment figure and paving the way for his entry into the very establishment he had been denouncing. Lyman remembered Heywood Johnson as a young black in dashiki and jeans. The Heywood Johnson who stood behind a broad mahogany desk as Lyman and Garraty came into his office was a matured politician in a gray-striped three piece suit. The

Afro haircut was gone, too, Lyman noted. "I know you gentlemen are very busy, so I thank you for taking the time to come down to see me, and so promptly."

"What can we do for you, Mr. Johnson?" Lyman asked, delining an invitation to be seated.

"The news media are saying that the Apperson case has homosexual overtones."

"It does."

"As you may know, part of my responsibility to the Mayor is to be a liaison between City Hall and the gay community. Gays make up a sizeable proportion of the voters in this town. I don't need to tell you that, I suppose. They are very conscious of their status, and I would hope that in your handling of this case you will be aware of the larger issues that may be touched upon."

"Mr. Deputy Mayor, I've been in this business a long time. I am very tuned in to the feelings of all the minorities with whom my cases may bring me into contact."

"That is excellent. I've been told that you are a uniquely sensitive police officer, Mr. Lyman. I assume your partner shares your sensitivities."

"He does," said Lyman.

The Deputy Mayor smiled and when he spoke again, his tone was light-hearted, gossipy. "The newspapers say that this murdered man may have been a call-boy. Is that the word?"

"It will do," nodded Lyman.

"A call-boy whose clients may have been drawn from certain select circles?"

"Yes, sir."

"Yes. That is an area that could be as sensitive as the area of the gays and other groups, hm?"

"I imagine some of the men Lawrence Apperson knew are men who have some considerable clout in this town, sir. Witness this very meeting."

Garraty uttered a low, almost inaudible groan.

The Deputy Mayor's eyebrows arched up. "What do you mean by that, detective?"

"Excuse me if I'm wrong, Mr. Deputy Mayor, if I've jumped to a wrong conclusion here, but I suspect that the thrust of your intention in meeting with me and my partner is in the direction of telling us to keep in mind that we may be dealing with some very important people on this case. Perhaps we might even stumble onto *one* name in particular?"

"That's an unwarranted assumption, Lyman."

"Well, I am glad to hear that."

"The interest of this office is strictly one of fairness, of sensibilities. I speak of the Gay community. We have been working very hard to improve relations between the city government and the Gays and I wouldn't want this case to derail those efforts."

"This is a case of murder, sir. I hope you're not asking me to handle this murder case differently than others?"

"Of course not. It's just that there are aspects of this murder that. . . ."

"Murder is murder, sir, and that's all I see."

"All I'm asking is that you keep us informed."

"Oh, I thought maybe you might be asking me to do something else, such as back off if this murder case turned into a difficult public relations problem."

"Not at all."

"Good. Glad to hear it. Good day, Mr. Johnson."

7.

Garraty had never seen Lyman so angry. "Easy, Shel. Easy."

"The nerve of that guy," Lyman growled as they came down the steps of City Hall and crossed the parking lot to their car. "Can you believe that he's worried about upsetting the Gay community when what we have here is a case of homicide? Jesus! The nerve. What am I supposed to do, drop this case just because the Mayor might have to have a meeting with Gays who are pissed off about publicity?"

"They have a point, Shel. There are sensibilities to consider."

"No. There's murder to consider. Nothing else!"

Garraty glanced at City Hall, shook his head, then started their car and edged it from the plaza parking area onto Broadway. He drove the circling route that would take them away from City Hall, then back toward it, and, at last, onto a ramp for the northbound lanes of the F.D.R Drive. Brooding, Lyman was silent going uptown.

At the turnoff, he announced, "There will be real hell to pay if anybody messes with this case!"

The statement was a period, a verbal punctuation mark on the incident.

Immediately, Lyman's mind was back on the case while Garraty threaded their car through the needle's eye narrowness of crosstown streets, then through a swifter sunken road that cut across Central Park to the west side.

Through the open door of Frederick Sloan's Central Park West apartment, the detectives had a panoramic view of snowy Central Park and the imposing march of buildings along Fifth Avenue at the other side of the park. A huge picture window framed the scene, which was Currier and Ives in its wintry beauty. To the right of the window, as Lyman and Garraty saw it, stood a splendid grand piano, its top propped open and looking rakish. The room was stark in its lack of other furnishings, merely a few music stands, a stool, and two black-leather-and-chrome directors chairs. "This is my rehearsal room," explained tall, gray, handsome Frederick Sloan as he admitted the detectives to his home. "We'll be more comfortable in my sitting room, just down this little corridor."

The room was a sharp contrast to the emptiness of the music room. Crowded—stuffed, Lyman decided—with memorabilia festooning the walls, bric-a-brac on every table, large, soft chairs and couches arranged around a fireplace, the room had a delightfully warm coziness. Lyman's eyes settled on a portrait above the fireplace and the signature of Conrad Ames signed with a flourish in the lower right hand corner. The painting was of Frederick Sloan at a piano in his prodigal youth. Lyman did not have to ask when it had been painted. It showed twenty year old Sloan with the 1955 Moscow Tschaikovksy Competition's Special gold medal about his neck.

"You've come about Larry," said Sloan, settling into one of the large chairs. "I have been expecting you. Neal Davis phoned and told me he had let my name slip. I do hope you won't think wrongly of Neal. It was a friendly gesture. Now, about me and Larry."

THE FREDERICK SLOAN TAPE

I was told that this new boy whom Neal Davis wanted me to meet was, how did Neal put it, divine.

Neal was notorious for his extravagant praise for his boys, even those who were very close to being common, but when I met Lawrence Apperson, I saw immediately what Neal meant, and the description was apt in every way.

He came to my door and knocked so quietly that I wasn't sure if someone was there. Opening the door, I was stunned by the beauty of that face, but I was immediately touched, won over, by the shyness apparent in his eyes, in a little smile that was part embarrassment, part fear, part amusement. 'My name's Larry,' he said, softly. 'Neal spoke to you about me?'

Wordless, because I was so overcome by his personality, I simply stepped back and held open the door and let him in. He had on a very handsome tuxedo, which I knew had come from the tailor whom Neal used regularly to outfit his boys, but none of the others had seemed so perfectly natural, so right, in formal dress. It was a very elegantly tailored, subdued. Most of Neal's boys wore blue tuxedos with satin lapels and those ruffled blue shirts. Not Larry. He chose his tuxedo himself, I was later told, and he showed impeccable taste. It was black, perfectly fitted, and with no cumberbund. It may seem ridiculous to say that a plain black tuxedo could look princely, but his did. Of course, it was the boy who brought the regal touch, not the clothes!

We went to Carnegie Hall for a recital by an old friend of mine and then had supper in The Russian Tea Room next door. I was delighted to discover that Larry appreciated music. He was alert and attentive during the concert and spoke about music with understanding afterward. I was amazed because I believed that young men his age were conversant with only the Beatles and Elvis Presley. With such an amazing boy I could only be immediately infatuated. In all candor, he was even more exceptional in bed. I am not a man who goes off the handle over a beautiful boy, but I loved Larry very much and even invited him to come and live with me.

He didn't, but he was very gentle and kind in refusing. He made me see that it was important to him to be himself, to seek out who he was and what he ought to be doing about his life. I could not agree more, I told him. He also had the extraordinary insight to see that had we lived together the delicate fabric of our relationship would be made common merely through familiarity. It is one thing to be enchanted with a boy in a tuxedo, quite another to go around picking up his socks and underwear for the laundry. Not that Larry was unkempt. He was very clean and neat. For him there was a place for everything and everything in its place, as the cliche goes. We saw each other once or twice a week for several months.

When he left me and took up with someone else, I was hurt, of course.

Especially, I was hurt because Larry had an affair with a dear friend of mine to whom I had introduced him. His name is Marty Gould. I have no reticence about telling you his name. If you have mine, you probably have his. Besides, I blamed Marty for the breakup between Larry and me. I could never blame Larry for anything. I surely could never bring myself to murder him!

As had others who had spoken to them about Larry, Frederick Sloan uttered his final words with tears in his eyes. Lyman was hesitant to ask another question, about whether Sloan knew about Larry writing a book. Sloan's face opened into a smile. "No. Was he really? How exciting."

"We need to know where you were Thursday night, Mr. Sloan," asked Garraty.

"I was here, rehearsing."

"Would your neighbors verify that?"

"Not really. You see, my apartment is soundproofed, not just to save the neighbors' nerves but to keep their noses away from me. When I am here at my piano I am as silent at Tut's tomb."

"We appreciate your honesty."

"What good would it do to lie?"

"None whatsoever," smiled Lyman.

"You said that Thursday was the night Larry was killed?"

"Yes."

"Then perhaps I can save you some effort and time. If you are going to check into where Marty Gould was Thursday night, I can tell you. He was in Los Angeles. I know because I met him at the airport the next morning. He came in on the Redeye flight, which leaves there in the evening and gets here before dawn. I would think that leaves Marty out as a suspect?"

"We'll have to talk with him anyway," Lyman replied.

"Well, he's now in Bermuda. Marty travels a lot, I'm afraid."

"Do you know where he's staying there?"

"One of the hotels."

"Thanks, Mr. Sloan. You've been very helpful."

"It's too bad you never knew Larry, gentlemen."

"Why?"

"Knowing Larry was having a little sunshine in your day."

8.

A little sunshine in your day! Only a queer could say that!"
Lyman chuckled at Garraty's disgust. "Oh, I don't
know, Terry. You always put a little sunshine into my day."

Getting around the city was easier, although many streets
were still unplowed. By staying on the avenues and the main
crosstown streets, they had little trouble reaching the loft
building in the Chelsea section where Conrad Ames had his
studio.

Ames had been a boy-wonder of New York art in the
turbulent 1960s, shocking art connoiseurs with his boldly
innovative styles of painting. Sharing the pioneering and
inconoclastic views of other artists, especially Andy Warhol,
Conrad Ames had reaped a fortune for paintings that some
critics denounced as nothing more than advertising illustration
work. Besides the popular work which brought him a fortune,
Ames had also been opening new vistas in special art for those
who shared his homosexual preferences and had the wealth to
afford to buy his paintings. While the straight world was
buying Ames paintings of Lucky Strike posters, Pepsi signs
and Coca Cola bottles, gay New York was snapping up his
almost-photographic renderings of naked boys. As far as
Lyman knew, Ames had never moved into film making, as
Warhol had.

The door to his studio was open, but Lyman knocked on

the edge of the door anyway. Peering inside the studio, he saw Ames in a gray sweatshirt and blue jeans, a palette in one hand and a brush in the other. Before him was an enormous canvas on an easel. The apparently nearly-finished painting was of a naked boy reclining on an antique chaise lounge. The model for the painting reclined just beyond the artist. Ames answered Lyman's knock without looking away from his work. "Come in, whoever you are!"

"We're the police," Lyman answered, stepping into the chilly studio.

"Police? How fascinating! What can I do for you?" Ames still did not look at them, but at the boy. The young model was not more than fourteen, Lyman figured. He held his pose resolutely despite the chill. "I hope this is not an arrest. I assure you this fellow is a professional model and we are not doing anything pornographic." Ames turned as he said the word 'pornographic' and flashed a smile.

"I'm not one to interfere with legitimate art," Lyman responded. "That is an exquisite painting, sir."

"Thank you. If you promise not to arrest me, I will add that the model is an exquisite inspiration. His name is Mark. My name I assume you know. You are?"

"Sheldon Lyman. My partner, here, is Terry Garraty. We're from Third Homicide."

"Ah," sighed Ames, putting down his brush and palette. "You are here about Larry."

"Yes."

"You've come to ask about the portrait?"

"That and about your relationship with him generally."

Ames spoke to the boy. "Mark. Take a break. Warm up by the stove. The heat went off in the studio this morning, Mr. Lyman, and we've been shivering all day. I opened the studio door in the hope of receiving some heat from the hallway. I would not have worked today at all but the client who ordered this painting is eager to have it. Mark has been absolutely stoic about posing in the cold." Lyman glanced at the boy as he crossed the studio, picking up a robe from a nearby chair, and putting it on. "Perfect grace and innocence," Ames said about the boy. "He is the son of the man who ordered the painting. Truly. He *is* the man's son, not a kept boy. He appreciates that his son is absolutely magnificent and wants to have something to remember him at this age of splendid beauty. He believes no photograph could do him justice and I, as a painter, concur."

"How does the boy feel about it?" asked Garraty, clearly displeased by what he'd seen and heard.

"Ask Mark yourself," Ames said, pointing to the boy.

"Do you go along with this painting you naked?" Garraty asked.

Mark shrugged. "Sure. Why not?"

"Why not!" Garraty muttered, letting the subject drop.

Going back to the chaise lounge, Mark stretched out in almost the same pose he had been holding for the painting. He wore the robe untied, letting it fall open to reveal a wide swath of his gently curved chest, the smooth slope of his belly, his flat abdomen with a small patch of dark pubic hair around genitals which were more man's than boy's. He waited, his large brown eyes fixed on the detectives who had interrupted him and the man who was catching his essence so perfectly for all time in canvas and oils.

"Extraordinary boy," Lyman said to Ames, "but I wonder if he should be present while we talk about Larry."

"Mark is quite mature, I assure you. What is it you wish to ask me?"

"About the painting of Larry and your relationship with him."

THE CONRAD AMES TAPE

I painted Larry late last summer at my place on Cape Cod. I always spent part of my summer at the Cape in a house that sits back from the water but has a clear view of the sea and its own beach. I had not expected to paint Larry at first, but as I got to know him, I realized I had to try to catch him on canvas. He thought I succeeded and so did many of my friends. Larry was proud of the work, which pleased me, because a lot of love went into it. I took Larry to the Cape because I was in love with him and wanted some time with him when we would not be constantly interrupted by others.

We were a pair those two weeks, but generally we stayed close to my house, keeping to ourselves and working on the portrait, which we did in the mornings. Evenings, Larry would sit in a big chair by the fireplace with his bare feet on a stool, a book in his lap, his shirt open. He was incredibly seductive even when he was reading! In those quite hours he was very introspective.

I knew he was giving a lot of thought to what he was going to do with himself. 'Good looks don't last forever,' he used to say.

As we worked on the painting, he made remarks about how much he wished that my painting of him could be like the one of Dorian Gray. I told him that he could not expect his evil to be transferred to the portrait because there was no evil in him in the first place. That usually provoked something scandalously erotic by way of answer. There were a few times when we simply had to leave the painting because we were on fire to possess each other.

He posed naturally, as though born to it. I often thought he had to have been the model for a Greek statue or a Roman god in a previous incarnation. He certainly could have been a Hermes for any classical sculptor. Naked, lithe, handsome, seductive, he stood for hours effortlessly while I tried to catch his essence on canvas. I am not sure I totally succeeded, but I got a bit of that special quality that is . . . was . . . Larry.

Out of Larry's patience and native ability to pose emerged that almost life-sized naked youth, washed and warmed by the sun, caressed by zephyrs from the ocean, the green sea at his back, and above him the heavens from which he certainly must have come.

It was his idea, his insistence, to show him sexually aroused.

When I argued that it might turn a work of beauty into a mere erotic picture, he pleaded with me to do it his way, and to my amazement, I discovered he was right. If painting him that way did anything to change the mood of the painting it was to make it more human, more vulnerable, more true to life, and—I mean this sincerely—more innocent.

Painting Larry and being with him for those two weeks was a turning point in my life. He was so young, so full of optimism and verve, that I could not help but become affected. I am much closer to the end of my life than to the beginning of it, yet since those two weeks with Larry, I have felt younger, more involved, more forward-looking. I had quite a bad reputation in this city's gay circles as being cynical and bad-tempered. I've been known as the George Sanders of the gay community—a nasty snipe, a scoundrel, a man with never a good word for anyone. I don't hear those things about me since my summer with Larry.

Of course, I was madly in love with him.

For two weeks we were incandescent in our passion, but, looking back, I don't believe I ever expected what we had to last beyond that flashing, pyrotechnic fortnight. We were a comet blazing across the Cape Cod heavens, but it was bound to burn out.

Finally, one day Larry met Joey Shaw, and it was no longer Conrad and Larry, Larry and Conrad. It was Larry and Joey.

By that time I had completed the portrait and was letting it dry thoroughly before giving any thought to framing it and getting it back to New York. I had intended to keep it, to hang it in my apartment, but Larry asked if he could have it and I was never one to refuse him anything. I said he could have the painting but got him to promise to allow me to have an unveiling of it, properly, with all our friends invited, when we returned to New York.

The event was a sensation.

'Anyone who knows paintings at all can see the love of the artist for the subject,' someone said. It was all very flattering but very true. I was quite the tragic artist at the unveiling because everyone knew that Larry had a new lover in Joey. It was Neal Davis who consoled me, 'Conrad, we must all be content in having had Larry to ourselves even for a short time. Obviously he is a spirit that is not to be contained. He is beyond permanent possession. Yesterday it was you, before that it was me and Freddy and Martin and Everett and all the others and now it's Joey. Who knows who will be next to be smitten, to succumb? We are travelers to his Mecca. We linger a time at his side as if he were a quenching pool of water on a hot day, but he is a special pool from which all who pass by may drink . . . but just a little.'

'It hurts to lose him,' I replied, watching Larry smilingly accepting compliments as he stood by his portrait at the unveiling.

'Of course it hurts, Conrad,' said Neal, patting me soothingly on the arm. 'But isn't it worth the hurt to know that you loved that boy, if only for a little while?'

'I have never been able to easily accept being dropped, even by ordinary mortals. This . . . this is a pain I never expected.'

'Well, Conrad, I can't say you will get over it entirely, but you will survive.' Neal brightened with a light-hearted laugh. 'One day we shall read all about ourselves when that divine creature writes his memoirs!'

At the moment, it seemed a delightful jest, and I laughed. I found out later that Larry had been giving a great deal of thought of writing a book. He told me he would make it into a novel, changing names, but it would be an honest portrait of all his experiences. 'I don't think I could write a portrait as beautiful as the one you painted, Conrad, but I have a feeling that writing may be what it is I was intended to do in this world.'

Relating this remarkable comment to Neal Davis, I expressed my opinion that Larry might, indeed, be able to write a very good book. Neal waved the possibility aside. 'Larry is always brooding about what it is that he is supposed to do in this life, as if God has given us all a script to follow. I don't know about heavenly scenarios, but if there are such things, Larry's role is the one he has so admirably performed to date—a beautiful boy who men must worship.

"Where were you last Thursday night, Mr. Ames?" Lyman asked.

"Here. Working. I have no one to verify that. No alibi."

"Did you ever see anything of a manuscript of the book that Larry was working on?" asked Lyman.

Conrad Ames shook his head. "But I do believe he was seriously pursuing that idea of his to write. Whether he had an actual novel in progress or was just keeping a diary or notes, I haven't the slightest idea."

"Have you gotten over being dropped by Larry?" Lyman asked.

Conrad Ames shook his head, then smiled. "No one does get over being dropped by Larry. I don't believe I'll ever get over the fact of his death."

"Do you know any reason why someone would want to kill him?" Asked Garraty.

"No. I have never been able to understand people who murder beauty, such as people who capture butterflies for collections or men who go out and shoot deer. I am an artist. I believe in creating and preserving beauty, not in destroying it. So, if your question is really intended to find out if I was hurt enough or bitter enough at being dropped by Larry to kill, I would tell you that I was deeply disturbed. Enough to feel the primitive human urge to kill, but my artistic temperament would never have allowed it."

Interview ended and on their way out, the detectives turned back a moment when Conrad Ames called to them. "One thing, Mr. Lyman, if I may?"

"Yes, Mr. Ames?"

"The portrait of Larry. What will become of it?"

"That will be up to Larry's next of kin. His brother."

"I would like very much to have the portrait."

"That's between you and the brother, Mr. Ames."

"Have you any idea where I might contact him?"

"We're trying to locate him ourselves."

Ames smiled. "If you would tell him to give me a call at a convenient time?"

"Sure thing." He waved at Mark, who waved back and smiled.

Garraty wore a look of displeasure on his face as they drove uptown. "For people who say they loved this kid so much, they're all damned concerned about themselves. Imagine this guy Ames wanting to bother Apperson's brother at a time like this because he wants his fucking painting back."

"The status of the deceased's estate is always the prime topic for discussion at funerals, Terry."

"It's ghoulish."

"Merely human, is all."

"I don't like that Ames guy. And I don't for a minute believe that kid he has up there is the son of a friend. I wanted to bust that sonofabitch when we found that naked teenager there with him."

"Terry, you are a case," Lyman laughed.

"Do you believe that story about him being some friend's son?"

"Yes, I do."

"Jesus. Why?"

"I don't know. I just believe him. I can usually spot a liar."

"Cops bust guys for getting kids to undress and pose for pictures."

"*Pornographers*, Terry! I don't think even you would call that painting of that kid pornographic."

"Hell, I wouldn't."

"I'll wager that you wouldn't be upset if we'd found Ames painting a picture of a naked girl."

"Of course not."

Lyman smiled and changed the subject. "We've been

going without let up for quite a while on this case. Maybe you'd like to go home and see if your family's still there?"

"Nah. Let's keep up the momentum."

"Good," smiled Lyman. "We'll check in at the squad and then look up Joey Shaw."

9.

The questioning of Joey Shaw would be delayed.
Garraty slammed down the phone. "We've got another fag killing, Shelly!"

Lyman spun around from his desk, his brow knitted in a frown, his eyes narrowed. "Where?".

Garraty handed him the note he'd scribbled while on the phone. "An address over in Brooklyn Heights. There are a lot of similarities."

On the drive at top speed down F.D.R. Drive, they monitored the tactical frequencies on their radio, picking up the fragmented jargon of calls related to the killing in Brooklyn. As they swung around the cloverleaf approach to the Brooklyn Bridge, a station wagon belonging to Channel Two News barreled past, flying up the ramp from the direction of City Hall. "Fuck," Lyman muttered. "We're gonna have to wade through a gang of newsmen when we get there. The bastards will right away connect this case and ours! Damn! The city ought to force those guys to stop monitoring our radio calls."

Garraty didn't reply.

They came off the bridge, threaded through traffic around the Cadman Plaza apartments, then made a series of left turns until they were at a complex of apartment buildings across from the Federal Court House. It was easy to find the right apartment. A sea of flashing gumball-lights and an armada of news units clogged the street in front of the murder address.

Lyman shoved through the newsmen without a word.

Lieutenant Brad Morton of Brooklyn Homicide shook hands with Lyman and said hello to Garraty in the hallway outside the apartment where the body had be found in a pool of blood in the middle of the living room. Morton's eyes were red, his square-jawed face drawn. His voice betrayed how tired he was. "This is my second murder in twelve hours, and my ass is dragging, I have to tell you. I read about your Apperson case in the papers and when I arrived on the scene here I wondered if you might be interested in some similarities."

The naked body was that of a young man. Lyman figured the victim to be on the far side of twenty-five, but barely. Blond, muscular, and probably handsome—the battered face left the question of his features open. "What was the weapon?" Lyman asked.

Morton tucked his hands in his pockets and shook his head. "We haven't found it. That's one similarity that struck me. The lack of a murder weapon. It was heavy and blunt. The killer took it with him. Just like your case."

"Anything stolen?" asked Garraty, his searching eyes surveying the expensively furnished living room.

"There was no ransacking. Of course, it's too early to know if anything was taken. My instincts tell me that this wasn't for profit. The condition of that face indicates rage if it indicates anything."

"Our victim was surprised coming out of the bathroom," Lyman noted.

"Maybe there's no connection at all, but I thought you'd want to have a look. The victim is named Cecil Walters, and he's gay. He was open about it. One of the gay libbers. He took part in several of those community-involvement deals we had last year. He came into the precinct along with a bunch of other gays and had bullshit sessions with the men who work the gay life. It was very constructive. Walters was quite eloquent."

"His days of eloquence are over now," Lyman said, looking down at the corpse. "Could it be that his lover did this?"

"We're open to all the possibilities, but I have that feeling in my gut that Walters picked up the wrong hustler."

"In our case, it looks as if the murderer could have been a close friend of the victim."

Morton nodded. "Well, I'll see that you get copied on all the paper on this."

"That'd be great, Lieutenant."

"You can hang around if you care to."

"For now I'll settle for whatever information you send over."

"You got it!"

On the way out, Lyman anticipated the newsmen waiting in the street and asked one of the uniformed officers to show him and Garraty the back way out. "Well, what do you think?" asked Garraty as they made it to their cars without reporters seeing them.

"It looks like an imitation to me."

"That's what I thought."

"Hell, if I were gay and wanted to get rid of a lover, I'd club him to death, too. The trouble is, if this city gets another gay killing in which the body has its face bashed in, the press is going to turn it into a crime wave, all perpetrated by the same guy."

They sped back to Manhattan over the Brooklyn Bridge.

10.

They caught Joey Shaw on his way out. Short, boyish, and dressed outlandishly for the disco dancing he and his friend planned for the evening, Joey Shaw wondered if the detectives could come back at another time. With a glance at the boy with him, Joey Shaw explained that if they didn't get to the door of the disco early they'd be standing in the street all night just waiting to get in. "This won't take long, Mr. Shaw," Lyman replied. "If your friend could spare you for just a few minutes?" Lyman smiled at the boy. He was slender and across the line into effeminacy, but there was a flinty look in the eyes and a set to the jaw that told Lyman the boy could be hard to handle when angry. The boy left the apartment slowly, reluctantly, his anger beginning a slow burn.

"It is really an imposition!" Joey Shaw exclaimed. He made no move to invite the detectives to be seated in the living room. The apartment was an L-shaped studio, the bed tucked away in the alcove behind an oriental screen. The rest of the furnishings were an amalgam of expensive art deco and Woolworth's plastic. "Am I a suspect?"

"We're just checking out the friends of Larry Apperson to see if anyone can help us get started with the investigation of his murder," replied Lyman,

"I can't be of any assistance. I haven't seen Larry in months."

Joey Shaw toyed with the sequined collar of his disco

outfit, a second skin of double-knit powder blue with a plunging neckline that advertised smooth flat pectorals. The bunching of double-knit at the juncture of his thighs left little to the imagination regarding the size and shape of Joey Shaw's genitals.

THE JOEY SHAW TAPE

I was his main attraction at the end of last summer. Since, there have been two other loves that I know of. You should talk to Lonnie Harris, who came after me. No pun intended. And Ellis Marsh, the current favorite. Not to mention a prime list of numbers in that chic crowd that Larry was attracted to, the South Hampton, Cherry Grove, Park Avenue, Bloomingdale's bunch. Me? I'm Alexander's all the way, and I have been known to scrounge around in May's department store, picking my wardrobe from the irregulars while fighting off Puerto Rican boys for just the right cut of jeans that might pass for Calvin Klein, even though they were made in Korea!

You sound kind of bitter.

Bitter? No. It's just that I was almost over the Larry Apperson experience, and now it's as if he just walked through that door again. He's dead, but his dying has brought him back to life for me. You see, I loved him, and I was deeply, deeply hurt when he left me. Once that crowd of rich fairies got a look at the portrait that Conrad painted last summer, Larry was suddenly the rage. I assume you have seen the painting? Larry kept it above his bed. He said he got a thrill out of it above him while he was making love.

Anyway, the painting was a second debut for Larry in the chic gay society that always attracted him. He was hardly a new face! He'd been an available-boy in this town for at least five years and had had sex with some of the men who suddenly acted as if he had just stepped off a UFO from a planet where all the inhabitants were beautiful young men. In the legends and mythology of New York's gay world, last fall will be remembered as 'the autumn of Larry Apperson.' He took gay society in triumph the way Lillie Langtry conquered Victorian London. The princes and princesses of homosexual New York were at his feet. Had we had a poet, as the Jersey Lily had Oscar Wilde, a great ode might have been written. We did have an artist, Conrad Ames, who saw in Larry something angelic.

Your affair with him lasted only a few weeks, then?

Yes.

What ended it?

Larry's affairs never had endings, Mr. Lyman, they just dissolved. One day you woke up and realized he wasn't calling you anymore. He was swept up in that mad wish to be courted by the people Conrad Ames showed the painting to. Next thing I knew, Larry was all the rage and getting ready for a stage debut, thanks to Ray Bonner, the director. During the show, Larry met Lonnie Harris. Have you met him?"

Lonnie found Larry's body.

(Laughter.) I bet Lonnie wept real tears.

Yes.

I never understood Larry taking up with Lonnie, who was really very common. I knew it wouldn't last. It didn't. Ellis Marsh was next.

Did Larry ever speak to you about a book he was writing?

A book? God, was it not enough for him to be a social success, a dramatic success, and the subject of the most talked about painting since the "Mona Lisa?" He was writing a book?

That's what we've heard. You know nothing about one?

No, but if it's ever published I'd like to read it.

Where were you last Thursday night, Mr. Shaw?

All night?

After dark.

I was here with the number you gentlemen are forcing me to keep waiting.

Is there anyone else other than that boy who can vouch for your whereabouts?

(Laughter) I never have an audience when I'm fucking, Mr. Garraty. (Pause) I was not like Larry, who never minded an audience.

What do you mean, Joey?

You didn't know that Larry made a really hardcore tape?

No.

Oh, but you should see it!

Do you have a copy of the tape?

No, but Larry had one. I would have thought you would have found it among his effects.

What was so special about the tape?

Oh, gentlemen, it is something. It stars Larry and the one and only Nelson Royce. I can see that this news has raised your eyebrows. Larry made the tape at Neal Davis's apartment.

Did you say *at* Neal Davis's apartment?

That's where Larry and Royce got together when Royce was in town. Royce was nervous about anyone knowing young boys came calling on him.

How do you know about this tape?

(The partners glanced at each other, both aware of what Joey Shaw was saying to them—the meaning of it: Neal Davis had lied about not letting his apartment be used for sexual liaisons between his boys and their clients.)

Larry told me about the tape. It was made as a joke. Royce was totally stoned when it was made on the video equipment that Davis keeps in his bedroom. That guy gets off by watching tapes that he makes when he is, shall we say, auditioning talent for his service? Anyway, Royce was stoned and Larry was in one of his playful moods, so he surreptitiously made a tape of what the two of them did in bed. He was going to show it to Royce and then erase it. Larry said something happened and he and Royce got into an argument, with Royce storming out. Then Davis came back and there was another big argument and Larry got thrown out. He hadn't had time to erase the tape, and he sure as hell didn't want Davis to see it, so he snuck it out with him when he left.

So Davis didn't know about the tape.

Larry never told him. Whether Royce did or not, I don't know. Royce probably forgot all about it, he was so stoned.

I gather that you viewed this tape?

Yes. When Larry told me about it and that he had it and was probably going to burn it or something, I begged him to let me see it. Just for laughs. I have a friend who's in television, and he has one of those BetaMax machines. We looked at it at my friend's house. It was, like, triple-X-rated!

Does the tape still exist?

I haven't the vaguest idea. I know Larry took it home with him that night. A few days later he discovered Lonnie Harris and that was the end of my affair with Larry.

Were you very upset when he dumped you?

Of course. But I didn't kill him.

We're going to ask your friend to verify your story about him being here with you the night Larry died.

Go ahead. Lance will tell you that he and I were here fucking like champions.

Waiting impatiently in the hallway as the detectives came out of Joey Shaw's apartment, the boy asked, "*Now* may we go dancing?"

Lyman asked about the night Larry Apperson died.

"Oh, Joey and I were here screwing, officers," said the boy.

"You'd lie for your friend, wouldn't you?" asked Garraty.

The boy laughed. "Sure. But I'm not lying. Now I want to dance." He shook his hips suggestively. Like Joey Shaw, he wore blue, tight-fitting disco clothes. With a smirk, he turned and said, "When things really get groovin' the shirt comes off, and Joey's too, and we are really something to see! We give all the guys hard-ons!"

"That's two things among the missing," Lyman said to his partner as they sat in the car watching Joey Shaw and his friend working hard to hail a taxi at the corner of West End Avenue and Sixty-sixth Street. "This thing about a pornographic video tape starring Nelson Royce could be a break in the goddamned stonewall we've been up against. The tape and the book."

"If there is a book," Garraty pointed out. "Nobody has ever seen it."

"Yeah, I know, but I have a feeling that there is a book of some kind. A real sizzler, probably, naming names." Lyman took out the folded, typed list of names from Larry Apperson's address book. It was proving an interesting vein of information to mine about Larry Apperson but the names had produced no paydirt, only the sparkling, alluring, heady glint of what, so far, had turned out to be fool's gold.

Joey and his friend climbed into a cab and were gone.

"Guys like that could give queers a bad name," Garraty announced.

Lyman chuckled and kept on looking at the list of names.

The list had been greatly reduced in its potential, dwindling from nearly two dozen names to a handful, most of whom he and Garraty had already interviewed. An initial check of the book's addresses, names and phone numbers had quickly indicated that many of the persons listed had long-since ceased to be factors in Larry Apperson's life. Some of the phone numbers now belonged to other parties. Other persons on the list had moved quite awhile ago. A few had moved to other cities. As an active working list of a call-boy's clients, the address book had proved woefully out of date. That Larry had made no effort to keep in touch with most of the names on the list was obvious because the book had been allowed to lapse into virtual uselessness as a client list.

There remained only three current listings yet to check: Ray Bonner, Donny Wills, and Emil Denziger.

Tonight there remained time to see Bonner.

In the morning, it would be Denziger.

Locating Wills would be a problem.

And, they would be going back to talk to movie star Nelson Royce to follow up on the information Joey Shaw gave them about the pornographic tape.

More importantly, Neal Davis was going to be asked to explain a couple of lies.

11.

"What the hell is there about fags and the theater?" asked Garraty.

"What?"

"Have you ever met a fag who wasn't in the theater or planning to be in the theater?"

"Christ, where do you get these ideas?"

"Well everyone knows that the theater is full of fags."

"The world is full of fags, partner."

They were heading downtown to the off-off-Broadway theater where director Ray Bonner's latest production was on the boards. It was the play that had briefly featured Lawrence Apperson.

The theater nestled on the ground floor of a loft building in SoHo, that slightly seedy sprawl of bleak structures south of Houston Street which once was a manufacturing area but was now being taken over by galleries, theaters and rebuilt lofts made suitable for people to live in. At most, the auditorium of the theater would hold a hundred people, Lyman figured, as he watched the play. The actors nearly out-numbered the audience. "An experiment in the theater of the senses," said a sign outside. A quote from a review said, "Daringly erotic!" it was that. Everyone on stage was naked except a handsome young man who had most of the lines in the scene—an angry tirade against the "straight establish-ment." Lyman assumed this was the role Larry Apperson had played, recalling that Larry had not been required to take off his clothes for his theatrical debut.

Garraty watched with mingled fascination and disgust. He was fascinated by the fact that actors would willingly go on stage naked and that audiences would pay to see them and believe they were watching drama and not a skin show. He was disgusted because it was a performance that, once upon a time, the police would have closed down for obscenity—his disgust rooted in his disapproval of the changes in the law that kept the cops away. First Amendment! A license for smut!

They waited until the end of the play to talk to Ray Bonner who, an usher whispered to them when they inquired, was the handsome older actor at stage left. Noting Bonner's nudity, Lyman quipped, "I see he has nothing to hide as an artist." The usher groaned and turned away. He reappeared just before the final line of the dialogue to tell them that if they would follow him he would show them to Mr. Bonner's dressing room.

The term was charitable, Lyman decided.

Bonner knew there were cops in his dressing room, thanks to the usher. He guessed why they wanted to see him. For their sensibilities, not his, he put on a robe, then sat, lit a cigarette, crossed his legs, and said, "You are here to talk to me about Larry. What a tragedy! He had so much promise.

"We've lost a talent, believe me. Larry had been just wonderful in this production when I first opened it a few months ago. He inspired me, I admit, to be even more daring in mounting the show. You see, the script originally called for all the actors to be nude. But I thought, wouldn't it be a funny twist to take the most beautiful of all the cast and have him fully dressed throughout? It worked! That is why the young man in Larry's role tonight was dressed to the hilt, although, as good looking as Warren is, he couldn't approach Larry for sheer beauty. Ah, Larry! To be that beautiful *and* be able to act! A miracle! Who killed him, by the way?"

"That's what we're trying to find out, Mr. Bonner," said Garraty, leaning against the wall just behind Bonner, who sat at a small dressing table, turned, so he could face the detectives. Garraty was trying to decide if the bristled mustache was really Bonner's or fake. It was a shade or two darker than Bonner's sandy hair. All in all, it was difficult to know how much of the man's face was real and how much was makeup. Having seen Bonner on stage, nude, however, Garraty knew that everything below Bonner's neckline was real, as well as abundant.

THE RAY BONNER TAPE

I have no idea who killed Larry. I only know that whoever did it has deprived all of us of a future star.

Indeed? Larry was that promising?

I was working on getting him a really good agent, and a certain mutual friend had managed to introduce Larry to a very important movie actor.

That would be Nelson Royce.

You know about that, do you?

Why did Larry leave your play if he was so successful in it?

Impatience to get on with what he believed was the career he had been looking for for so long. He came in for a Friday evening performance and told me that he had a chance to go to Hollywood and so was leaving the play after the Saturday night show.

How did you feel about that?

Upset, but I calmed down and wished Larry well. I offered to help him get an agent.

That was very generous, Mr. Bonner.

Ray, please.

Ray.

I try to help young actors get started. I do it for the theatre. If you know anything about theatrical people you know that there are certain things that you just do for the good of the theatre with all personal considerations aside.

Forgive the directness of this next question, Ray, but I have to ask it. Did you and Larry have sexual relations with each other?

You are direct, Mr. Lyman. The answer is yes, but only once. The first time I met him we had sex. Very innocent. I blew him and that was it. I found I was much more interested in him as an acting talent than as a piece of ass. There's plenty of ass around but not much acting talent, I mean to tell you.

Where were you last Thursday night, Ray?

Here.

You can prove that?

Ask anyone in the cast and, if you can locate them, any of the fifty-five people who were here that night watching me act! Sorry to be a wash-out in the suspect category. Melodrama was never my bag.

I understand that Larry met his friend Lonnie Harris at this theatre.

Um. It was backstage on opening night. Lonnie had come in with a gentleman-friend. A sugar-daddy if you must know. There was something electric between Larry and Lonnie. I saw it right away. It was pure sexual attraction. They got together after that and I understand became roommates.

You sound as if you find it hard to believe they could get together.

Not really. Lonnie adored Larry from the very first, and Larry always enjoyed that kind of slavish adulation. They were not precisely master-and-slave, because Larry was never into the S&M bag. But he could dominate Lonnie and he seemed to enjoy knowing that he could even if he never put it into practice. The difference between Lonnie and all the others who adored Larry was a fundamental one. All the others wanted to posses Larry. Lonnie wanted Larry to possess him. Get the difference? Rumor has it that Larry finally asked Lonnie to move out. They had quite a row, according to the gossip at "Charlie's Aunt."

That's a gay bar. Excuse me, Mr. Garraty, but have you ever thought about becoming an actor?

Garraty was startled and straightened abruptly. "An actor? Me?"

"Yes. You have a certain raw quality. Rough. Like Burt Reynolds without the smooth edges. Or Charles Bronson. If you ever want to get into acting, you come around and see me."

"I like my work," Garraty replied firmly.

Bonner shrugged. "What else can I tell you about Larry?" he asked, looking at Lyman again.

"Did you know he was writing a book?"

Bonner smiled. "Do you actually believe that story? It's hogwash. Take my word for it. I know because I understand what deeply motivates people, and Larry Apperson's motivations were far more visceral than intellectual. Larry was a sensual youth. He couldn't sit still long enough to write a book. He'd get antsy or horny or both and he'd be up and out, looking to get laid."

"Ray," Lyman concluded, buttoning up his overcoat and turning to leave, "thanks for talking with us. Good luck with your show."

"Luck I don't need. I need customers. Bring your friends."

"We work nights mostly, Ray. Not much of a chance to get out to the theatre."

"Too bad," Ray Bonner smiled. "Goodbye."

It was near midnight as the detectives settled into their car and moved uptown.

Much of the following day Lyman would be working alone while Garraty went downtown to Centre Street for a court appearance on an old case, which was expected to be called around eleven o'clock. The court date required some planning between them as to what Lyman would do while Garraty was testifying. "First thing in the morning, the two of us will look up this man Denziger. I'll drop you at court, and then I think I'll have a chat with my old pal John Fagleton in Public Morals to see if he knows the whereabouts of Donny Wills."

"I have a feeling there's going to be a plea bargain settlement of this case in court, so I shouldn't be gone long," Garraty said. He hoped there would not be any bargaining. The case involved an assault on an eighty-two year old woman during a robbery. The old woman wanted the kid who did it put away forever. Garraty agreed. But the D.A., the defense, and the judge would decide.

Lyman looked at his watch. "We might as well hang it up for tonight. Drop me at my house. First thing tomorrow we'll talk to this Denziger guy."

After Lyman got out of the car, Garraty lingered a moment, watching him go through the revolving door into his apartment house. A deep, warm wave of affection flowed through him as he watched his partner. He looked very tired, very alone, and very vulnerable, Garraty thought. When they had a better handle on this case, he decided, he would bring up the suggestion of Lyman taking a vacation. It would set off an argument, he knew, but he knew even better that Lyman was a man in desperate need of a long, purging, restorative break from his job and, more importantly, from the lonely routines of his life.

12.

The emptiness reached out through the open door of his apartment and drew Lyman into it. When he flicked on the switch, the glare from the ceiling lamps made the apartment hard and uninviting. Lyman snapped the lights off immediately. He turned on a small lamp on top of his color TV console, transforming the apartment into the soft, warm place it had been when Betty was alive. Feeling at home, Lyman went to the kitchen and poured a glass of beer. The refrigerator was empty except for part of a six-pack. Filling it the way Betty used to fill it had proven a wasteful exercise. He'd tried to run his house the way she had, but soon after her death he spent less and less time in the apartment, finding the human contact he needed with the men of the squad, with his partner. He sat in a large chair that faced the TV set but did not turn on the set. It was the chair Betty sat in watching TV while he was at work. Television was for her what the men of the squad and his job had become for him.

He got up from the chair and stood by the window of the living room, looking down on the rooftops, white and clean with snow. Empty, silent, the roofs were unpeopled in the winter, but in summertime they were alive with sunbathers and kids from the neighborhood who made playgrounds of them.

Going into the bedroom, he sat on the edge of his bed and

knew he would not be able to sleep. Draining his glass of beer, he decided he might as well work.

He took a cab to Greenwich and Seventh Avenue and walked the half block to Neal Davis's address. His detective's shield and the threat of arrest persuaded the young overnight doorman not to signal ahead, so Neal Davis was surprised at the arrival of Detective Sheldon Lyman at his door. "This is an outrageous intrusion, Mr. Lyman," Davis protested.

"I was in the neighborhood, Davis, and I thought I'd drop by."

"I have guests!"

"Well, tell them to put their clothes on and leave us alone for a while because you and I have a few little misunderstandings to straighten out."

"I will not speak with you without my attorney present," replied Davis, closing the door.

Lyman's foot and hand kept it open. "Let's keep this on the pleasant side, hm? Do I come in or do I take out my shield and my trusty .38 and prove to you that I'm a police officer here in the legitimate pursuit of my sworn duty?"

"Interrogations at *two in the morning*?"

"A conversation is all I want. Make it easy on yourself, Davis."

"May we talk elsewhere? It would be very inconvenient for me to interrupt my guests. In your car? There's a coffee shop nearby."

They both had a fleeting remembrance of an interrogation ending with Mike Brown slugging Davis. Both smiled ruefully at the memory, but neither mentioned it.

They walked slowly in the cold along Greenwich to the coffee shop on Sixth Avenue, a brightly lighted, noisy, bustling establishment. They found a booth in the back. "You told me a couple of little white lies, Neal," Lyman said for openers.

"I lied? How did I lie?"

"For one thing, you told me Nelson Royce met Larry

Apperson at the Plaza. Royce says they met at your place. Which is it, Neal?"

"My place."

"So why the lie?"

"I wanted to keep out of this Apperson thing, as best I could. What difference does it make where they met? Larry was killed at his own apartment, so what's the big deal?"

"Veracity, credibility, *mendacity*, Neal. What am I to think when I find out you've lied to me, not once but twice?"

"Twice?"

"You said you didn't know Larry was writing a book."

"Whatever I said, I said because I never believed him when he talked about writing. I don't really know if he was writing one, but even if he was and you told me he was I still wouldn't believe it. Do you have any idea how many stories I hear from boys about how they're really, finally, getting their acts together?"

"But Larry was not your usual run of the mill hustler."

"No, he wasn't, but he had the same flaws, the same maddening characteristics that you find in all hustlers. He was never able to establish a lasting relationship. Some people say that is the curse of being a homosexual. Maybe it is. Larry was a very whimsical boy. He could be madly in love with someone one day and fall madly in love with someone else the next. He was flighty like that in his relationships and it was natural for me to assume that he would not have any more success in sticking to something as challenging and demanding as writing a book."

"Wasn't it possible that Larry was not just like all your other boys?"

"I deal with probabilities. I'm like an insurance company. I could admit that a man might live to be two hundred years old but the life insurance policy I'd sell him would be written on the probability that he'll die in his sixties. I listened to Larry talking about reordering his life, about writing, about acting, about getting a job in the movies, and I put my money on the probability that he'd do none of those."

"That's a crummy attitude for a man who says he loved the kid."

"Look, Lyman, what the hell is this? You've got a murder on your hands. You've had hundreds of murders on your hands. This one's no big deal. Larry just picked up the wrong guy one night, probably. You're not going to find Larry's killer among his friends or even among his former lovers. There is no deep dark crime hidden in this case. If you ask me, Larry made a pickup somewhere and it turned out bad. How many times has that happened? What the hell is the big deal, anyway?"

"I don't like being lied to on a case. It makes me nervous. And suspicious."

"You know your problem, Lyman? You don't really understand what Larry Apperson's life truly was. You don't know, except what you get from police manuals and Lord knows where else; you don't know *anything* about homosexuals. You certainly don't know anything about hustlers, even when they have the luxury of being call boys. If you knew anything about hustling and the shit that those boys go through, you wouldn't be going around this town harassing frightened men who happened to have been clients—maybe lovers, even—of Larry Apperson. It's too bad you're not gay, Lyman. Then you'd understand. May I go now? I do have guests."

Lyman let him go.

When he, himself, left the coffee shop, he was shaken. Perhaps Davis had discerned a truth about him—a truth that he did not understand about Larry Apperson. He did *not* understand about Larry the hustler, who always managed to beguile and enchant and charm and win men who possessed money and style and all the graces but who always left them, on a whim, for boys who had little, if any, money, charm or grace. The Larry Apperson he knew was a portrait in oils: beauty, seductive eyes, a comely smile, a sense of humor that demanded that one of the world's foremost portraitists paint an erotic picture. The Larry Apperson he knew—and liked— existed in his head.

Perhaps, he decided, walking, I ought to get a little perspective on what Larry Apperson's life was really all about. By the time he reached the corner of Sixth Avenue and Eighth Street he'd made up his mind about what he had to do.

He found a bar called "Denver." It was a new gay bar and strived to catch the flavor of the Rocky Mountains in its decor, but with only a little more than an hour to go before closing the sparse clientele looked steadfastly Greenwich Village. Lyman went to the bar and ordered a Heineken's. With beer in hand, he turned, leaned against the bar and surveyed "Denver" with his eyes. Unless by some miracle it caught on with trendy gays who could adopt a new bar and make it a gold mine, "Denver" would not stay in business long. The customers paid no attention to him as he looked them over. They were older men. None looked like a hustler. Deciding that he'd picked the wrong bar at the wrong time and probably was being a damned fool to even consider it important to get to know the victim in the case he had to solve, he set down his untouched beer and prepared to leave.

At that moment, out of the men's room in the rear of the bar stepped a boy whom Lyman recognized immediately—the boy who'd been drinking Heineken's in "Charlie's Aunt". The boy leaned with one foot propped against the wall and hooked a thumb in his belt. In his other hand dangled a bottle of beer. He had on the imitation flight jacket, jeans, a red flannel shirt, and boots. He had the eagle-eyed look of a young John Wayne in an old John Ford western—alone, wary, ready.

Lyman walked toward the boy, a knot of nervousness

forming in the pit of his stomach and spreading hotly, like liquid fire to his chest. His mouth went dry when he saw the boy watching him as he approached. In the eagle-eyes Lyman thought he saw a flicker of recognition. The boy shifted his booted foot to the floor, lifting his whole body upright. Lyman expected the boy to drift away, but instead he smiled. "Still drinking Heineken's," he observed. Lyman stopped, caught dead in his tracks with surprise and confusion. "I never forget a face," the boy said. "I know I've seen you, but I don't think we talked."

"Not about anything except how good Heineken's beer is."

"Now I remember. Hello! My name's Ned," the boy said, holding out a hand.

Lyman took it. "Sheldon. Friends call me Shelly or Shel."

His cop's instinct was to tell the boy who he was and to show him the photograph of Larry Apperson, to ask questions, to work the case he was on, to develop it, but he did none of these things. Instead, he relaxed, slipping his cold hands into his pockets because he realized in a moment of amazement and confusion and embarassment that they were trembling. "I thought maybe you were waiting for someone that night we spoke."

"No. That place was just too crowded. I don't like to feel crowded. I wasn't waiting for anyone."

Lyman studied the boy's face. The eyes were brown and flecked with green and caught the flicker of the little electric lights which the decorator of "Denver" hoped would simulate gas lamps. His was an angular face, as if it had been rudely shaped from a square piece of clay, unlike Larry Apperson's face which had been smooth and polished. This boy's face had deep dimples and a cleft in the chin. The lips were thinner than Larry Apperson's full ones. Larry's lips could pout. This boy's would draw into a line of anger.

With an amused but slightly nervous chuckle, the boy said, "You have a way of looking at someone as if he had no clothes on."

"Maybe that's because I'm a. . . ." Lyman caught himself at the word "cop." Instead he said, "Maybe that's because I'm a man who's interested in really getting to know people."

"That's nice," the boy smiled.

"I, uh, don't usually go to, uh, gay bars," Lyman said.

"I haven't seen you before, I know."

"It's just that tonight I thought it might be interesting to come out to a bar."

"Are you looking for someone?" The question was direct, spoken openly, not as if the boy thought it was a question that ought to be whispered. It was an invitation, and it left Lyman stammering for an answer. The boy laughed. "You are a nervous one! You seem like a nice man to me."

"You're a nice boy."

"Nice man. Nice boy. Nice combination. What's a nice couple like us doing in a place like this? Shall we go somewhere?"

Blinking in disbelief, Lyman did not know how to answer. He knew from years on the police force, in Vice, that this was how easily contact could be made among gays. He knew that this was the familiar dialogue of casual liaisons which characterized the notorious promiscuity of many homosexuals, and, finally, he knew that there had to have been dozens, perhaps hundreds, of solicitous conversations between Larry Apperson and the men from whom he earned a living or simply sought love. If it hadn't been for the brutality of murder intruding into Larry Apperson's life at midstream, this boy smilingly waiting for an answer to his proposition might be Larry Apperson.

"I live uptown," Lyman answered, finally.

The boy beamed a joyous smile. "Great!"

Only when they were in the street looking for a taxi did

Lyman think that there might be money involved. Self-consciously, he asked, "How much?"

The boy laughed. "It's late and I wasn't expecting to score this late, so you can make it whatever you think it's worth."

The boy hailed a cab and held the door open for him.

This was how it must have been, he thought, in those numberless times when Larry Apperson went to bars to meet the men who provided whatever it was Larry Apperson happened to be seeking. Until this moment, the boy in the painting had been a creature of his intellect. Beside him in a taxi bumping uptown was a boy who could have been Larry Apperson, and suddenly the carefree and gay boy—in the old sense of the word—was nearer to flesh than ever before. In the form of a boy named Ned who had unwittingly let himself be picked up in a bar by a cop, Larry Apperson had at last assumed recognizable human dimensions. It was as if Larry had come down from the painting in his bedroom to take the form of this boy in the phony flying jacket. In the cab swinging into Third Avenue and moving nearer to Sheldon Lyman's home sat a surrogate Larry Apperson, a boy who bore little resemblance physically to the beautiful boy in an oil painting but who was Larry's kinsman, his brother, in a unique and dangerous and bewildering trade which Sheldon Lyman, until now, thought he had understood. Glancing at the angular profile of the boy beside him, Lyman realized he understood nothing of how Larry Apperson's life must have been. This boy named Ned knew; at least he knew the generality of what it must have been like for Larry Apperson making it in the world with his beauty and wits and body.

For all those reasons, Sheldon Lyman did not tell Ned who he was as the cab came to a stop, as they crossed the white marble floored lobby, as they rode up in the elevator, as they went into the apartment, as Lyman sank into a chair in his living room without taking off his jacket because it would reveal the .38 special holstered on his hip. The boy was amused. "You are really a shy one!"

Ned placed himself in the center of the living room where the soft glow of one lamp painted shadows in the angles and clefts of his face. The light danced in his green-flecked brown eyes. It rippled upon him as the boy moved his hands to his clothing and slowly, teasingly, unbuttoned buttons and un-zipped zippers, peeling off the layers of clothing—the jacket, the shoes, the shirt, the blue jeans, the socks. Finally, he posed in the middle of the room in only his briefs, looking like a kid in a bathing suit getting ready to make a mad dash across the beach to the surf.

Lyman had not moved. He had watched as the boy undressed and imagined it was Larry.

Ned's body was not Larry's. Like his face, the body was roughly hewn, all angles and protrusions of bones, and hard muscles; not like Larry Apperson's body, which seemed in the painting and the Polaroid to be that of a much younger boy. Larry's body was classical in its form, like statues of boys in ancient Greece or Rome, all roundness and suppleness and voluptuousness.

Without taking his eyes off Lyman, Ned removed the shorts, rolling them down his hips until, proudly, defiantly, and invitingly, his hard penis sprang free. The boy kicked off the shorts and stepped forward, crossing the room, his penis swaying hard as he walked. Lyman sat frozen, mute and mesmerized with only his eyes moving, seeing not Ned but Larry Apperson advancing relentlessly toward him.

At last, Ned was in front of him, directly, and Lyman stared at the erection so close to him. "Go ahead," said the boy.

Lyman looked up across the rough landscape of the boy's torso into his smiling face, looking down.

"Come on, Shel. It's what you want, what I want. Suck my cock."

Lyman reared back. "Ned," he blurted, "I'm a police officer."

The boy jerked away as if he had been tugged by a rope. "A cop?"

Urgently, Lyman tried to reassure the boy. "I'm not going to arrest you! I didn't do this to entrap you."

"What the hell is going on?" the boy cried, angrily, clutching frantically at his clothes and pulling them on.

"I don't know why I brought you up here, why I let you think that we were coming here for sex. You see, I'm working on a case, and. . . ."

"Jesus Christ! A cop!"

"I can explain, Ned."

"You better explain it to a shrink, mister, because you are really sick."

Lyman sank deep into his chair watching the boy scramble into his clothes. When the boy was gone, Lyman sat with his chin against his chest, his eyes closed, his hands trembling.

13.

Just before nine a.m. they went looking for Emil Denziger.
Emil Denziger was in.

He was a small man, gray, professorial, speaking with a charming accent—possibly Austrian, Lyman thought. He courteously let the pair of detectives into his modest apartment on the twelfth floor and led them into a living room made cozy and warm by thousands of books which climbed to the ceiling and filled three of the room's walls. "I knew," he said, sinking forlornly into a chair that was positioned to catch the light from the window, a chair for reading. "I knew you would come. I knew when I read about the murder of the boy. I hoped you would not come. But I knew you would. Sit down, please, sirs."

"What was your relationship with Lawrence Apperson, Mr. Denziger?" Lyman asked, taking a corner of a couch.

"I believe you know already, sir."

"You paid him for having sexual relations with you?"

"Yes."

"How often?"

"Perhaps once a month. He visited me on Sundays always, but, do you know what, sir? Do you know this about that boy? That he had a *mind*? Oh, he admired my library. Sometimes, after we did what I asked him to come here for, he would stay and have lunch with me, and we would talk, and I would tell him about the books he ought to read to develop that mind of his. Sometimes he would ask if he could stay here and read some of my books, and I let him do it because I wanted to encourage him to learn. He told me he had dropped out of school and ran away from home. What a pity that was. A boy his age should have been in school learning. Now, he has been trying to make it up. He has a long list of books that I wrote out for him, and he has even taken out a library card to get some of the books. He is working very hard to improve his mind. That is the kind of boy Lawrence is. Oh! I have been talking about him as if he was still alive! In my mind, in my heart, he is. It is so sad. So sad. After a while, he became like a son to me. Although the people in the building, the doorman, my neighbors—they believe Lawrence is my nephew. They do not know that he came here for . . . for. . . ."

"I assure you, Mr. Denziger, that there is no need for any of these people to know about your relationship with Larry Apperson."

"There has been so much publicity, I am afraid someone will figure it out."

"Mr. Denziger, we have come here to ask you to tell us what you can about Larry. I am sorry to say that we don't have much to go on in investigating his murder, except the names of his friends."

"There is nothing I can tell you, gentlemen. I am sorry."

Lyman and Garraty exchanged glances. Emil Denziger was obviously not their man. They each knew that. "Mr. Denziger," said Lyman, "you are a man of letters, an educated man, and the interest you showed in Larry's mind is admirable. Do you recall Larry ever mentioning to you that he was thinking about writing a book?"

"Oh, my, yes! He talked about that a great deal recently. He said he was going to write a novel about his experiences. He saw my alarm at the possibility of finding myself in its pages and he immediately assured me that he would not write about me."

"Did he ever actually produce anything for the book?" Garraty anticipated Lyman's question.

"Oh, I saw several pages, different pages, at various times. It showed promise, although the pages were better described as notes rather than finished writing."

"Mr. Denizger, this is very important to us. Until now we've heard only that Larry was always talking about writing something. You actually saw some of the material. Do you know where that manuscript is?"

"No. I'm sorry. I wish I could help you. It is that important?"

"It could be why Larry was murdered."

"Oh, my God!"

It was clear that Emil Denziger could be crossed off their list of suspects, they agreed, sitting in their car and going over all they had learned so far. Larry Apperson had accumulated a lot of people with reasons to do him in. However, Denziger was not one of them.

"What'll you be doing while I'm resting my ass in court?" asked Garraty as they drove downtown.

"I'm going to visit John Eagleton in Public Morals to see if his guys have a line on the infamous 'Chicken' Wills. I'm also going to enlist the help of Morals in picking up any street talk about this case."

Curving off the F.D.R. drive and wending their way through twisting streets, they came onto Centre Street and slid to a stop in front of the gray-slabbed monolith of the Criminal Courts Building. Lyman wondered, momentarily, if their efforts would result in bringing Larry Apperson's murderer to trial in the building. Garraty got out, waved, and headed into the court.

Sergeant John Eagleton, a burly gray-haired cop whom most people mistook for an insurance salesman rather than a policeman, greeted Lyman in his office, set off in a corner from the larger space devoted to the Central Obscenity Unit, whose current main mission was the investigation of boy prostitution. Eagleton and Lyman were friends going back to Lyman's years with Vice. They chatted about old times for a few minutes and told each other how great they looked for cops their age, then got down to business. "I've got a drawer full of suspects, but they are either the world's greatest liars or the world's most innocent men. These are men who've had connections with the victim because they are men with a taste for boys. Young ones. It's a remote chance, but if one of these men did the job on Apperson he might get talkative with another boy and some of that talk might get back to the ears of your men out working the streets. I'm grabbing at straws."

"I'll be glad to put the word out. You'll give me the names of these men?"

"I brought them with me." Lyman slid the list across Eagleton's desk.

"He was a friendly young man, apparently."

"You've heard his story a thousand times, John. He got into hustling when he was chicken. Thirteen years old."

"Hell, by today's standards that makes him a late bloomer. Kids today start at eight, nine years old."

"Larry was broken in by our old nemesis Donny Wills. I believe the two may have run into each other recently. A neighbor says he saw Larry having a hassle with a black man. I think it could have been Wills. I'm hoping to unearth the bastard. I thought you could help."

"Wills is at Rikers Island."

"Since when?"

"We arrested him last night. All the usual charges. Wills never changes his tune."

"Was he out on the street at the time of the Apperson killing?"

"If the victim died before last night then Wills was walking around."

"Did you guys have him under surveillance by any chance last Thursday?"

Eagleton hunched up his broad shoulders. "Sorry, but we didn't have an around-the-clock on him. We knew where he was when we wanted him."

"Then Wills could have committed the murder."

"Yeah, but, as you know, Wills is a pimp and a pander, and he doesn't really have a record for violence."

"Except for the kind of violence that is visited on kids he hooks into his kiddie-pros business."

"Yes," shrugged Eagleton. "But murder? I don't think Wills is capable."

"As Paul Parker says, 'We're all capable of murder under the right circumstances.'"

"So true, Sheldon."

"I appreciate the help you're going to give me on this one, John. You want a report on what I get out of Wills when I talk to him?"

"Love to have it, Sheldon."

Donald Jackson "Donny" Wills, a.k.a. "Chicken" Wills! Age: 32. Black. A yellow sheet running five pages, from his first arrest for purse snatching when he was eight years old to his latest bust for engaging in the prostitution of young boys, a second offense.

Lyman remembered "Chicken" Wills very well.

At the time of his first arrest on charges of promoting prostitution, "Chicken" Wills had pleaded not guilty, claiming that he had simply been friendly and helpful to scared, hungry and homeless boys who happened to wind up on his doorstep. Lyman, as one of the arresting officers from Vice, testified at the trial:

DISTRICT ATTORNEY: Officer Lyman, will you be kind enough to tell the court what you know, in general, of the trafficking in boys for purposes of prostitution in New York City?

DEFENSE ATTORNEY: Objection! There is no basis for admitting this testimony.

JUDGE: Overruled.

DISTRICT ATTORNEY: Officer Lyman?

LYMAN: In New York, as in many cities, there is a flourishing business in boys for sex. On the street, the boys are known as "chickens." They range in age from about twelve years to eighteen. The men who hire them are called "chickenhawks." Many of the boys work on their own, free-lance. But many are initiated into the business by pimps and work for them, either on the streets or in call-boy operations. The pimps are skilled in spotting potential talent, usually in bus stations or in game arcades that abound in the Times Square area. The boys are induced by the money. But many of them are just so starved for attention, for affection, for love, that they go with men for these reasons. The money is a nice extra.

DISTRICT ATTORNEY: The defendant, Mr. Wills, is charged with being in the business of prostituting young boys. Do you have any direct knowledge of his alleged activities in that area?

LYMAN: Yes, I do.

DISTRICT ATTORNEY: Tell us about it.

LYMAN: I arrested Mr. Wills when he was engaged in the process of arranging for a man to buy the services of a young boy.

DISTRICT ATTORNEY: How old was the boy?

LYMAN: Twelve.

DISTRICT ATTORNEY: Tell us the circumstances of the arrest.

LYMAN: My partner and I, Detective Brown, were working undercover in the Times Square area. We had a backup team of four other officers. I was wired.

DISTRICT ATTORNEY: Wired?

LYMAN: I was wearing a hidden microphone and transmitter.

DISTRICT ATTORNEY: For what purpose?

LYMAN: So my partner and the backup team could hear what was transacted between me and the suspect.

DISTRICT ATTORNEY: What was transacted?

LYMAN: We negotiated terms for me to have sex with the boy.

DISTRICT ATTORNEY: You negotiated these terms with whom?

LYMAN: Mr. Wills.

DEFENSE ATTORNEY: Move that this testimony be stricken on the basis of entrapment and the illegal use of listening devices, violating my client's Constitutional rights.

JUDGE: Motion denied!

Lyman glanced across the courtroom at Wills and cracked a slight smile. "Gotcha, Wills," he thought, while the defense lawyer argued futiley to have the testimony barred.

"Chicken" Wills turned his head, noticed Lyman's smile, and gave a win-some-lose-some shrug.

The face of the boy had looked like something out of a Norman Rockwell "Saturday Evening Post" cover. The hair was yellow as hay, the face freckled, the nose upturned, the lips full, the brow puckered into a frown as the boy batted his hands against the sides of a pinball machine in the game arcade in the middle of the block between Times Square and Eighth Avenue on Forty-second Street.

Lyman and Brown had watched the white boy and the tall black man for quite a while, from a distance, and had seen the black man—Donny "Chicken" Wills—give the boy his instructions: go into the arcade, play a machine, and if a man comes up to you and looks as if he's watching you, or interested in you, ask him for a quarter to play another game. If the man gives it, be friendly to the man. If the man keeps giving you quarters, be nice and talk to the man, and if he asks you to go with him, do it. I'll catch up with you and the man and I will decide how much he's going to pay you.

The man who approached the boy—Eric, he had said his name was—had been Sheldon Lyman, wired for sound.

He and Brown and the backup team arrested Wills near the Nedick's stand at Forty-second and Seventh.

Petrified with fright, Eric had tried to run, but Lyman caught him, being gentle with him and assuring him that he would not be hurt or be sent to jail. Later, after Wills was booked, Brown and Lyman took Eric to dinner and then turned him over to Juvenile, who ultimately delivered him to his frantic, worried parents in the Bronx.

Wills got a year on a plea-bargain.

Lyman never knew what happened to Eric.

Driving to Queens on his way to Rikers Island for a reunion with "Chicken" Wills, Lyman imagined that Larry Apperson at thirteen had looked a lot like Eric. Tragically ironic, he thought, that, like Eric, Larry had run across Wills at that age. How their paths crossed, Lyman did not know. That was just one of the things that he was going to get out of Wills.

At each of three checkpoints on the road and bridge from Queens to Rikers, Lyman slowed his car almost to a stop to show his shield to the guards, who waved him on. He drove over familiar roads to the entrance to the main building of the Men's House of Detention. Parking, he crossed an ice-slicked parking lot. Beyond the prison-island sprawled the tantalizingly close La Guardia Airport where thousands of travelers freely came and went every day, their huge planes flying low above the prison's cellblocks.

He waited for Wills in a room reserved for prisoners to talk to their lawyers. A guard waited outside the locked room, looking through the small window occasionally at Lyman and Wills, seated at a square, battered table.

THE DONNY "CHICKEN" WILLS TAPE

You have a right to have your lawyer here, Wills.

What for? That sucker ain't done nothin' for me so far. Lyman, what you doin' back on a Vice case? Thought you was Home-ee-side?

I am.

Hey, man, I ain't killed nobody.

I didn't say you did.

An' I sure as hell didn't kill Larry Apperson.

Do you happen to know who did?

Probably one of those fancy fruits he hung out with.

I heard you and Larry had a shouting match shortly before he was killed. I hear you went to see him just before he died.

You heard right.

What were you shouting about?

I told him he was a piece of shit, is all.

Why'd you tell him that?

'Cause that's what he was.

You don't see the kid for years, then you come up to him out of the blue and tell him he's a piece of shit?

Yeah.

Why?

I heard he was writing' a book about me.

A book about you?

Yeah, man.

And?

And I wanted him to know that if I was gonna be in his mother-fuckin' book I expected a piece of the action.

And what did Larry say?

He told me to fuck off, man.

And you called him a piece of shit.

Damned straight.

And that was it? You and he had an argument over literature?

That was it.

Why in hell should he cut you in on any money from a book he might write?

'Cause without him gettin' started with me he'd have been nothing', man. Mother-fuck, I started that kid when he didn't know his ass from a hole in the ground much less what his ass was for. Fuckin' dumb chicken fresh off the bus from Philly! Man, the vultures in this town could have had him for supper if it wasn't for me bein' there in the Port Authority when he hit town.

You did him a real favor. Turning him into a hustler.

Didn't hurt him none, did it?

It killed him, creep.

Didn't kill him when he was with me.

He started dying then, whether you knew it or not.

Oh, Lyman, get off my case.

They got you this time, Wills. No plea bargaining this time. Things are tougher now than they were when I busted you years ago. Decent people are sick of what you do, and guys like you do hard time these days.

Sing your tune, Lyman, but I ain't hearin' it.

You'll get ten to twenty, sure as hell.

Now what? You gonna come onto me about how if I cooperate with you in the Apperson case you can get me a break with the D.A.?

I'm not saying anything like that. Just expressing my opinion on what kind of time you'll be doing.

I don't know nothin' about who killed Apperson, 'cept that I didn't kill him!

Can you prove that?

Don't have to. You gotta prove I did.

You'll be doing hard time anyway.

*So what you doin' here? You know I didn't waste that dude. You
knew that when you came all this way to Rikers. What is this jive
anyway? You came to pump me about the kid, is that it?*

You know how we cops operate, Wills. Talk to everybody. Even slime like you.

*Shit. What's so special about this Apperson dude? He was nothin'
special, no matter what those Village and Park Avenue fags tell you.
Apperson was no different from any other kid who ever peddled his ass.
He liked what he was doin' and he liked the bread it brought in. I had
myself a damned good laugh when I learned that those gay snobs had
flipped out for Larry Apperson. They acted as if he had just suddenly
appeared here on earth. Hell, I fucked Larry Apperson when he was a
thirteen year old cherry.*

How many young lives have you corrupted, Wills?

*Never corrupted nobody that didn't want to be corrupted,
Lyman.*

I'd love to hang a murder rap on you. I'd just love it.

*You're somethin', Lyman, you really are! You get off on this
reputation you have for you you-man-i-tee. Humanity, shit! You
may not beat up on people like that partner you used to have. Brown.
But you beat up on people other ways. You and your little mind
tricks! You think you're hot shit, better'n everybody else. Mr.
Morality in the flesh. Well, shit, Lyman, I've had your number for
years.*

Indeed?

*Ever since that day you busted me in that set-up with that little
piece of chicken in that Times Square arcade!*

You've had my number since then, eh?

*And I still got it. You know what I think, Lyman? I think if
you hadn't had all those cops with you and you didn't have that wire
on you, you'd've liked to have gone somewhere with that neat little
piece of chicken to bang him in his sweet little ass! Just like any old
chickenhawk!*

14.

There was a hard, slate-gray, hateful frigidity in the streets as Lyman drove into Manhattan over the Triboro Bridge, cutting across the northern end of the island, Harlem, and then moving south on west side streets.

His destination was the area around the Port Authority bus terminal, the port of entry where Larry Apperson had slipped quietly into New York and quickly into the life of easy sex, easy money, and easy pickings.

The rattle of west side traffic could not drown out the ugly, vicious parting remark of "Chicken" Wills: "You'd have liked to have gone somewhere with that neat little piece of chicken to bang him in his sweet little ass! *Just like any old chickenhawk!*"

He knew such men. *Pederasts*! Men who paid consenting boys to have sex with them. They didn't use force. They were not rapists. They were buyers on the open market from men like Wills and scores of others who worked the midtown streets. They had always been repulsive to him. They were men to be arrested, prosecuted. In Ancient Greece such men might have been named Plato or Socrates or Aristotle and they might have been great and respected men, but in modern New York City they were child molesters. *Chickenhawks!* The word turned in his stomach.

He parked his car and crossed Eighth Avenue to look up an old friend, a man who knew as a good cop, a hero cop, a friend. Lyman had long been a supporter of the exceedingly good work of Father David Rogers, who ran a shelter for runaways, abused kids, and children who had been caught up in prostitution. The shelter was on Eighth Avenue, close to the Port Authority bus station which disgorged so many kids into the New York maelstrom. Lyman and Father Rogers had met during the child-pros investigations. The priest was surprised and pleased to see Lyman, so many years later, coming into the shelter. "How's it going?" Lyman asked.

"It's always like going upstream." Father David Rogers was a young man, balding, open-faced, the kind of man decent people in decent communities wanted to have as their parish priest. Father Rogers wore a tee shirt emblazoned with "I Love New York." He had on blue jeans and jogging shoes. "I've been reading about your case," he said, leading Lyman upstairs to the small office from which they could look out on the human flotsam of Eighth Avenue. "It's a tragic case, from what I've read, but it would seem that the boy came to an inevitable end. He started as a teenage hustler, correct?"

"Yes. He debuted with Donny Wills."

Father Rogers' face crinkled in anger. "How old when he started with Wills?"

"Thirteen."

"Typical," grunted Father Rogers.

"The boy prospered," Lyman noted. "He was dealing with very rich men, very important men."

"To what end? The boy's dead. One of his rich clients did it?"

"It's possible. Tell me, Dave, about the men who deal in this kind of thing. I don't mean deal, I mean participate."

"The Johns? What can I tell you that you don't already know by being a cop?"

"I deal with what they do. You deal with the why of it."

"Why do men buy boys? For the same reason men buy women. Loneliness. Affection. Attention. Someone to talk to.

Someone to be nice to. Someone to fill up the time with. Homosexuals who obtain sex from prostitutes aren't any different from heterosexuals who deal with hookers. Around here I confront the trading of the flesh of minors. As a priest, I should care about men who engage in sex with other adult men, but I don't have the time. And frankly, Shel, I'm not sure that's anybody's business but the adults themselves. Society is re-examining its whole attitude toward consenting adult homosexuality, and Lord knows the Church has been grappling with the question of homosexuals for centuries. So with the whole question an open one, I just concern myself with what everybody agrees is wrong—the use of kids in sex."

"I just came from talking with Wills. He's at Rikers Island."

"Praise be to God for that. What did you talk about?"

"His connection with Larry Apperson—the murdered boy. But Wills said something to me, a personal thing, that's been preying on my mind. He referred to a young boy who was involved in a case in which I busted Wills a few years ago. A kid named Eric. Wills said that he knew all along that if I had had the guts to admit it I would have liked to have had sex with that kid."

"Oh, Shel, that's nonsense. How can you let something that Wills said bother you? He's scum."

"Yes, but if I've ever been anything with myself, Dave, it's been honest. I would hate to think that I'd been living a lie all these years. You know something about men with that kind of nature, so I thought I'd talk to you."

"There are men who are homosexual but never confront it, probably never even suspect it. There are men who know all along and only come out later in life. Whether a man is gay or not is not really the central question. The question is, can that man function in society? Is he able to do all the necessary and expected human things, or does he let his sexual hangups dominate him, immobilize him, make him disfunctional? I would say that whatever your sexual persuasion may be, Sheldon, you are managing to function very well in society."

"So what difference does it make if this good old cop turns out to be not as straight as he thought he was?"

"Obviously it makes a great deal of difference to you, but I tell you, Sheldon, that there are millions of gay people who are getting along just fine in this world. Being comfortable with oneself, being well-adjusted, being able to function is what matters. Being happy! If a man knows himself, functions, and is as happy as men ever can be, then he ought to get on with life. You'd be my friend and trusted fighter against the bad guys whether you suddenly turned out to be gay or not."

"There are plenty of bad guys to keep us busy, eh, Dave?"

"The Devil's Legions are legion, Sheldon. Keep the faith, my good friend."

Lyman went downstairs through the noisy knots of children taken off the streets by Father Rogers, shook hands with the priest again, and then stepped out onto Eighth Avenue. He walked south, looking at but not seeing the flow of humanity along the avenue at its intersection with Forty-second Street. Lyman was facing inward as he paused at the busy corner, seeing a parade of faces from his past: the boy at the Spanish Steps, Jim in junior high school in his shorts and no shirt doing stunts on the gymnastic equipment, his best buddy in the Marines, boys playing roof games beneath his apartment windows, Terry Garraty developing his keen edge in the police gym, and, finally, Larry Apperson nude and compellingly attractive in his portrait.

Lyman shook off his thoughts and decided he was simply tired. Terry Garraty was always after him to have a vacation, to take all the time he had accumulated and to get away from the job. Paul Parker was on his case increasingly about all that piled up vacation time. It was an administrative problem for Parker, but it was also a personal concern. "Get your ass out of here, Shelly. Go bake in the sun and get all the dirt and sadness and loneliness out of your system. Crissakes, go get laid, if nothing else!"

Lyman looked up Forty-second Street awash in people.

He shrugged his shoulders, casting off his ridiculous thoughts, and walked into Forty-second, his mind on the case again.

This was a block of porno films, book stores, strip houses and sex-filled sidewalks. This was a street Larry Apperson walked when he first came to New York. Lyman could picture him on the bus up from Philly, in the back, shrinking with fear and tingling with excited anticipation, heady with the freedom he had proclaimed for himself by running away. He probably carried a suitcase of some kind. A few dollars in his pocket, if he was lucky. He would have been in blue jeans, faded and thin from wear and clinging to his thighs and behind and crotch. In a little while he was through the Lincoln Tunnel and in the terminal, aswim in the crowds, lost, ready to cry. But in the crowd there was a pair of eyes which had latched onto the forlorn teenager the moment he came through the gate. "Chicken" Wills knew a good thing when he found it.

Lyman walked east on Forty-second, swimming against the stream of sex. Mingled with the adults might be detectives such as himself, working the street, looking for the men with chicken to market and the man who were eager to buy. Some of the buyers who walked this street searching for boys may have been on the street looking when Larry Apperson made his debut, and Lyman could imagine the gleeful anticipation of the chickenhawks who encountered him: new and fresh, young, with that appealing yellow hair and the earnest, trusting eyes.

This was the block of available boys attracted to the glow and the glitter from rows of movie marquees and flashing signs above porno places, and it was on this block where they put themselves up for sale in their tight boyish clothes by hanging around seductively in game arcades or in front of them.

God, Lyman thought, Larry must have been terrified the first time. Or had he, as Neal Davis believed, already rid himself of the fear of being an available boy for men in his hometown? Lyman paused and stood on the curb a quarter of the way up the block. He closed his eyes tight at the thought of Larry being initiated into man-boy sex in the backseat of a car on a dark rural road. He opened his eyes to the flash of Forty-second Street. Maybe it wasn't in a car. Maybe it was in a warm and luxurious house with a big bed and candy and a TV to watch and a man to hold him. Boys who went out and sold themselves, said the experts on boy prostitution, were looking for the kind of love their fathers never gave them. They were out there for love when all they really ever got was money.

Lyman moved on, an anger and a sadness welling in him. He could not understand how a father could not love his child. He had adored his daughter; he even spoiled her. Betty had complained. Had he had a son he would have adored him, too, and the boy would never had had to seek a substitute for a father's love by offering himself for sex. The sadness came when he thought of Larry starved for love.

In the middle of the block, an extremely handsome young black boy with skin as rich as mocha lounged in a doorway and looked invitingly at him as Lyman strolled the sidewalk at the edge of the curb. He turned his eyes away so the boy would not think he was returning his come-on look.

A few feet away, a white blond teenager had the same look in his eyes. Nearby, hovering, Lyman spotted a middle-aged, portly man watching the boy. Suddenly, there was eye contact between the boy and the man, and each moved slowly and casually away, not speaking to each other but moving together toward Seventh Avenue. Damn, Lyman raged, I ought to bust that sonofabitch! But he knew he couldn't. No crime had been committed. He had no partner, no backup, and this was not his job. He looked around in hope of finding a police undercover team whose job it was to catch chickenhawks. He saw no one even closely resembling a cop. The man and the boy were getting into a cab. For a moment, Lyman permitted himself to imagine what was going to happen to that teenager. In a room somewhere in the city the boy would undress and lie down and the man who was paying for him would undress and slide into bed beside him. At the touch of the man's hands the boy would have gotten what he came on this street for: love or money. Tomorrow, both would be spent, and he'd be back, hustling.

Lyman stopped at Seventh Avenue and looked at the old *Times* building. The moving news sign that used to brighten the corner was dark, shut down by its owner because he said he wanted to protest the decline and fall of once-proud, decent, beautiful Times Square. The shutting down of the sign, Lyman believed, had given another push to the downward slide of the area into decadence.

Before stepping into the street to continue walking east, Lyman wondered how many taxi cabs Larry Apperson had gotten into with strangers.

By the time he reached the opposite corner, he was wondering how much Larry received from the man who bought him and whether the money had been all he was after. Had it been love he'd sought, then it was obvious he had not found it in the time he had spent on the streets.

Probably, he thought, moving rapidly east toward the quiet, decent dignity of Fifth Avenue, Larry Apperson had never found the love he was looking for. Not a lasting love. He had bounded from one man, one boy, to another. His little book listed them. It was likely that there had been many who never made it onto the narrow lines of that neatly inscribed roster.

It now seemed possible that someone whom Larry Apperson once hoped would be the lover he had spent a lifetime looking for turned out to be a killer.

At Fifth Avenue, Lyman used a public telephone to call

the squad to see if Garraty had come back from court. "Nope," said Brown, sounding bored. Lyman asked Brown to tell Garraty to wait at the office, he was on his way in. "You got it," said Brown, hanging up.

Walking purposely east, planning to turn at Third Avenue for the northerly walk to the Seventeenth, Lyman discovered Larry Apperson rampaging in his thoughts. He knew almost everything there was to know about the boy—except who killed him. Nor did he know the sound of Larry Apperson's voice. It must have been a pleasing one, he decided, if Larry had proved promising as an actor, even though the play Lyman had seen had not risen to great dramatic heights. He had never heard Larry Apperson laugh and wondered what kind of laugh it was. There were countless personal facts he did not know and could never know—his favorite color, what movies he liked to go to, if he cared for sports, if he was addicted to rock-and-roll music as so many of his peers were. He did not even know what Larry looked like, except in the ugly bloated death of his bathroom four days after he was murdered, and in the Polaroid shot found in Ellis Marsh's room, and, of course, in the portrait. These merely were Larry's form in the stillness of death, photography and an artist's view of him in oils. What Larry looked like alive was a mystery that would, he knew, be ever fathomless. He could only imagine him.

Lyman's imagination turned to a beach, and he saw again the form of a boy lying on the sand with a huge towel covering him—the shroud-like towel and the boy beneath it with his feet sticking out which had startled him at the beach last summer as he feared for a moment that he had chanced upon a corpse. In his thoughts, he remained on the beach to look at the boy and the towel-covering until the boy flicked the towel aside and smiled up at him with that winning smile Conrad Ames had put into the portrait. "Hi," said the boy on the beach. The voice was rich, young, floating between boy and man, clear as a songbird's.

"Hello," Lyman replied. "You're wise to keep covered in this hot sun. You could get a bad burn."

The boy stood up, smiling, and held out his hand. "My name's Larry Apperson."

"Sheldon Lyman's my name."

"You live around here?"

"I have a little cottage just a few blocks away."

"You're lucky to live near the beach. I love the beach." He grinned his pleasure in being where he loved to be. He stood barefoot in the warm soft sand, the ocean at his back, the sky arching clear and blue above them. He stood with his hands on his slender hips. The pressure of his hands drew down the edge of his membrane-thin racing trunks, showing a pale stretch of skin in contrast to the rich tan of the rest of his body. The tight blue bathing suit curved voluptuously at the juncture of his thighs. "Hot day," he said, raising a slim muscled arm to wipe the sweat from his forehead. He shook his head, tossing his long blond hair.

"How about a cool drink at my place?" Lyman asked.

The boy grinned. "Great!"

"My wife and daughter are shopping," Lyman explained as they walked toward the cottage, Larry in his bathing suit, the towel slung over a shoulder, Lyman feeling foolish in a suit—a cop's suit. They found a bottle of lemonade in the refrigerator and drank it seated on the cushioned wicker chairs in the living room. Larry drank two glasses before he was filled. "There's more," Lyman pointed out.

"I've had plenty," Larry said.

They sat silently gazing at each other for a long time. At last, Larry pushed himself from his chair and stretched, drawing taut all the muscles of his body. When he relaxed, he smiled and said, "You seem like a nice man."

"I try to be."

"There aren't many nice men in this world, I can tell you."

"You're a nice boy."

He flashed an amused grin. "Nice man. Nice boy. A nice combination."

Lyman said nothing more. He could not speak. His mouth and throat were suddenly parched, his tongue immobile. Only his eyes had life as they roamed the vision of the boy standing barefoot before him, his body browned from the sun, eyes blue as cornflowers, hair as yellow as straw. When he smiled, the straight white teeth flashed pearl-white against the tan face. The boy stood absolutely still, as if he were a painting. Lyman studied him, the way a man would examine a work of art displayed in a gallery. Then, the boy seemed to come out of a trance, rousing himself from what must have been a faraway daydream. He threw back his head and shook his hair. His proud chest swelled with life-giving air. The muscles of his belly drew long, taut and flat. They bunched into hard brown squares as the boy relaxed again. He smiled contentedly, but there was a mischievous look in his blue eyes that was prelude to the slow, graceful hypnotizing movement of his arms and hands from the sides to his waist. The fingers brushed the taut skin of his bathing trunks as the thumbs hooked beneath the top edge. Slowly, as if performing a sacred rite, he rolled down the blue trunks, pushing them lower and lower on his hips until, proudly, defiantly, invitingly, his penis came into view nestled in a downy cushion of yellow hair. The boy kicked off the trunks and stepped forward, crossing the room slowly while smiling a bewitching smile. Lyman sat frozen, mute, mesmerized with only his eyes moving, following the boy as he advanced.

At last, the boy stood before him, and Lyman's eyes drifted down from the angelic face to the long clean sweep of his neck and down the curve of his chest and the slope of his belly to the thatch of straw-like hair around the penis. There, Lyman's eyes rested.

With a quick, easy, knowing sweep of his hand, the boy touched his penis which quickened and rose and lengthened as if it had just been born.

Lyman stared at the erection, so close to him.

"Go ahead," said the boy, his voice soft and inviting from above as he stood looking down at Lyman in the chair.

Lyman raised his eyes and looked up into the smiling face across the rugged landscape of the boy's torse. "I don't. . . ."

A frown clouded the boy's face for an instant. He pushed it away with another smile. "Please."

Lyman lowered his eyes, then closed them as he leaned forward, his lips trembling.

When the lips parted, taking the boy in, the boy sighed and put his hands atop Lyman's head. "Thank you. It's wonderful that you love me as you do."

The sudden blaring of a car horn jolted Lyman.

He blinked his eyes and found himself at the corner of Third Avenue and Forty-second Street.

He turned north and walked fast uptown toward the Seventeenth.

15.

Routines. Lyman plunged into all of them. The flow of paper was increasing. Names of men in Larry Apperson's address book which no longer could be traced in New York were traced to wherever they had traveled. To the police in Bermuda went a request for an interrogation of Martin Gould and with the request went a list of questions to be answered. The same questions went by Telex or letter to cities and towns all over the country and to Scotland Yard asking help in interviewing a man who was in London on business. All of the routines, the requests, the in-and-out paper were handled at his desk in Third Homicide. Waiting for Garraty's court appearance to be over provided Lyman the time for the routines.

When Garraty phoned at noon and said his case had not yet been called and would not be until the afternoon session, Lyman decided to break for lunch. At the coffee shop on Third Avenue he joined Brown and Hadley, who were just finishing. "How's the case coming?" Brown asked.

Lyman answered with a shrug.

Hadley, who was about Garraty's age, and eager, tossed back a strand of his long blond hair and said, "I figure we ought to treat fag killings like Mafia killings. As long as they only kill each other, let 'em."

"I see your partner's learning well from you, Mike," Lyman joked.

"I read your report, Shel, and I don't think you've got felony murder in the perpetration of burglary. I agree with Garraty on this one. A fag murder, pure and simple."

"Mike, I wish I had your certainty. We've been talking to a lot of people who had motive, means and opportunity, but it isn't adding up. Right now it makes more sense to me for a burglar caught in the act to have done it rather than some wrought up jealous old queen."

"A pickup could have done it," suggested Hadley.

Lyman nodded.

"Are you gonna solve it?" Brown asked, his long narrow face wrinkled with his own doubts about Lyman's chances of solving the murder.

"We'll give it the old college try," Lyman smiled.

When the waitress came to take his order he decided on a cheeseburger, fries and a chocolate milk shake. For a moment he was glad Garraty wasn't there to chastise him for his menu.

A little before two in the afternoon, Garraty phoned to read him the headline in the *Post's* afternoon edition. "Quote: Cops Quizzing Customers of Slain Gay Hooker; end quote. Guess who wrote the article that accompanies that piece of shit?"

"Our old nemesis Donnelly."

"That fucker ought to have that headline crammed down his throat. Worse, he somehow found out who we've been talking to and names names. Including that nice old man Denziger."

"Jesus Christ!"

"I thought you'd want to know about this, Shel. I don't know where this Donnelly got the names of the people we've talked to, but he's got all of them in the article. He also quotes some people he says we haven't talked to yet, although the sonofabitch doesn't name them. 'Sources told the *Post*,' he says about *them*! And in the fourth paragraph he has a beauty of a bombshell, again without attribution. Listen. 'There are indications that the slain call-boy had sexual relations with very important personalities in showbusiness, industry, and politics, including one high official in city government.'"

Lyman whistled through his teeth. "Now we know why Deputy Mayor Heywood Johnson was so antsy."

"Do you think Heywood's the quote high official unquote?"

"No, but he knows who the guy is. Damn! Where's Donnelly get all that stuff?"

"Maybe we should talk to Donnelly?"

"Hell no. That bastard would be screaming First Amendment from the top of the Empire State Building."

"You know somebody in Department Headquarters is going to want to know if we've been leaking stuff to Donnelly."

"Why the hell can't it be easy?" Lyman groaned.

"I gotta go. Court's convening. Later!"

Lyman slammed down the phone loud enough for everyone in the squad room to hear it.

16.

Deputy Commissioner Felix Hogan of the Manhattan Detective Area convened a conference at 201 East Twenty-first Street, a building that looked more like a school than a police station, although no one would have mistaken Hogan for a kindly principal. With a face forever scowling, he was every inch a cop. The only time he smiled was when he stepped off to lead the St. Patrick's Day parade up Fifth Avenue where he was always sure of a wave and a shout from the Cardinal on the steps of the Cathedral.

Hogan's Executive Officer, Inspector Vincent Howe, was by far the more scholarly looking in owlish glasses and civilian jacket with suede patches at the elbows.

Captain Joe Campana, spit and polish, braided and blue in his uniform, completed the top brass contingent at the conference in Hogan's office around a long elliptical conference table.

From Third Homicide came Lyman, Garraty and Parker.

Uptown from Headquarters had come Theresa "Scoop" Finley, a television reporter who had taken on the thankless task of Deputy Commissioner in charge of handling all her former colleagues in the news media. Pert, intense, but always with a ready smile, and with reddish hair that had more curls than Shirley Temple's, "Scoop" Finley was, by everyone's estimation, an asset in handling the Department's public relations. Under her arm as she came into the conference she carried a folded copy of the *Post*. She winked at Lyman and sat at the end of the table near Hogan, who promptly opened the meeting.

"We have a multi-faceted problem before us. First and foremost we have a homicide. Next we have a problem in that a reporter is getting confidential information from someone in the Police Department, information which may have a very serious negative effect upon the homicide investigation, what with the details of that investigation showing up in a newspaper before the investigating officers' reports show up in the squad commander's office. Next, we have a public relations problem with the gay community. I have had two calls from the Commissioner reporting contacts by leaders of various gay groups wanting to know what we are doing to solve the Apperson case. Last, there is an interest in this case from persons outside the Department but in city government. I just wanted to put these facts on record so that the men on the line know that we do not have an ordinary homicide on our hands. Commissioner Finley is here because from now on it will be through her that all contacts with the press are to be made. I do not mean to imply that I believe any of the officers on this case have been feeding information to the press. This is a case that necessarily needs the help of other squads, and there could be leaks from those units not directly connected with the investigation. At any rate, anything official is to be given out by Commissioner Finley. No one else. Now, before we proceed, I would like Detective Lyman to bring us all up to date on the status of his investigation."

"First, sir, let me get into the record that neither I nor my partner, Terry Garraty, have said anything to the news media about the nature of the material that showed up in Donnelly's article. My only comment to the news media was at the scene of the crime and it amounted to nothing more than a 'no comment.'"

"I was not saying that you had leaked anything to the press, Sheldon."

"That was the way it seemed, sir."

"Not intended that way."

"May I say," said "Scoop" Finley, leaning toward Hogan, "that Dick Donnelly is a hell of a good reporter. He has contacts in the Department, sure, but I would bet that Donnelly has just been doing his own legwork. He probably picked up that list of names from someone he dug up on his own—one of this Apperson's friends, probably. I don't think we should rush to judgment and say that there are leaks in the Department when what we are probably observing is good old fashioned reporting."

"I hope that is the case," Hogan replied. "About the status of the investigation, Sheldon?"

"We have interviewed the people Donnelly names in the newspaper, and we are continuing to interview either directly or through police departments in other areas, talking with people whose names were in Apperson's address book. Most are men he dealt with professionally. He was a male prostitute, but he appears to have been not as active as previously. Most recently his attentions were directed to another young man, Ellis Marsh. We can't locate him, and we regard him as a suspect. Larry also kept in touch with a very small circle of older lovers who were men of wealth and status. These men certainly had means and even some motives, that's for sure. Donnelly's article mentions someone in city government. We have uncovered no one who fits that description, although there was an oblique inquiry in that direction from Deputy Mayor Heywood Johnson. I had the impression I was being told to go easy if I came across anything leading me to an unnamed city government personality."

"The Commissioner is aware of that incident and is handling it," Hogan said.

"That's good, because I certainly am not going to sit still for any political messing around with my case."

"Certainly not," nodded Hogan.

"There are three possible motives in the Apperson death," Lyman continued, "The most obvious one at first was homicide in the perpetration of a burglary. A wallet and a camera were missing from the young man's apartment. There next arose the possibility of a blackmail victim committing murder, although I have serious doubts about whether this kid could have been an extortionist. More likely, someone was worried about a book that Apperson appears to have been writing, naming names and so forth. a kiss-and-tell-book about rich New York gays. Finally, we have learned that Apperson may have had a video tape of sexual relations between himself and the motion picture actor, Nelson Royce. We do not have the tape and have only statements of one person we interviewed that there was such a tape. We have no idea what it might show. All of this is very sketchy and a long way from any grand jury presentment."

"Which of these motives seem most likely to you?" Hogan asked.

"Burglary, sir, but my partner thinks we have a homosexual murder in the classic sense, death from a lover, whether a chance pickup or a long-standing relationship."

"What about the Brooklyn Heights murder?" asked Inspector Howe, pushing back his glasses on his long sharp nose. "Could it have been done by the same person?"

"That was a copycat killing, I'm sure," Lyman replied.

"We don't have a gay Son of Sam on our hands?"

"No."

"Thank the lord for that," Howe said.

"This Apperson," asked Captain Campana, "what sort of person was he? I mean, was he one of those fellows who was asking to be beaten to death?"

"Not at all, Captain. He was loved. Everyone we've talked to spoke of the young man in the most glowing terms. He was greatly admired by some very discerning and choosey men. I've been trying to understand the young man as best I can from the interviewing Terry and I have done. In some ways he was a casebook study of a runaway youth, but some quality in him lifted him above the level of the streets. I could know more about him if I could read the book he was supposed to have been writing. Yet I think I can say that he was a very likeable youngster, very good looking, fun to be with, and commanding of personal loyalty even from men he had left for other romances."

"He sounds quite extraordinary," Hogan commented.

"That he is. Uh, was," nodded Lyman.

"Well, the poor kid is now a major headache for the whole Department and for our command in particular," added Inspector Howe. "The byword is going to have to be 'kid gloves' in this case, and that's what this meeting is about. I speak for Commissioner Hogan and for the Police Commissioner when I say that we've got to keep each other informed on a daily basis as this case develops. There's nothing we can do about Donnelly, but if we at least keep our internal information flowing, Donnelly won't surprise us."

"Thank you gentlemen, and lady," nodded Commissioner Hogan.

A few minutes later in the car, Lyman turned to look at Lt. Paul Parker in the back seat to ask, "What the hell was *that* all about?"

Parker tugged his lower lip. "That was us being told that we have a hot potato."

"There is some biggie in City Hall who's scared?"

"Yep."

"Who?"

"I don't know. I really don't, Shelly. But he's got clout."

"Obviously."

At the Seventeenth, they let Parker out and proceeded to the west side, planning to scour the gay bars which were, for the most part, earthier, grittier, raunchier, and more dangerous than the sophisticated bars on the east side. Lyman expected them to come up with nothing, but there was always the chance. While waiting for evening when the bars would be filled, they decided to have dinner at Joe's Pier 52, where, over the chowder and lobsters and coffee, they let themselves begin to imagine a scenario in which Lawrence Apperson had been murdered for political reasons.

That Larry Apperson may have been murdered to cover up his connection with a City Hall official seemed ridiculous, but there was intense interest by someone at City Hall in the case, and it was that interest which opened the door, however slightly, to the possibility that Larry Apperson had been killed because he was or was potentially a political threat. If he had been killed for the sake of someone's public image, then the exercise of prowling the rough gay bars of the west side of Manhattan seemed, at the least, an exercise in the absurd.

By four in the morning, as the bars closed, they had come up with nothing to move forward the case of Lawrence Apperson's homicide.

17.

Lyman couldn't sleep much and was up before the clock radio switched on to tell him that New Yorkers were finally getting dug out after the snowstorm. Turnpikes were open again, letting New Yorkers with the desire go to New England for great skiing. Likewise, New Englanders, who were also dug out, could come south if they wished. Alternate side of the street parking regulations remained suspended to allow snow plows to work. Lyman shut off the news and went to the bathroom.

In the morning he was always aware of his mortality. All the bathroom things he had to do served as reminders of the complexity of the human apparatus which, like all apparatuses, would fail sooner or later. Death was a living reality in the bathroom.

It had been a tragic reality for Larry, he thought, looking at his stubbled beard in the bathroom mirror.

He remembered the boy's bloated, naked corpse draped over the edge of a tub, his face water-logged and battered by the death blow, almost recognizable, except for his portrait in the bedroom.

Larry's death turned Lyman's thoughts again to his own inevitable dying. He supposed his would turn out to be damned inconvenient for someone unlucky enough to bump into the fact that Sheldon Lyman had passed away. He would probably collapse in a public street or perhaps over a cheeseburger in the place across the way, in the middle of one of Eve's flirtations. There were so many ways to go, a lot of them violent, unpleasant, embarrassing, bloody, body-shattering ways. The way Larry had died. Probably poor Doc Dock would have to come in and clean up after the death of Sheldon Lyman.

The phone interrupted him in mid-shave. "Gonna be a little late," said Garraty. In the background, Lyman heard Garraty's kids crying and his wife trying to quiet them. "Domestic crisis," sighed Garraty.

"I'll meet you at the office," Lyman said. "I'll go up by cab."

Inundated by childish squealing, Garraty said, "Thanks," and hung up.

Dressing, Lyman drew up the venetian blinds in his bedroom and looked down on the rooftops of the lower buildings next to his apartment house. On the roof of one of them were two boys having a snowball fight. They were young teenagers. Thirteen or fourteen, he figured. One boy, blond under his knitted blue sailor's cap, had on a gray jacket, open to show a slash of orange sweater above American youth's omnipresent blue jeans. The other boy was hatless, brown haired, in a blue jacket—one of the puffy, quilted kind that look like inflated life preservers—and blue jeans. Presently, the boys stopped throwing snow at each other and leaned over the parapet of the roof, brushing snow aside and watching it cascade like miniature avalances toward the street.

Leaning over the edge side by side, their shoulders touching and their hips brushing, they were laughing at the snowfall they had created. Soon, Lyman expected, they would start making snowballs and dropping them toward unwary pedestrians on the sidewalk below. Often, he had seen the boys playing on the roof during the previous summer when they were shirtless and barefooted, sneaking smokes and an occasional bottle of beer to their hideout on the roof. They spotted him, once, and waved and he waved back and they laughed as he shook his head and gestured that they were too young to drink. The blond impishly held up the beer as if to offer him a taste. The brown haired boy was shorter, more compact, a tighter human machine than his friend. The blond was loose, his arms and legs a little longer, almost gangling, his body about to blossom forth in growth that would leave him a tall, lean, ambling, long-muscled youth who might be a good swimmer if he had the chance. The brunette would make a good boxer, probably. The blond boy reminded Lyman of his junior high school friend, Jim.

Lyman moved away from the window to finish dressing, knowing that no matter what he wore he would have the word cop spelled out all over him. He decided against a suit and chose from his closet a tan tweed sport jacket and brown wool slacks, an outfit Betty had bought for him the year before she died. It was looser on him, now, he noted.

Putting on a brown tie to go with the outfit, he looked out the window at the roof boys as they moved away from the edge, grown bored with their assaults on people below. He wondered if the boys went swimming in the summertime and where, if they ever had a chance to swim naked in a country stream. There were public pools all over Manhattan, but they were crowded and chemical laden and poor places for boys to have a real swim. It was possible, of course, that the boys were not swimmers. That idea saddened Lyman as he watched the long ambling stride of the blond boy. Neal Davis said that good-looking boys always knew they were good-looking. Clearly, the blond boy on the roof knew. Lyman watched as the boys crossed the snowy rooftop, opened a door, and went inside.

Lyman looked over the rest of the view from his window: empty rooftops, empty sidewalks, an empty slate-gray sky. Motionless, his view had lost all its life, as if the city had suddenly died.

He was surprised when he arrived at the squadroom to find a message to call a lawyer by the name of Jason Baxter. A phone-message notation on his desk in Mike Brown's hand-writing said, "Baxter says he has a client who knows something about the Apperson case." Lyman dialed the Manhattan phone number immediately and waited patiently while an operator put his call through to Baxter's office. The voice was young, obviously a very junior member of a distinguished law firm. "This may be nothing at all, Mr. Lyman, but it may be something. I have a client who is over at Riker's Island waiting trial on a charge of assault with a deadly weapon. His name is Kennedy Forster. He's black. Young. Scared. Frankly, he may be grabbing at straws, looking for a deal to lighten the penalty he could receive on the charge. Anyway, he contacted me and asked me to put him in touch with someone who was handling the Lawrence Apperson murder. That, I discovered, is you. Anyway, Forster says he knows who may have committed the murder and he wants to talk to you and to a District Attorney. The young man has plea bargaining on his mind, as you can see. Shall I arrange a meeting?"

"Hell, yes, counselor, and I'll bring along a D.A."

Putting down the phone, Lyman tightened a grip on the surging elation that sprang up in him. This could be the lucky break that he hoped they would get, but he knew about prisoners sitting in their cells looking for a way to get them off the hook. He called Garraty and told him about the call to Baxter. Garraty yelled with delight and surprise. Sure, he said, "Baxter is setting it up and I'm about to line up an Assistant D.A. to go along."

They came together outside the main entrance to the Men's

House of Detention. Jason Baxter was a short, intense, bearded young lawyer with eyes as black as his beard and both as black as his briefcase. Baxter looked like one of the dauntless young men who worked on hopeless causes on behalf of the Legal Aid Society. Assistant District Attorney Mel Shapiro was also young, but he looked like someone from the D.A.'s office. "I wish I could tell you gentlemen just what it is my client has to say, but he wouldn't go into details on the phone. I hope this is not a wild goose chase. I'd hate to think I cost the taxpayers a lot of money for nothing," said Jason Baxter.

They waited ten minutes in an interview room before Kennedy Forster was brought in. Tall, slender as a reed, his skin a rich reddish brown, the prisoner was in the clothes he'd been wearing when he was arrested in a street fight in East Harlem, knife in hand, standing over the groaning, bleeding, slashed figure of another black man. He suspiciously eyed the four men, the eyes of a young man who'd had a lot of dealings with police, lawyers and District Attorneys. "First of all I have to know if we can make a deal on my case," he stated, pulling out a straight-backed wooden chair and sitting at the table opposite the four men.

"First we have to hear what you have to tell us," said Mel Shapiro.

"How do I know you won't just walk out of here after I tell you what I know?"

"You don't," said Shapiro.

Forster looked at his lawyer. "That stinks, counselor."

"We can't make the rules, Forster," replied Jason Baxter, cooly.

"Yeah, well maybe I should ask the judge to give me 'nother attorney."

"You have that privilege. I happen to be the lawyer the judge named. That was because I happened to be there. I assure you I am representing you properly and well, witness the fact that I've brought these men here at your request. You can't expect and I will certainly not ask the District Attorney to enter into a bargain with you until he knows what it is you have to tell these men."

"It's about the killing of this Apperson dude."

"Yes," nodded Jason Baxter. "But *what* about it?"

"I know who did it."

"Who?" asked Assistant District Attorney Mel Shapiro. "What's the deal?"

"So far there isn't any."

"Fuck you all."

"Gentlemen," announced Shapiro, reaching for his brief case, "I suggest that we adjourn!"

"Hold it! Okay. I'm not jivin' you dudes, and I expect you not to jive me. When I tell you what I got, we deal!"

"Who killed Larry Apperson?" asked Lyman.

" 'Chicken' did it."

" ' 'Chicken?' ' " Both lawyers spoke the name simultaneously.

"His real name is Donald Wills and he's being held here on a child prostitution charge," explained Lyman. "I talked with Wills and he says he doesn't know anything about the murder."

"Well, he told me he was at that dude's apartment and that they had a real hassle over some tape of some kind and that he wasted the kid for not handin' it over. That's the truth, man."

Mel Shapiro looked at Lyman. "Does that have any ring of believability in it?"

Lyman did not answer. He asked Forster, "When did Wills tell you this?"

"Last night. He was braggin' about what a tough dude he is and about how he's got friends with money who are gonna see that he beats that pros rap. And I said he wasn't nothin' but a cheap pimp who hustled little kids' asses. I expected

Wills to go up-side my head but he got really sweet and said he kind of liked me and he could help me on my case on account of his rich friends was into him for what he done. And I said what could he have done to make rich friends come to his rescue? That's when he told me how he was approached by some fags he knows to get back some kind of tape from that Apperson dude. He said there was a row and he had to go up-side the kid's head."

"Did he *say* he killed Apperson?"

"He didn't come right out and say he did it but he sure was actin' like he done it."

The lawyers waited, looking at Lyman.

"I'll want to talk to Wills again," Lyman said. "Meantime, is it possible to isolate Mr. Forster from Wills?"

Shapiro nodded. "We'll move him to another wing."

"What about my deal?" Forster demanded.

"Mr. Lyman?" asked Shapiro.

"I'd say that Mr. Forster is an important witness at this time."

Forster broke into a toothy grin. "I told you I wasn't jivin'."

"Mel," whispered attorney Jason Baxter, "shall we talk deal?"

"We'll talk," nodded Shapiro.

"Mel," said Lyman, "let us know when Forster's been moved. We won't talk to Wills until we know Forster's been transferred."

"I'll handle it before I go back to the city."

"In that case, we'll hang around," smiled Lyman.

Donny "Chicken" Wills knew what was going down as soon as he came into the interview room. "So that mother-fucker Forster has a flappin' mouth!"

"You're the one with the mouth, Wills!"

"Get off my case, Lyman."

"Tell us about how you killed Larry Apperson."

"Man! Killed! That dude Forster said I *killed* that kid?"

"He said *you* said you killed him."

"Oh, that bastard's got his head where the sun don't shine. I never said I killed nobody."

"Look, Wills, you are Suspecto Numero Uno right now. We've got a witness who'll put you at the scene of the murder. We've got a witness who'll say that you went to Apperson to get back a certain tape. We have another witness who says he heard a big argument between Apperson and a black man in the hallway. That adds up to you, Wills. Motive, means, opportunity, put 'em all together they spell 'Chicken.' There's not a grand jury in the world that wouldn't just love to put your ass on death row on circumstantial evidence a lot thinner than what we've got. You are a bad guy, Wills. You mess around with little boys. You seduce them. You force them into prostitution. You are a menace to mothers and fathers all over this country. What do you think a jury of moms and dads— white moms and dads—will think of you when we haul your black ass before them and tell them you not only murdered a white kid but that you admitted it to a fellow inmate of this very slammer while waiting trial on a charge of kiddie prostitution?"

"I didn't kill Larry."

"Make me believe it."

"I went to see him, sure. I went to see about getting back a tape he had. It was a sex tape. Him and that actor, Nelson Royce, fuckin' and suckin' and all that stuff. The kid had it and I was to get it back."

"Who sent you to get it back? Royce?"

"Nah. Neal Davis."

"Ah ha. Davis. Why'd he send you?"

"Who knows? He calls me up and says he wants me to go see our old pal Larry Apperson and convince him to give up a tape he has."

"Why'd Neal Davis call you?" asked Garraty.

"Because Larry had always been a little afraid of me."

"Why?" Garraty asked.

"I guess he remembered how I used to beat his ass up when he was workin' for me and when he kept sayin' he was goin' to go out and start peddlin' his cute little ass on his own."

"What happened when you went to get the tape?" Lyman asked.

"Larry told me to fuck off."

"So that story you told me before about going to see Larry about the book he was writing was a lie?"

"Yeah. I went about the tape."

"Did you get it?"

"No."

"Why not?"

"Larry wouldn't give it to me."

"You could have beat him for it. Beat him up and killed him."

"I was thinkin' of usin' muscle but then that nosey neighbor looked out at us in the hall and Larry told him I was causin' trouble and the dude said if I didn't haul my ass out of there he'd call the cops."

"So you left."

"I split, yeah."

"Without the tape and without laying a hand on Larry Apperson."

"Exactly."

"And you didn't go back?"

"Hell no. I told Davis to get his own fuckin' tape."

"I think you went back, Wills."

"Look man, by that time I found out the Morals Division was takin' an interest in my case and I wasn't goin' to do nothin' to attract no more attention to me than I had to. Anyway, the cops picked me up on this fuckin' pros charge so I couldn't go back even if I wanted to."

"You were arrested *after* the murder."

"Well, I didn't kill that little fairy and that's that, and you got nothin' to prove I did, and that fink Forster's not gonna do you any good 'cause once the word's out he's a fink he'll be shit."

"I'm gonna check out all of this, Wills, and if I find out you lied to me again, I am coming back here, and the friends I have among the corrections officers are going to let me have some private time with you."

"You check it out, Lyman. You'll see that I'm givin' you the straight shit."

Both Lyman and Garraty had Neal Davis on their minds as they headed to Manhattan over the Triboro Bridge and sped downtown on the F.D.R. Drive. Lyman didn't have to tell Garraty to drive to the Village. "You believe Wills, don't you?" Garraty asked as they got out of their car in front of Neal Davis's address.

"His story jibes with Weinstein's, and Larry was alive after Weinstein heard the argument in the hallway with Wills."

"Wills could still have gone back."

"But I don't think so. He was uptight about the possibility of the prostitution bust. So if anyone went back to look for that tape it wasn't Wills."

"Davis?"

"He sent Wills the first time. I think he'd send someone else again. Davis is a middleman himself in his business. He knows about people using go-betweens. He'd not go himself. Not unless he had no choice."

"Which is possible. Royce could have been leaning hard on him to get that tape."

"We'll see soon enough. I'm not going to let Davis lie this time."

The doorman recognized them. "Officers, I'm sorry, but Mr. Davis is not in at the moment."

"Where is he?" asked Lyman.

"Boston."

"When'll he be back?"

"He didn't say."

"Damn!" grunted Lyman.

Turning and leaving, he decided to ask Lt. Parker to let them have a stakeout team.

18.

Calls. From the Bermuda Police to say that they were Telexing answers to the queries they had put to Mr. Martin Gould on behalf of the N.Y.P.D. A Bermudan police officer with a delightful British accent said it was his opinion on reading the transcript of the interview that Mr. Gould, unless he were a consummate liar, had an alibi, namely being on a jet aircraft between Los Angeles and New York City at the time of the homicide. "Of course you'll have the complete transcript to judge for yourself, Mr. Lyman." The Bermuda Police were very pleased to have been of help. The fraternity friends of Peter Apperson, on a call from Lyman, reported that Peter was not yet back from wherever he had gone, but he often went away for days and weeks at a time, so no one was worried. Garraty with New York Telephone Company officials learned that Neal Davis had put through an exceptional number of west coast calls, person to person, on the evening and at the hours Garraty was interested in. Yes, said persons Garraty phoned in California, they had talked with Neal Davis at times indicated by Garraty on that particular night.

Paper. Reports on the status of the case were dutifully sent to all commands concerned, including the brass who wanted up to date briefings on the case. "Scoop" Finley wanted copies of the photo of the victim and would be setting up a special public phone number that TV stations would announce in a bid for tips.

Theories. Felony homicide during a burglary. To get the Nelson Royce tape. To even a score. Jealousy. Fear of what might be in Larry's book, if one existed. A rage killing at the hands of a lover or former lover. A hustler's turning on his trick. A mysterious political big shot with clout.

Thoughts. That Larry Apperson had managed to assemble as large a group of prime candidates for potential violence as anyone Lyman had ever run across in all his years on the police force. That there were an excruciating number of dead ends to this case. That all they really had were hunches and theories and very little hard evidence that could persuade a D.A. to take the case to a grand jury. That it was all tragic, from the day that Larry Apperson picked up and left home for whatever adolescent reasons. That Larry's life might have been different if he hadn't run across the corrosive influence of "Chicken" Wills as he came off that bus from out of town.

Another frigid dusk clamped down on New York City as Sheldon Lyman worked at his desk in Third Homicide, shuffling the paper, thinking, trying to find a breakthrough. Garraty had gone home already. The night shift was coming in.

Leaving the Seventeenth Precinct, Lyman walked in the cold to the murder scene.

To his surprise, the lock on the outside of the building had been fixed and he had to use a key to get in. Larry's apartment key also served as a front door key. The building was deathly quiet as he went up to the third floor.

As he unlocked the door to Larry Apperson's apartment with the CRIME SCENE: DO NOT ENTER sign still on the door, the neighbor, Weinstein, poked his head out of his own apartment. "Oh, it's you, officer. I heard someone out here and thought I'd better have a look."

"You have good ears, Mr. Weinstein," Lyman remarked, pushing open Larry's apartment door.

"It's these damned New York walls. You can hear everything."

Lyman was interested. "You hear what goes on in the hallways in this building?"

"Most of the time."

"But you can't hear what goes on in the next apartment?"

"Rarely."

"Well, sorry to have disturbed you, and I appreciate your vigilance."

"I got used to being on my guard all that time when the front door was broken. You never knew who might come into the building."

"It's fixed now," Lyman said with a satisfied nod. "Mr. Da Capo finally got around to it."

"Not him. There's a new super."

"Oh?"

"Puerto Rican." Weinstein made a sour face. "Dumb."

"What happened to Da Capo?"

"The owner said he needs him at one of his other buildings. Up in the Bronx. But Da Capo's still here until he can break in the new guy. Da Capo's around if you want him. Just yell!"

"Well, the new super got the door fixed, at least."

"Thank God for small miracles." Weinstein waved goodbye and ducked back inside his apartment.

Lyman went into Larry's apartment and closed the door. He studied the rooms for a moment, unchanged since the day that the New York Police Department had arrived to label it a crime scene and to put it off-limits. He made a mental note to be sure the new super understood what the sign on the door meant.

In the going over of the apartment by the experts, there had been a lot of assumptions, mostly assumptions that the death had come during a burglary. The apartment had been gone over with an eye to what was missing, not what was there. Now, Lyman was looking for what was there. He had come to search for a small video cassette and he had come to look for the manuscript of Larry Apperson's book. He did not know if either actually existed, but he believed they did. He knew it, instinctively. It was a cop's hunch, which was supposed to be as much a part of a cop's arsenal of weapons as revolvers, handcuffs, notebooks, and legwork.

He searched the apartment with his eyes, still leaning against the door. He thought, Larry was a boy most at home in a bedroom, and it was to the bedroom that he moved to look for the tape and the book.

In the doorway, he paused as his eyes fell upon the portrait. When he stepped into the room he crossed to the bed and peered up at the painting. The eyes seemed to have followed him. It was a characteristic of the portrait he had not noticed before and it scared him—it made him feel as if the painting were living flesh.

Conrad Ames had created a magnificent painting. The fleshtones had an incredible plastic quality. The delicate articulation of muscle and bone and skin seemed alive. There was an expectancy in the portrait, as if the boy in it were merely day-dreaming and about to snap out of the reverie to take a deep breath and get on with living again. Lyman stepped back, his eyes fixed on the boy in the portrait. He imagined the boy suddenly coming to life after his long, far-away daydream, sudden animation showing in a throwing back of the head, a shaking of the long blond hair, a powerful expansion of the muscular chest and a tightening of the flat, hard, washboard muscles of the solar plexus.

Lyman drifted back to the portrait to stand close to it once more, gazing up at it. He reached out a hand to touch the smooth varnished surface to convince himself that this was a two-dimensional painting and not a living, breathing, fleshy youth about to quicken, as if startled. He placed his hand against the face of the boy in the painting but slowly his hand slipped down, tracing lightly over the boy's neck, moving delicately across his chest to the belly and down to the flourish of pubic yellow and the column of flesh that sprang from the painted hair.

Backing away, Lyman stumbled against the chair by the desk. He sat, resting an arm against the portable typewriter atop the desk, but his eyes were still turned toward the glorious painting above the bed.

He stared until he heard a noise: a key in a lock, and he realized that the key was sliding into the lock of *this* apartment.

He got up quickly, his hand flying instinctively to the holstered .38 belted to his right hip. When he saw who it was coming into the apartment, he was furious.

"What the hell are you doing here, Da Capo?"

"I came to look at the sink."

"What about the sink?"

"I thought it might be leaking."

"That sign on the door says this is a Crime Scene. You're not allowed in here. Where'd you get the key?"

"My master key."

"There's nothing wrong with the sink."

"Okay. But I had to check."

"Take my word. Now get out of here."

The flustered, trembling Da Capo backed away, pulling the door closed as he left.

Returning to the bedroom, Lyman could not keep his eyes from going directly to the painting once more. He wondered what would happen to the painting when this case was closed, if Larry's brother would want it, if Conrad Ames had any claim on it. That's not my concern, he said to himself, finally.

He went to Larry's desk and sat at it, laying his fingers

atop the typewriter keys as though he were about to type something. He looked at the desktop, at the idle, paperless machine, and asked himself where he would keep something he was writing.

Opening and closing drawers that had a layer of finger-print dust on the handles, he found them empty of anything Larry had typed.

He leaned back in the chair, utterly frustrated and angry.

He surveyed the top of the desk again: the typewriter, a calendar, a pencil, a typing eraser, a little white bottle of correction fluid and two ream-size boxes of typing paper.

Idly, he reached for the top box of paper and lifted the lid. It was a brand new box of heavy bond. There was a red and yellow paper band around it with the brand name of the manufacturer printed on it.

He lifted the second box, which had been under the full ream of paper. It was much lighter than the full box. The box's corners were ragged and worn.

Lifting the lid, he peered inside the half-full box.

"Ha!" he cried. "Eureka! Right in front of us the whole fucking time!"

He laughed. Was Larry Apperson as shrewd as he seemed? Was he slick enough to see the wisdom of one of the oldest saws in the literature of crime? Had he read Edgar Allen Poe, who first suggested that the best place to hide something is out in the open?

Eagerly, Lyman gently lifted out of the box the thick stack of paper whose title page got to the superficial fact of Larry Apperson's life:

"The Bought Boy"

The Bought Boy

Notes, Thoughts, and Other Items
for a novel, tentatively titled
"The Bought Boy," by L. Apperson.

Possible epigrams for front of book:

"My mother made me a homosexual."
"If I bought her the wool, would she make me one?"

"Show me a happy homosexual and I'll show you a
gay corpse."

It's funny about gays, how they make jokes about themselves.
Most of the jokes about homosexuals were made up by
homosexuals. I suppose it's a kind of self-hate. The way I see
it, God made me a homosexual.

My novel will be about a beautiful boy who has all the great
and grand men of his day at his feet. It will be a boy of today
like Dorian Gray in Oscar Wilde's time. (I even have a picture,
like Dorian, ha! ha!)

If they make a movie of my novel, who will play me? Warren
Beatty? Robby Benson? Henry "The Fonz" Winkler? I asked
Joey whom he thought should play me and he laughed and
said Bette Midler.

Flashback: the day the kid's old man accused him of being a

fairy and how he told him he wasn't and how the next day he split for New York.

*   *   *

I picked up Neal in a bar on Third Avenue. He thought he was picking me up, and I let him think it. I was amused at his nervousness, approaching me as if I might bite his head off. Later, when we were at his apartment, he treated me as if I were an ancient Ming vase, too delicate and precious to handle. Neal was a madame, although he made it sound better by telling everyone that he ran an escort service. He flattered me by telling me that he wasn't interested in meeting me just to add me to his stable, but because he liked me for myself and just wanted to love me. If I hadn't really been up against it financially, I would have liked to have become Neal's private lover, but I needed cash and Neal had all the contacts. What I didn't count on with Neal was being introduced to the best people in the New York gay scene. Because I was something special to Neal personally, he made sure I met the cream of his clientele. Sadly for Neal, he was naive enough to believe that I would not, inevitably, leave him and his escort service. When it finally happened, he took it badly. "Fucking traitor!" he screamed when I told him.

*   *   *

The thing about the fuss over that singer—Anita Bryant—is this: she has probably done more to unite gays than harm them. She's been a great friend of gays.

Working the streets as a teenager wasn't all that bad. There was a lot of money to be made, and not all of it was split between me and Wills. I saved quite a bit! Ha, ha!

*   *   *

Freddy had been around, even before he became famous for his music and began world tours to play concerts. Born and raised in a small town in Ohio, he was the youngest child in his family of six kids, and his mother's favorite. "You might say I was everything Doctor Freud wrote about when he drew up his theories on why little boys turn into men who want to make love to boys. I lacked a strong identification with my father. He was working all the time, so I didn't see much of him. My devotion to music and not to football did not exactly endear me to him. Yet I loved him very much. So I suppose when I go to bed with someone I'm really expressing my desire to go to bed with my old man."

"What do you look for in the boys you go to bed with?"

"Cocks," he laughed.

"Seriously, Freddy."

"I believe I look for innocence. Youthful innocence. You have the quality I seek. I cherish you for it, Larry. I hope you never lose that wonderful innocence that radiates from you. I don't know what I'd do if the day came when I looked at you with anything but adoration."

"But I'm not innocent. Hell, the things we've done in bed?"

"I'm talking about the purity inside. I can be making love to your body and still, in my mind, hold you up as chaste and pure and innocent."

*   *   *

On the morning I met Joey, I had gone swimming. I crept out of the beach house, leaving Conrad asleep in the warm bedroom. Something, perhaps a gull screaming or the ocean waves, brought me totally awake. Outside, the first traces of dawn were showing over the distant horizon of the gray Atlantic. The air was cool and damp and heavy with the smell of the sea. I inhaled it deeply, letting the wet coolness seep into me, and then, suddenly, I wanted to swim.

As I walked across the sand, thinking about Conrad asleep in the house, I knew it was over between us, that I would soon be going back to New York, back to look for whatever it was I thought I had to look for. I felt sad about it, but it was something that had to be done. The realization that I would leave Conrad had come to me even as I posed for the portrait, finished, now, and standing on the easel in his living room.

The icy water slapped at my body as I plunged naked into it. I churned in the surf and swam out beyond the point where the rollers broke, crested by foamy whitecaps, to rush to the beach.

I felt completely alone.

Naked, diving, splashing, gasping for breath in the breathtaking cold, I felt like a newly born sea creature. A dolphin, perhaps. I laughed at the idea and dove deep in the water, then emerged in an explosion of foam into the clean lung-filling air. Opening my eyes and looking toward the shore, I saw a boy standing ankle-deep in the slapping surf as it glided spent and meek on the hard wet sand. Intrigued, I swam ashore. "You take a lot of risks," said the boy. "My name's Joey Shaw."

Joey was eighteen, although he often looked sixteen, with his upturned nose crossed by a bridge of freckles. His eyes were cornflower blue. His body was slender and splendidly muscled. He wore membrane-thin racing trunks that left little of his sexual parts to the imagination. His eyes drifted down to my naked sex, and he looked up with a grin. "Do you always swim nude?"

"Yes, around here. You are the first person I've ever run into when I was skinny dipping."

"Shall we swim together?"

"Sure."

Slowly, he peeled off his trunks, and then we plunged into the sea, but we stayed only a little while in the water before we came out, crossed the beach, and settled in the wind-protected side of a dune where he was against me in a rush, throwing his arms around me and rubbing his hard young body against mine.

Somewhere in the frenzy of our joining, I knew that not only would I be leaving Conrad and going back to the city, but I would be going back with Joey.

*   *   *

Ray settled comfortably into a chair in his suite at the Pierre and began telling me about Nelson Royce. It was clear he was enjoying telling tales out of school about Hollywood's most famous macho star's real interests. "Nelse is always looking. He seems to depend more on his eyes than other people. If you watch his eyes, you will see that he never fails to look at even the most mildly interesting young man. He looks at them behind counters in stores, taking tickets in theatres, riding subways, sitting in buses, on bicycles, playing on rooftops, at the beach, surfing, on the backlot at the studios, in screening rooms. Nelse is always on the lookout for an exceptional young man. He saw you at the party which Neal gave last evening, and he wants to meet you."

I never met a movie star before. I was really scared. But he turned out to be like all the other Johns I knew. He was just another cocksucker.

I wonder what he would have said if I told him that's what he was: just another cocksucker.

*   *   *

Things for characters to say about being gay. (Things which

friends have said to me, so they are really good quotes for the book.)

What Neal said: "Sucking a cock is not something you do well by instinct. It is an acquired taste, a learned art. While everyone knows how to suck—it is a faculty born into us to get us through our childhood—the sucking of a cock is a delicate and challenging adult undertaking."

Nelse told me, "You wouldn't be the first kid to make it in Hollywood by opening his fly."

Ray Bonner, about the play and its reviews, which weren't very good: "That reviewer in the "Times" who said he was weary of plays about homosexuals doesn't understand that there will always be plays about homosexuals as long as homosexuality is looked on as wicked. Its very wickedness is its fascination. If homosexuality is ever accepted, it won't be wicked, it won't be fascinating, and we won't have plays about it."

Mr. Denzinger quoted Oscar Wilde to me: "There is no such thing as a moral or immoral book. Books are well written, or badly written. That is all."

*   *   *

The young man knew, of course, who the client was. He was on TV news all the time. It was not possible to live in New York and not know that man. If anybody stood for New York, that man did, and now there he was, standing in the middle of the room, waiting, just like any other "John." The famous man looked at the bought boy and said, "There isn't much time."

Less than half an hour later, the young man was dressed and sitting in the back of a limousine being driven home to his apartment. He could have told the driver to take him anywhere, the man in the room said.

The driver looked as if he had done this sort of thing often.

The young man passed the test, because less than a week later he was in the room again with the famous New Yorker, and he was lying back and watching the man's head bob up and down just like the others who'd done it to him—hundreds, maybe thousands.

It was an uncommon act that made this uncommon man common.

*   *   *

The Break

1.

For the first time in his career as a police officer, Sheldon Lyman suppressed evidence.

Laying aside the pages of Larry Apperson's manuscript, he sat very still in the rapidly failing light of the gray day. He felt for the first time since he began working on the case that he was beginning to understand something of the soul of the naked boy in the painting across the room. In the handful of pages he had scanned and the few he had read, he had encountered the living Larry Apperson. He had been admitted to the mind of a boy who until this moment had been an oil painting, a bloated corpse in the bathroom, a reason for gossip among the men he had loved and been loved by while he lived. Until he read Larry Apperson's words, Lyman had been dealing with a crafty, devious, hurtful, manipulative hustler. Suddenly, he had stumbled onto a boy who was thoughtful, serious, self-conscious, seeking to understand himself and others, questioning. In the fragmented and roughly worded pages of Larry Apperson's plan for a novel breathed the soul of the boy whose body Conrad Ames had captured on canvas.

Perhaps the clue to who murdered Larry Apperson would be found in the pages of the manuscript. If so, Sheldon Lyman would unearth that clue. But first—without anyone knowing he had found this vital piece of evidence—Sheldon Lyman wanted to discover all he could about the victim of as terrible a murder as he had ever investigated.

If Larry Apperson had been randomly killed by a vicious person whose heart was set on burglary at all costs, then Sheldon Lyman would see to it that that killer would be brought to book and made to see the terrible thing he had done.

If Larry died at the hands of one who knew the beauty of his body *and* his soul, Sheldon Lyman would not let that killer go unpunished.

In the meantime, he would keep the knowledge of the existence of Larry Apperson's book to himself.

Following the wise decision of Larry Apperson in choosing where to keep the precious pages, Lyman placed the manuscript back in its box and returned it to the desk, placing the box of typing paper upon it, and leaving it in exactly the place where it had been safe so long.

When he returned to the squad, Lyman found Garraty in a dither. "Where the hell've you been? The guys on the Davis stakeout called a few minutes ago. Davis is back from Boston."

Lyman cracked a smile. "Let's go ream that bastard's lying ass!"

Streets were passable so cars were more abundant, making going slower than it had been just after the storm, but Garraty was his usual great wheel man, and they made it downtown fairly fast.

They warned the doorman about sending signals.

Lyman shoved open the door when Neal Davis answered the bell.

"What the hell are you doing?" shouted Neal Davis.

"Sit down, Davis, and don't get out of line because we are in no mood to put up with any of your shit."

"Lyman, what the hell is going on? What are you so pissed about?"

"How come you've been lying to us, Davis?" Garraty

poked a hard finger into Davis's ribs, then flattened his palm on Davis's chest and shoved him into a chair.

"Lying?"

"You've done nothing *but* lie!" Lyman growled. "You lied about not knowing about Larry's book. And you've been holding back information, which is the same as lying! How come you didn't tell us about the video tape that Larry made with Nelson Royce? How come you didn't tell us how much Royce wants that tape back? How come you didn't tell us about your call to Wills to get the tape back for you? How come, Davis? How come?"

"It was a very sensitive matter that had nothing to do with Larry's murder."

"Nothing to *do* with it? I happen to believe it was the reason Larry was killed. And I have a strong suspicion that you had the kid killed just to get that tape back."

"You've got to be kidding!"

"That's the way it adds up."

"Look, sure, I sent Wills over there to get the tape back. I thought he might be able to scare Larry into giving it back. It didn't work out and I dropped the whole matter."

"You dropped the whole matter? I don't believe that, Davis." Garraty snapped.

"I spoke to Nelson Royce. I told him he was just worked up over nothing. I told him that Larry didn't have any intention of using the tape for blackmail or anything. Nelson dropped it."

"But what about you, Davis?" Lyman smiled.

"What *about* me?"

"Royce may have bought your little speech about Larry not being a threat to him, but you wanted the tape for yourself, didn't you? A little insurance for your retirement?"

"Bullshit and you know it."

"It adds up. Terry and I were trying to figure out your interest in this tape, which went far beyond doing a little favor for a client. We decided that you wanted the tape for yourself. Right?"

"No."

"When Wills failed, you kept after this little scheme, and you either went to see Larry yourself or you sent someone. We haven't found any tape in Larry's apartment, so it's obvious that whoever killed him took the tape; went there for that very reason."

"I don't believe you guys! This is wild conjecture! Pure conjecture. I told you I got Wills to go and see Larry, but when that didn't work I got Nelson Royce to forget the whole deal. That's the truth. I'll take one of your lie detectors to prove it."

"That can be arranged."

"Do it. You'll see."

"What I'd prefer to do, Davis, is send around our mutual friend Mike Brown to give you his kind of lie detector test."

"Get out, Lyman. Get out now and don't come back without a warrant of some kind."

"I think you killed Larry, Davis."

"Get *out*!"

"I'm gonna prove it, Davis. I'm gonna hang this one on you."

"OUT!"

2.

A little after three in the morning, five days after the body of Larry Apperson was found, Emil Denziger leaped from his twelfth floor terrace and splattered himself all over the sidewalk.

Responding to calls, Lyman and Garraty arrived in a few minutes, parking half a block away because the street was jammed with police vehicles, their gumball-machine lights whipping streaks of yellow and red over the fronts of the highrises, many of whose windows were up as the startled occupants of hundreds of apartments gazed down at the excitement in their block. "Think he killed Apperson and this was his way out?" Garraty asked, finally, as they pushed through the crowd around the police barriers. It was a question on his tongue since they'd gotten the call.

"Could be," Lyman grunted.

They showed their shields to the uniformed officers near the body, had a cursory look at Denziger courtesy of Murdock Flemming, who knelt on the hard pavement by the mangled corpse, and went inside and up to Denziger's apartment. Right away Lyman knew Denziger hadn't murdered Larry Apperson. Denziger wasn't a perpetrator. He was a victim. On the top of the wall of the terrace from which he had leaped Emil Denziger had left a message: a copy of the *Post* opened to the Donnelly article about himself and his having been questioned.

"A guy jumps off a terrace because a newspaper prints that he was questioned—*routinely questioned*—in a murder. Jesus, why?" Garraty shook his head and turned away from the spot where Denziger had climbed onto the wall and jumped.

"It wasn't the questioning that pushed him over the edge," Lyman replied. "It wasn't even the fact that the paper said he had been routinely questioned in a homicide case. It was because he was a homosexual and now everyone knew it."

3.

Parker was in uniform because of some kind of ceremony at One Police Plaza. The Lieutenant was impressive in his blues, but he came in making noises about being pissed off about having to give up important office time just to attend a dumbass ceremony made for TV at headquarters. Passing Lyman's desk, he tapped Lyman on the shoulder. "See you a second in the office, Sheldon?"

Parker was out of the coat and had his white sleeves rolled up even before he reached his desk. He sat, leaned back in his chair, folded his big hands across his belly, and said, "The owner of that building where you had the homicide of that kid wants to know when he's getting his apartment back."

"When I'm through with it," replied Lyman, tensely.

"Why are you holding it? Anything there's already been found."

"I'll release it by the end of the week, okay?"

Parker came down in his chair. "What's got you pissed off?"

"This fucking case. It isn't adding up. I've got a list of suspects as long as my arm. Plenty of 'em with motive, means and opportunity."

"And?"

"I can't figure out why anyone would *want* to kill the kid."

"You said you've got *suspects* with *motives*!"

"I do, but they come right out and make no bones about having reasons to kill the kid. Jealousy, fear of being blackmailed, anger over being jilted. The whole catalog."

"So?"

"They all *loved* the kid."

"Love is the number one motive for murder, Sheldon."

"They all talk about this kid as if he were some kind of saint."

"The kid was a hustler, right?"

"Yeah. He did it all."

"Yet he's a saint."

"Crazy, huh?"

"Well, one of your loving suspects has to be lying to you."

"I know."

"What about the burglary angle? The missing items."

"Could be red herrings. To make it look like burglary."

"Why are you hanging on to the apartment?"

Lyman shrugged. "Dunno. Maybe I expect the killer to return to the scene of the crime."

"That happens only in books, Sheldon."

"I'll release the apartment end of the week. Okay?"

"Sheldon, if you think holding onto that apartment for a year will help you break this case, I'm not going to tell you to release it."

"End of the week," Lyman waved, leaving the office.

He left Parker's office and walked directly to Larry's apartment. All the way, he told himself that he should have told Parker about finding the manuscript, about the things he'd already read in it that were ample motive for murder, but he was silent about the book, and he knew why.

The book was Larry Apperson alive, and he wanted to spend more time with the living Larry Apperson, going over the pages again and again, absorbing them, making them part of all that he knew about the murdered boy. There were a few pages yet unread, and therefore there was something of Larry not yet discovered. Perhaps when he believed he knew Larry Apperson beyond the cold facts of his cruel death, he could toss the manuscript on the litter of detail accumulated in less than a week of investigation and say, finally, "This is why he died and how." And, with God's help, "This is who did the killing."

Circumstantial evidence abounded to indicate that Neal Davis was behind the murder, driven by a compulsion to have the video tape showing movie actor Nelson Royce in homosexual acts. The tape was Neal Davis's ticket to a fat bank account and a worry-free retirement. Neal Davis had sent someone to get the tape, no matter what. That's how the case now shaped up. But there was no way that a D.A. could get an indictment. No way.

Walking up the three flights of stairs to Larry Apperson's apartment, Lyman was afraid he would never be able to close the case on Larry Apperson. It would go down as another homosexual murder for which no one would ever be arrested.

In the apartment, he went to the bedroom, took the boxed manuscript from atop the desk, and stretched out on the bed under the portrait of Larry.

A handful of pages remained unread. Fragments, pieces of a puzzle, they provided glimpses of Larry Apperson alive:

> "They sat on the balcony outside his room as darkness settled on the city below them. Somehow each knew that this night together was going to be something special, as if their one day of not seeing each other had been a deeply shattering experience for each of them and one which, curiously, brought them closer together than before so that now they were not simply a man who had picked up a boy and a boy who found a man willing to pay for making love to him. They had discovered that they needed each other."

Lyman could only guess whom Larry had written about. He hoped the passage was about Emil Denziger.

On the next page, Larry was thirteen again, untouched by New York, unspoiled, the little angelic kid who ran away from home because his father had called him a name. A moment later he was on Forty-second Street, hustling. The first man to pick him up took him into the dingy, dark balcony of a movie house.

> "Cigarette smoke hung like a gray ghost over the balcony, the eerie, oozing grayness dotted with shadow figures. The place stank of urinal disinfectant. I waited and soon the man's hand was in my lap and then he was onto me like a crazy person."

Lyman went over to the desk, half-turned to look at Larry's portrait, then opened the manuscript again, leafing through it, scanning the raw emotions of a boy's attempt to find himself in words. Honest, rough, pornographic, the pages were a soul on paper. He was describing Frederick Sloan:

> "He went down on me slowly, tightly, and warmly. The way a man does it when he likes it. With the steadiness and certainty of a carefully choreographed dance, his mouth and tongue and lips and hands urged me along, coaxed me steadily, wetly, smoothly, and easily onward and upward toward the hot, tightening squeezing hardening that I knew would become so excruciatingly tense that it would have to explode."

Lyman lifted his eyes to the portrait. It was still there— the innocence. Amused. Interested. Watching. Silent. Knowing. Angelic.

Lyman looked back at the page:

> "When it was over, I summoned the courage to
> tell Freddy that it was finished between us. He lifted
> himself onto an elbow and looked down at me.
> 'Don't say that,' he sighed. As he said it, he ran his
> hand down my body and took my cock into it. 'I love
> you, Larry. Don't tell me that it's over between us.'
>
> " 'But it is,' I said as gently as possible. I put my
> hand to his cheek and drew his mouth to mine, for a
> final, farewell kiss."

It was the last page of the manuscript. In all, there were
barely more than fifty pages. Not a book at all. Notes, really.
Jottings. Yet there was intent in them, a determination to take
the memories of a bought boy and turn them into a human
document, a book.

Lyman closed the box with the manuscript in it and made
up his mind to take it back to the office, to put it with the other
evidence, to add it to the pile.

Ironically, he thought, although so much had been made
of and said about the book that Larry Apperson was writing
there seemed to be very little in its pages worth worrying
about. If someone had killed for these few pages, it had been a
terrible mistake. A joke, almost.

Lyman looked again at the portrait of Larry. "Kid, I'm
sorry about everything," he said. "Sorry you never had a
chance to write the book. Sorry that someone did that awful
thing to you. And I'm sorry that I'm probably not going to be
able to find the sonofabitch who murdered you!"

He waited, his eyes on the portrait, listening to the
silence, as if the portrait could answer him.

He heard a noise.

The soft sliding of a key in the lock of the door to Larry's
apartment.

He thought, *That bastard Da Capo is creeping in here again! I'll kick that sonofabitch in the ass!*

No, he realized, it couldn't be Da Capo because the super had been moved to his boss's apartment in the Bronx.

Lyman sat straight, listening, as the key turned slowly in the lock and the bolt fell open.

A shaft of light from the hallway cut into the dark living room. The silhouette of a man moved into the widening light as the door opened.

Reaching for the butt of his .38, Lyman deftly and silently snaked through the bedroom door into the living room and flattened himself against the wall. He could see the shadow of the intruder moving out of the slant of light and into the grayness in the middle of the room. He could hear him breathing shallowly, nervously.

Lyman drew his .38, curled his hands around it in a combat grip, and laid his finger alongside the trigger. "Police! Don't move!"

"I won't! Don't shoot!"

Lyman found a wall switch and snapped on the ceiling light.

"Please! Don't shoot! I can explain!"

The young man was terrified, near to tears.

"You see, there's been a mistake!" the young man pleaded.

Lyman stared. His jaw fell slack. A cold tingle rippled down his spine. He could hardly speak. "My God, Peter, you look just like your brother."

"No, you don't understand. I'm *not* Peter."

Lyman lowered his .38.

No, he realized, you're not Peter. You're. . . .

"I'm *Larry*. There has been an *awful* mistake!"

4.

I can't believe you're alive!"

"Please. Put away the gun. Please."

Lyman holstered his special. "I'm Sheldon Lyman. I'm in charge of the case. The murder. Your murder. Oh, Jesus Christ, this is something!"

"I've been out of town. Skiing. Up in New England. We got snowed in because of the blizzard, in a private house in the mountains. The phones were out. It was terrible. I just got back."

"You didn't know about the homicide?"

"Only today in a Hartford newspaper on the way back."

"We've been investigating *your* murder, Larry!"

"Mr. Lyman, I have to find out who it was. I have to find out if it was Petey."

"Oh, Christ! Your brother?"

"He was staying here while I was away. Was it him?"

"I've been trying to locate your brother since, since. . . ."

"He was staying *here*."

"It must have been him, Larry. I'm sorry. He looked just like you—the build, the hair. We couldn't tell it wasn't you because the face was. . . ."

"Oh, dear Christ!"

"Sit down. You don't look good. I'm going to call my office." As he dialed, he studied the boy. Drawn, ashen, shaken, he was a sad case. Boyish in his ski jacket and pants and boots, his camera slung around his neck—the missing Pentax!—Larry appeared ready to collapse or cry or both.

It took a moment for Garraty to come on the line and another moment before Garraty understood exactly what his partner was telling him. He agreed to find Lt. Parker and bring him along to the Apperson apartment. When Lyman put down the phone, he looked at Larry Apperson, who sat stiffly upright at the edge of a chair. "You want a drink or something, Larry?"

"No. What I want now is to find out if it was Peter who was killed."

"In a couple of minutes my partner and my boss will be here and we'll decide what we're going to do, how we're going to handle this. The case has become a sensational thing in the newspapers and on the news, Larry. I wish it hadn't, but there was the sex angle."

"Sex angle?"

"About your being a hustler. I'm afraid one of your neighbors shot off his mouth and then one of the newspapers did a lot of digging around."

"I don't care about any of that."

"We'll go to the morgue in a little while and find out if it was Pete."

"God, what a terrible thing to happen."

"Why was Pete here, Larry?"

"He always liked New York and when I called and told him that Ellis and I were going away for a few days, he asked to use the apartment."

"Ellis Marsh has been with you?"

The boy nodded. "We went to a place in New England to see if we could work out our problems."

"What problems?"

"Problems."

"Lovers' problems?"

"Yes."

"Did you work them out?"

"No. It's over between Ellis and me. Why are you so concerned about Ellis?"

"He was a prime suspect."

"Ellis would never harm anyone."

"Well, you were dead and he was among the missing. It added up. Although I was onto some other leads that made a lot of sense."

"What other leads?" asked Larry as the doorbell rang.

"We can talk about all of that later," replied Lyman, going to the door and admitting Garraty and Parker.

Garraty stopped short, his eyes on Larry Apperson. "It's him. Alive. Sonofabitch."

Lt. Parker moved to the center of the room and looked down at the boy. "You're Lawrence Apperson?"

"I am," he replied, looking up.

"Do you have any idea who was murdered in this apartment?"

"My brother, I'm afraid."

Parker turned to Lyman. "Does this make sense?"

"Yes. We'd been trying to get in touch with Peter Apperson but didn't have any luck. Now we know why."

"But you have no positive I.D. yet?"

"No. I called you and Terry first. I thought we'd better get our heads together. This is going to make an already sensational case a lot more sensational. I thought we'd want to decide how to handle it."

Parker nodded. "I'll get on the horn to Commissioner Finley and see what she recommends on handling the press. And I'll let all the other brass know so all those who've had an interest in this case can promptly get off our backs. You and Garraty take this young man downtown for an I.D. on the victim. I'm sorry, young man, but you'll have to look at your brother's body."

"I understand. May we do it now? I have to know. I'll have to make arrangements and all that sort of thing."

Garraty drove. Lyman sat in the back seat with Larry.

There was no doubt. Identification of the body of Peter Apperson was made instantly by his brother despite the bruised and battered face of the corpse, rebuilt as best they could by Doc Dock and his assistants. There was a one inch scar just in back of the hair line on the right forehead, the result of a wildly thrown pitch in a sandlot baseball game when they were kids, Larry told Doc Dock. Peter also had a scar on his right wrist made by a Boy Scout knife when he was six years old. Because the young man wanted to know, Doc Dock related how Peter had died and the medical evidence that sustained his deductions. Doc Dock finally advised Larry on how to go about obtaining assistance from a funeral director in arranging for the burial of his brother. "There were just the two of us," Larry said as he watched one of Doc Dock's assistants roll Peter's corpse into a vault. "I'll probably just go for a cremation."

"When you feel up to it, Larry, we're going to have to talk to you," explained Lyman as they left Doc Dock's morgue and got into the car. "While it was your brother who was killed, there is strong evidence to indicate that you were the intended victim."

Larry smiled. "Someone wanted to kill me?" He laughed. "You have to be kidding."

"I'm not."

"Who the hell would want to kill me?"

"A lot of people. Friends. Clients."

"Officer Lyman, you are mistaken. This has to have been

an accident, a mistake. Someone breaking into the apartment."

"That is a possibility, but Terry and I have come up with a lot of information that points to premeditated homicide. That's why we have to talk."

"Can we do it now?"

"Of course.

"There's apt to be press at the Seventeenth if we go there," Garraty pointed out. "And they'll probably stakeout Larry's apartment."

"Go to my place," Lyman decided. "Is that all right, Larry?"

With a nod, he replied. "Anywhere, because at the moment I would rather not go back home."

"When the story gets out that you're not dead the news media are going to want to talk to you," Garraty said.

"I don't want to talk to them."

"You don't have to, but they'll come looking for you."

"My place is probably the best spot right now,' Lyman said.

"I can stay with friends."

"Some of your friends have pretty good motives for wanting to harm you," Garraty reminded the boy.

"I don't believe that."

"We'll fill you in on what we've learned in the past few days, Larry. Meanwhile, it would be better if you steered clear of some of those friends for a while," Lyman explained.

Larry nodded as a puzzled frown clouded his face. "Okay."

Lyman and Garraty decided that Garraty should go back to Third Homicide where he could keep Lyman informed of developments there once the news was out that in the most sensational sex-and-murder case in recent years, the wrong victim had been chosen.

In his apartment, Lyman poured Larry a scotch on the rocks and fixed one for himself. Larry took off his ski jacket, kicked off his boots and sat on Lyman's couch. His face was freshly tanned from two days of sun before the blizzard hit. He wore a blue sweater with white stripes, dark blue ski pants and white socks. He was remarkably calm as he sipped the scotch. Lyman watched Larry's eyes—those blue eyes—for signs of shock, but Larry seemed totally adjusted to the fact of his brother's death. He had to make funeral arrangements, but he had been told it would take a day or two before Doc Dock could release the body. "There's time for you to get yourself pulled together," Doc Dock had told him. Larry sipped the scotch, keeping his eyes on his hands and the drink, for a few moments. At last, he put down the glass and looked directly at Lyman. "You've been very kind and considerate, Mr. Lyman."

"Sheldon. Or Shelly. Or Shel."

"I appreciate the hospitality of your apartment. I couldn't have faced that place of mine just now. I suppose I should call Ellis. He's got room. I could stay with him. He'd be hospitable even though. . . ."

"Even though it's over between you?"

"The drive back from New England was very grim, even before I picked up that Hartford newspaper and found out what had happened back here while I was away. Ellis was very nice after we read the paper. I think he hoped that somehow what happened might fix things between us. He'd wanted to come in to the apartment when we got back, but I insisted I go in alone. I'm sure Ellis will put me up."

"You may stay here as long as you like, Larry."

The boy smiled in surprise. "I wouldn't want to intrude."

"There's no problem. I'm alone. A widower. I've got room. Besides, I should remind you, not to alarm you, of course, but just remind you, that it's very likely that the person who killed your brother intended to kill you. We haven't found out who that person is."

"My life is in danger?"

"It may be."

"Well, that's something to think about."

"That's why it may be better if you stay here. In addition to which, there are a lot of questions I have to ask you. There's much about you and your friends that only you can tell me. This may sound cruel, but I don't mean it that way. You see, a police officer never has the luxury of interviewing the victim of the murder he's investigating. Although your brother was the one killed, you were meant to be the victim. Understand?"

"Yes. What can I possibly tell you? I wasn't there."

"For instance, you had an argument in the hallway with a black man. Was it "Chicken" Wills?"

The boy was astounded. His eyes widened. His jaw dropped. "Yes. How did you know that?"

"Wills is a suspect. He was after a video tape?"

Larry shook his head. "God, you know so much! Yes. A tape I made as a joke. Do you know who it was with?"

"Nelson Royce."

"Damn! You're very good as a detective, aren't you?"

"It's not hard to put together the facts of someone's life. In your case, you left a lot to go on. Your address book. The manuscript of the book you were working on."

Larry blushed, and Lyman was touched. "You've read my book?"

"It says a good deal about you, Larry."

"That makes me feel a little uncomfortable, I have to admit."

"It was important for me to get to know you as well as I could. By knowing you, I'd have an easier time figuring out who wanted to kill you. Who *did* kill, uh, your *brother*."

"You almost said, who *did* kill *you*."

"It's not easy sitting here talking to the boy I've thought dead for most of the past week."

"I can see how difficult that would be."

"Larry?"

"Yes?"

"I have to tell you that I'm very glad it wasn't you. I'm sorry it was your brother. I'm sorry anyone had to be murdered. But I'm glad it wasn't you."

5.

The Funeral Syndrome.
Lyman recognized it in Larry Apperson.

In The Funeral Syndrome, as Lyman called the phenomenon, there comes a great rush of words, a monologue, by the survivor—or survivors—of the person who died. The words tumble forth in a stream of consciousness. When Betty died he had talked to Garraty for hours. He remembered when his father died how his mother had told the details of her husband's fatal heart attack again and again, using the same words, until the awful event was completely talked out. The Irish institutionalized The Funeral Syndrome in wakes. Jews had similar rites. He supposed all societies had them. The dead were conducted to their eternal rest on a river of words.

THE LARRY APPERSON TAPE

When my parents were killed in a car accident, I was thirteen years old. Peter was ten. We were taken in by my father's brother. Uncle Robert was a wonderful man with kids of his own. Poor Uncle Rob. He never realized that he had homosexual tendencies until I moved in with him and his family. He was very shocked and guilty the first time we had sex. He was afraid he had seduced me. Hell, I seduced him. After that, he got to be very fatherly. I suppose he thought he could make amends, straighten me out. He started becoming very much like my father—strict, suspicious. That's when I split for New York. I knew what I was doing. I wasn't exactly innocent. I'd had a long-standing relationship with a man in my hometown, a school teacher. I talked it over with him before I left. He offered to let me live with him, but I told him that would only get him into trouble. He gave me some money and I came to New York.

Donny Wills met me at the Port Authority bus station. I guess he saw that I was bewildered and even a little scared. He offered me a place to stay, but I knew right away what he was up to. I've had men hitting on me all my life. Even at thirteen I knew when I was being hit on. Before long I was on to what Wills was doing. I let him be my pimp. Donny knew a lot of men with money, and I was very popular. After about a year, I had a client book of my own, so I split from Wills. He was pissed about it, but mostly I think he was angry because he was in love with me. We never really lost contact. He'd come back every now and then and try to get me to live with him, but I was on my own by then.

I met Neal Davis in a bar called 'Charlie's Aunt.' I'd heard about Davis and knew he ran a very exclusive service. Frankly, I wasn't doing as well as I wanted to, and I decided to look Neal up and go to work for him. It was easy because Neal fell for me. I was working for him for quite a while and met a number of men who went beyond being customers to being friends. When I got out of the business, some of them stayed my friends.

Realizing that I wasn't getting any younger and knowing that there would be a day when I wouldn't be able to make it on my looks any longer, I started thinking about what I could do. I guess I was looking for a meaning to my life. I discovered it. The theatre. At the same time I met Ellis Marsh. He came backstage to see another member of the cast, and we were introduced. Right away something clicked between us. That very night we became lovers.

It had to end between Ellis and me because he was very, very possessive.

I've seen and done it all, and I haven't regretted any of it. There were plenty of times when I was on the verge of disaster, but something—someone—came along and saved me. What is it that Blanche DuBois says in 'A Streetcar Named Desire?' I have always gotten along on the kindness of strangers.

Pete was never into what I was into. I did my best to save him from it. He knew what I was doing, how I was earning my living, but he loved me and trusted me and when I told him in no uncertain terms that I'd kick his ass and have nothing to do with him if he ever got into hustling, he believed me. He was doing very well in college. He never got on my case about what I did. He was a very good brother. I remember once when we were little kids . . .

Lyman listened and watched. The stories rolled from Larry's lips: funny, touching, boyish tales of games and brotherly love. Lyman listened to the harrowing tales of men Larry had met in New York and of what he did with men and what they paid him and how so many of them loved him. He listened to Larry speak with affection and admiration for Conrad Ames and the portrait Ames had painted. He listened to Larry tell about all the other men he'd met through Neal Davis and subsequently through Neal Davis's clients. He listened while Larry talked about Joey Shaw. Finally, he let Larry talk about Emil Denziger. When he learned that Emil Denizger was dead, a suicide, Larry broke into tears. Lyman got up from his chair and went to the couch to sit beside the sobbing boy, to put an arm around his shoulders, and to hold him closely in the long, agonized minutes of Larry's grief.

Presently, when tears and the talking ceased, Lyman decided he could not proceed with the other questions he had to ask. It was past midnight and Larry was obviously tired, spent, talked out. In the morning, Lyman decided, he could ask about the video tape, about the argument with Wills, about the broken hearts which littered Larry Apperson's recent past, about what men in Larry's life might want to even a score by killing him. He suggested they get some sleep. "I've got twin beds in the bedroom."

While Larry showered, Lyman called Third Homicide and spoke to Garraty. The news was out, Terry reported, and reporters, especially Donnelly, were clamoring for an interview with Larry. "No way. Not until we're finished," Lyman replied. Garraty asked when that would be. Lyman said, "In the morning, I guess."

Larry was in bed under the covers when Lyman came in. He lay with his blond head cushioned in his cradled hands, the hair curling onto the pillow. The sheet and blanket were drawn up to his chest. The paler flesh of his muscled arms and shoulders curved to frame his suntanned face. His blue eyes were flecked with dots of reflected light from the lamp between the beds. His body was so slender, so straight, so flat that the blanket was barely disturbed. He lay with his legs parted beneath the covers which curved in a small mound at the juncture of the thighs. The boy watched as Lyman came into the bedroom. Suddenly, he smiled. Transfixed, Lyman thought no one should be allowed to smile like that. He turned away and sat on his own bed with his back to the boy to take off his shoes and to begin to undress. When he looked back, Larry was asleep.

When Lyman turned out the light he realized that this was the first time anyone had slept in the same room with him since the death of his wife. He listened in the darkness. The boy's breathing was shallow, barely audible. With a sidewards glance in the gray dark, he could see the boy as a darker shadow in the center of the bed. He had not moved since he fell asleep. The blond head still rested in the cradled palms. A faint light from somewhere painted the silhouette of his profile with a thin outline in soft pink.

Lyman looked up at the ceiling. He tried to concentrate on the case, listing all the questions he would have to ask Larry in the morning. Had there been any threats? Of all the men he knew, which would Larry say might be capable of murder? If Larry had to pick one man, which one would he pick as the most likely to want to murder him? Where was the Nelson Royce video tape? Could "Chicken" Wills have harbored murderous intentions? Who would want to kill you, Larry? Who?

Larry moved in bed and Lyman looked at him. He'd turned onto his side, his cheek resting on an arm, the hand thrust beneath the curly blond head. He lay on his other arm, his body diagonally across the bed, the hand dangling over the edge. The covers slipped, baring his shoulders and chest and the slope of his sides and belly to the waist. The covers draped his hips loosely, leaving a dark cavern of shadows between the gray slash of the edge of the sheet and the swath of flesh of belly and abdomen.

Lyman stared at the ceiling again, aware of how dry his mouth was and how parched his throat was. He was very conscious of his heart trip-hammering in his chest.

He said to himself, "We do not have enough evidence in this case to make a grand jury presentment. We are certain that a murderer intended to kill Lawrence Apperson, but he killed Peter Apperson instead, and how can we allege that murder had been premeditated while the intended victim lives?"

The appearance of Lawrence Apperson had knocked the case of murder into a cocked hat.

Lyman's eyes drifted to his right to the sleeping form of Larry Apperson. He thought, Who would want to murder that boy? How could anyone come in the dark of night with the sinister intention of killing that beautiful boy?

In the distance, Lyman heard a siren. He lived near hospitals and sirens were commonplace, but the sound touched Larry's ears and stirred him. He moved little at first, then rolled partly onto his back. A frown creased his forehead. He moved again, struggling against the bed covers. He shifted his legs, kicking in his sleep at the confining blanket and sheet until, at last, he thrust one leg free. Turning slightly again, he rolled flat, his arms and legs akimbo, his head tilted deeply into the pillow. Suddenly, he started with a quick, violent jerk. He fell silent and motionless again, slipping back into the deep sleep which the distant siren had molested.

Lyman wondered if Larry had been dreaming, if in his sleep which began so peacefully and had become so fitful he had been dreaming about his brother, about the murder, about himself as intended victim. Looking at the boy's face, now so serene, Lyman was pleased to see that whatever had disturbed him so violently was now past.

His eyes moved from the placid face to Larry's neck and muscular chest. His gaze wandered down the slant of his belly to the gentle rise of his abdomen. Through gray shadows he saw the flurry of yellow pubic hair and, lying heavily against the abdomen like a fallen tree, Larry's penis. Tangled covers slashed across his legs at mid-thigh.

Turning quietly onto his side, Lyman stared across the space between the two beds.

Presently, gray winter-morning light peeped through narrow cracks in the drapes at the window, and the room took on a ghostly glow. Lyman had not moved. He had lain through the night with his face turned toward the silhouette of the naked boy in the bed that used to be his wife's. In the dawning slant of light Lyman saw specks of dust glinting. He forced himself to think of menial problems. The windows needed washing. His laundry was piling up. If he had a maid he wouldn't have to worry about windows and laundry. Or dishes. Or sweeping the floors. He considered a maid, once, but rejected the intrusion of a stranger into his life.

An hour passed. Daylight was bright outside the drawn shades of the bedroom. A shaft of sunlight had come through the opening in the drapes, crossed the room, and thrown itself upon Larry's bed. Lyman had watched the shaft of light as it nosed into the room, making its way from a wall to the floor and then onto the foot of the bed, creeping upward, climbing the slope of Larry's covered legs until it tumbled between the edge of the covers to the juncture of Larry's thighs. At last, the sun nestled in Larry's hair and, like a tongue, slid up the firmly risen column of his penis.

Lyman looked at the time.

Garraty would be calling soon, he knew.

6.

In the morning, a press confrontation was unavoidable. The reporters thronged the sidewalk outside the Seventeenth Precinct, crowding around Larry Apperson as he stepped from the car beside Lyman, who was trying to push a way through the noisy mob. Garraty hurried around the car, pushing and shoving with as little success as his partner. "We just want to talk to the kid," complained one reporter. "Hey, Larry! Who'd want to kill you?" The question boomed across the heads of reporters from the rear of the crowd. "We have nothing to say!" Lyman answered angrily. "No. It's okay," whispered Larry. "You don't have to," Garraty said. Larry shrugged. "It's okay."

Lyman thought the questions were cruel, insulting.

Finally, he seized Larry's arm and led him through the mob. "You got enough!"

"Hey, Lyman. You have any leads in this case?"

Lyman turned and looked into the face of Donnelly of the *Post*. "No. No leads."

Succeeding at last in reaching the lobby of the precinct Lyman realized he had probably written the headline for Donnelly's story: "Cops Baffled as Murder 'Victim' Shows Up Alive."

They went to Parker's office where another crowd waited—police brass: all the brass who had been at the conference in Deputy Commissioner Hogan's office. Hogan waited by a window, the cold sun glinting on the brass and gold braid of his uniform. Inspector Vinnie Howe sat on a chair in his jacket with the patches at the elbows. Captain Joe Campana stood against a wall in uniform. "Scoop" Finley sat quietly in a tweedy, mannish suit that was very unbecoming to her. Lt. Parker was at his desk in shirt sleeves. All turned to stare as Lyman, Garraty and Larry Apperson came into the office. A few minutes later, Assistant District Attorney Mel Shapiro came in, breathless and angry from having had to fight through the news media outside.

Commissioner Hogan made a speech about how sad they were about the death of Larry's brother, ending with a pledge to solve the case. He regretted the notoriety. If there were anything the New York Police Department could do for him, just ask. Larry answered quietly. "Mr. Lyman and Mr. Garraty have been very considerate. I thank you all for your kindnesses." The boy was obviously uncomfortable about all the attention. Hogan muttered another promise of support, then turned to Lyman. "Sheldon, please bring us up to date."

Hesitantly at first, conscious that Larry was present, he reviewed the case and what they knew. Noticing that Larry was as attentive and interested as the others, he relaxed, presenting the details of the investigation, the futility of the canvassing of the gay bars, the alibis of men who seemed to have motives, and, at last, the most plausible explanation for what had occurred. "I believe we can make a case around the Nelson Royce tape. That Royce wanted to get it back appears uncontestable. He went to Neal Davis for assistance. Davis sent Wills. When Wills was unsuccessful, it appears that Royce might have given up. Davis, however, saw an opportunity for possible extortion if he could get his hands on the tape. I believe that Davis could have sent someone—maybe Wills, again—to get the tape by breaking-and-entering. Whoever went into the apartment found it was not unoccupied, as he may have expected it to be." He concluded by telling about the amazing reappearance of Larry. "In sum, I'd say Neal Davis is the man we want."

"But you have no evidence to back up that theory?" asked Mel Shapiro.

Lyman slowly shook his head.

"We can't indict anyone on theories, Sheldon."

"That is all we have right now. Maybe later we'll have the evidence."

"Where is the tape?" Shapiro asked Larry.

"I burned it. Right after Wills came around asking about it."

"Did you tell anyone that you'd burned it?" Lyman asked.

Larry shook his head. "I was going to let Nelson know when I got back from my trip to New England."

"So we don't even have the tape," said Mel Shapiro dejectedly.

"What about Wills? Can we lean on him?" asked Hogan.

Shapiro made a face. "He's facing a prostitution rap, plus endangering the welfare of minors. If this weren't a case of murder, we could bargain with him."

"How about granting Wills immunity from prosecution?" asked "Scoop" Finley.

"Wills would never go for it," answered Lyman. "Why should he admit to murder, even if he wouldn't be prosecuted for it?"

"I would hate to see this case remain open," announced Commissioner Hogan.

"We're at dead ends all around," Garraty answered.

"Stay with it. Maybe something will break. After all, Mr. Apperson is now a new factor in the case," Hogan stated. "His showing up alive may shake up the murderer. He may slip. He may give himself away."

"We'll keep on top of the case," Lyman promised.

" 'Scoop,' " said Hogan, "you handle the news hounds,

okay? We're working on the case. A break is near. It'll take time. We want to be sure. The usual."

With that, the meeting ended.

On the way out, Larry whispered to Lyman. "You're not going to solve this, are you?"

Lyman said, "It's a hard case, Larry. I'm not going to lie to you."

"Am I in danger?"

"I don't know."

"From what that one officer said, about my showing up shaking up the killer, I got the feeling he was almost hoping the guy would come after me again. Do you think he will?"

"Do you want police protection?"

"No."

"I can arrange it. Maybe you should have it for a while. Maybe you ought to stay at my place for a while."

"I've imposed on you enough already."

"Well, for a day or two it would make it easier for me to go over the case with you. You might spot something that we've been overlooking. You stay awhile, until you figure out what you're going to do with yourself."

Larry chewed on his lower lip, thinking. "Yeah," he said, following Lyman across the squad room to Lyman's desk. "I do have to think about what I'm going to do."

7.

Neither Garraty nor Lyman wanted to admit what they both feared. They were at an impasse. All the procedures, routines, leg work, calls, bar canvassings, interviews, tough words, brave words, hopes, expectations of an imminent break had not panned out. After more than a week of intensive investigation they were no closer to breaking the case. After the flurry of headlines and press attention to the startling appearance of Larry Apperson, newspapers and TV newscasts began paying less and less attention to the case, a sure sign that they knew an immediate break was unlikely.

Doc Dock released the body of Peter Apperson. That same day, the body was cremated by a funeral director on Madison Avenue. The cremation was private. Only Lyman and Garraty stood at Larry's side as he said goodbye to his brother.

Filming ended for Nelson Royce, and the movie star flew back to Hollywood. He did not see Larry, but Larry sent him a note promising him that the tape had been destroyed. "It was just a joke, anyway, Nelse," the note ended.

A grand jury indicted Donny "Chicken" Wills on eight counts of prostitution, eight counts of endangering the welfare of a minor, and an assortment of other charges which Mel Shapiro put together to be sure Wills did a lot of time.

A week after the cremation of Peter Apperson, Neal Davis telephoned Lyman. "I've been trying to reach Larry, but he's not at home. Would you tell him, if you see him, that I'd like to talk to him?" Lyman made no promises, but he passed along the message to Larry.

Larry was amused. "Did he say he wants me to go back to work for him?"

"I didn't ask."

"You despise him, don't you?"

"I think he tried to have you killed and failed only because he got your brother instead."

"Don't worry. I won't see Davis again."

"Have you decided what you're going to do?"

They were seated in the kitchen of Lyman's apartment. A yellow and red sunset streaked the broken overcast above midtown skyscrapers to the north of the kitchen's window. Larry sipped a cup of coffee. "I can't go on doing nothing. You've been wonderful to let me stay here. But I have to get on with my life."

Lyman smoothed the table cloth with the palm of his hand and kept his eyes averted from Larry. "Are you going to hustle again?"

"It's a quick way to get money. I need money."

"I've got money."

Surprised, Larry deliberately set down his cup. "I couldn't take money from you, Shel."

Lyman looked up, hard. "You take it from other men."

"That's different."

"What's so different?"

"They're gay."

Lyman looked down at the tablecloth. "I'd feel a lot better if you'd let me help you out instead of you going to those men in your little black book."

"I couldn't just take charity, Shel."

"Charity? Hell, it's not charity!"

"I can't expect you to do something like that. You've got your own life, your own concerns."

"I don't have any other concerns except my job. I'm on my own, just like you. I'm alone, Larry. There'd be no problem."

"It wouldn't be right for either of us. You're a cop. A straight cop. I'm a gay hustler."

"I enjoy having you around. I like you, Larry. I like you a lot."

"You'd only get hurt. I have a way of hurting people who like me too much. You ought to know that, what with all you've found out about me during your investigation. Somebody was hurt enough, hated me enough, to want to kill me! You said it yourself. You're a very nice man, Shel. One of the nicest men I've ever met. I don't want to mess things up for you."

"How would you mess them up?"

"Shel, what would your partner think? What about those cops you work with? Your friends? What would they think if you let me move in here with you? I'll tell you what they'd think. They'd think that you'd gone off the deep end. They'd start to think you were making it with me."

"I don't give a damn what they'd think."

Larry waited. He was afraid to say what he was thinking, wondering, asking.

Lyman shifted nervously, self-consciously in his chair. "I like you, Larry," he said, presently. His voice was thick, choked.

"You don't know what you're saying. This case has got your head all fucked up."

"You understand what I feel better than I do. You've known men before. You recognize them in me. Don't you?"

"I haven't the slightest idea what you're getting at."

"It's taken me a long time to even admit to myself the *possibility* of it."

"Possibility of *what*?"

"I kept saying to myself that it was okay because what I

was dealing with was someone who was dead. I was dealing with a boy who had been murdered, and that was what made it okay in my head, you see? It was the fact that Larry Apperson was dead that made it okay for me to feel the feelings that suddenly came out in me."

"What feelings?"

"I don't have to tell you and you don't have to pretend that you haven't suspected how I feel."

"I'm not dead, Shel. I'm *alive*. You've got to deal with that reality."

"Yes, you were just a portrait hanging on a wall. You were a victim. A face in a photo. The boy that everyone talked about in the past tense."

"Exactly, and now it is the *present* tense."

"Nothing is changed in how I feel."

"Shel, be sensible."

"I love you, Larry."

"That's crap. A figment of your imagination."

"No."

"It can't be that way between us."

"Why not?"

"Because it's not what you are. You're a cop, Sheldon. You can't suddenly become like me."

"I don't know about any of that, but I know how I feel, what I feel. I know what it's like to be in love. I know that I've been fooling myself all my life. The lies I've made myself believe! I'm closer to you than you know, Larry."

"I don't love you, Shel."

"You've gone with plenty of men you didn't love."

"That's over. I'm changing my life. I'm looking for a commitment. I thought I'd found it with Ellis. It didn't work out with him, but it will with someone. I'll find someone and it will be something great and permanent."

"A young man?"

"I don't know. Not necessarily. But I'd have to love him.

I'm sorry, Shel, but I don't love you. I admire you. I have great respect for you. I want to be your friend. But we can't be lovers, Shel. Not even for money."

"You can be cruel. I knew that."

"I don't want to be cruel to you. I just want you to know that it can't be what you *think* you want between us. I believe I'd better go back to my own place."

"Yes, you'd better."

"I want us to be friends, Shel."

"Sure."

"I *am* sorry."

"I know."

8.

A murder case is never closed until arrest and conviction. But a lot of them are dormant.

Some get solved quickly.

"It looks like those detectives in Brooklyn have all the luck!"

Lyman looked up from his work as Terry Garraty came in and stopped by the desk. "What are you talking about?"

"That Brooklyn Heights copycat killing? They got the guy. It was a pissed-off lover. He admits he got the idea about how to do it when he read about the Apperson case. Those lucky bastards in Brooklyn got a *confession*."

"Maybe it's not luck. Maybe they're better cops."

Then it looked as if they were about to get a break. Central Park Precinct called to tell them they'd arrested two Puerto Rican teenagers for assaulting gays in the Ramble, a thickly grown remote area of the park frequented by cruising homosexuals. "One of the kids admitted to beating up a queer and killing him during an apartment break-in about the time of your case," Central Park reported.

It turned out the break-in had been on the west side.

A more promising lead came when a frightened caller asked to speak to Detective Lyman. "I was the person with Joey Shaw the night you questioned him about Larry." Lyman shut his eyes, trying to recall. He remembered an effeminate boy named Lance in blue disco clothes, grinning unashamedly and admitting he would lie about his lover's whereabouts. "I remember you," Lyman answered. "I have to see you," the boy whispered. "Can you meet me at the Arch in Washington Square in an hour?" Lyman asked what this was about. The boy paused, and Lyman heard him gulping for air. "I know who killed that Apperson boy by mistake!"

Lance Bentley was pacing nervously beneath the George Washington Arch and puffing on a cigarette as Lyman and Garraty slammed to a stop in their car and crossed the sidewalk to the park. A day like spring had broken through winter's skies, and the park was crammed with strollers, bicyclers, and frisbee throwers. Lance had on tight-fitting jeans and a nylon windbreaker. He kept looking at the people in the park, wondering if anyone he knew would see him. "I'd like to talk to you in the car, riding around," he told the detectives. As they drove to Sixth Avenue, he turned to Lyman, who sat in the back seat with him. "It was Joey that did it!"

"Joey Shaw? How do you know?"

"He told me he did it."

"Why did he admit this to you?" Garraty asked, studying Lance through the rearview mirror.

"We had a hell of a fight last night, and he was getting really physical. I could show you the bruises. He said he wasn't going to let me dump him the way Larry Apperson did, and if I did I'd get the same thing Larry got."

"That's hardly an admission of murder," Lyman pointed out.

"I laughed when he said that and he got very serious and told me that he'd gotten really pissed at Larry and went up there that night and beat his face in."

"You said you were with Joey that night."

"I lied."

"Why'd you lie?"

"I figured that if you wanted to know where Joey'd been on that night you asked about he probably ought to have an alibi. Besides, he once told me that if at any time cops asked where he was I was to tell them I was with him fucking."

"Where is Joey now?"

"I don't know."

"Where does he hang out?"

"He goes to a couple of bars and late at night he goes to one of the baths. The one on Twenty-eighth Street."

"Do you figure he'll be there tonight?"

"I guess so."

"You stay around where we can reach you if we need you, Lance."

"I'm staying at the Y on Thirty-fourth."

"We'll leave you off there."

"Thanks."

The detectives were exultant as they sped uptown. They knew a break when they saw one. Suddenly, it added up. Suddenly they had a case again.

They could hardly wait for night to come.

The fire had broken out in the early evening, but it was much later when Lyman and Garraty found out about it. They'd made a turn from Twenty-ninth Street onto Fifth Avenue, a block away from the baths where they expected to find Joey Shaw. They saw a mass of fire equipment blocking Fifth at the corner of Twenty-eighth. A huge rolling pillar of black smoke smudged the red sky above the fire. With their gold shields flapping against their chests, they walked to the corner to get as close to the inferno as possible.

It would be days before the fire department dug out the last charred body in the ruin of the baths.

Some weeks later, on the wooden fence built around the

burned out hulk someone would write in spray paint: "Closets Kill!"

No one would ever know how many homosexuals died in the fire.

Lyman and Garraty were convinced Joey Shaw had been one of them because no one ever saw Joey again.

9.

Larry was circulating but the publicity—the notoriety—had made former friends shy. Standoffish. Leery of him. They seemed embarassed when he called. Men who had been eager to be with him now were offering excuses. Some offered him money ostensibly to help him out but really to buy him off, a payment to go away until the unfortunate situation blew over. He took no money from them. Neal Davis thought it would not be a good idea for him to work again. "Later, when things cool down, we'll talk," Neal said, Then with a laugh, he added, "But you never had any trouble turning tricks, Larry!"

He did better in bars. In bars, men who fancied him did not know about the famous murder case in which he had been the central figure. To men in bars he was a good looking boy. An easy pickup.

When the bars were slow and he needed money he went out on the streets. He knew how to work the streets, but it had been a long time and the streets were meaner, rougher, and flooded with more blacks and Puerto Ricans than when he first worked them. He kept to Third Avenue, where the hustling had always been excellent, but he found far more hustlers than previously. He was also older, now. Streets were better for the very young, as they had been for him at thirteen. Night after night he went up and down Third Avenue in the handful of blocks where hustling happened. He took his place among the boys waiting for hungry men to come to look them over, to find someone appealing, to make an approach. He stood in doorways or walked or sometimes dropped in on a hustling bar to get out of the chill or to have a drink or to take a leak. He studied faces.

Hustling was a matter of eyes. Looking for a held-glance, the lingering look, the man turning around after he'd passed to have another glimpse. Success was a matter of returning an interested look, talking with a man who stopped, playing the game, acting out the charade, keeping an eye out for a cop, moving on when one came along. Sometimes, scoring. Not as often as he would have liked. Some men took him to hotels and impersonal beds. Some took him to apartments, some lush and rich, many modest and meager. Some took him in cars to quiet streets in Brooklyn or Queens. Some drove into Central Park. One let him drive and the man did what he wanted while the car went around and around the park. It didn't matter what or where.

Money was coming in. When he had money he went out for himself, going to bars that he liked but not to ones where he could be picked up. With money, out for himself, he shunted aside the approaches, the come-ons, unless they were from young men and boys he took a fancy to. There were many in tight jeans and open shirts whom he liked and who liked him. Sometimes he went to discos, occasionally dancing, but mostly to watch. He went to the theatre to see Ray Bonner's show, the one he'd been in briefly. Ray was pleasant but embarassed and Larry did not stay long backstage, where he'd met Lonnie and Ellis. Lonnie had moved and was out of touch. Ellis was over. They saw each other across a room at a party where a pickup had taken Larry, but they did not speak.

Days, Larry slept late then went out and did New York things—shopping for food, browsing in bookstores, cruising the salesboys at Bloomingdale's. Sundays he went out and got the *Times* and spent the day reading it. For four straight

Sunday afternoons he met a man from Lindenhurst, New Jersey in a room at the City Squire hotel on Seventh Avenue. On the last Sunday, the man said he wouldn't be coming to town on Sundays any more. One day he took two subways and a bus far into Queens and visited the cemetery where Emil Denziger was buried. He mailed copies of his incomplete manuscript to publishing houses and began growing impatient until a boy he knew who worked for a publisher said it would take months to hear because his book probably landed in the slush pile that editors read only when they had absolutely nothing else to do. The boy said he would ask an editor he knew to have a look at the manuscript.

A photographer he met in a bar offered him a job posing for a gay magazine. The money was good and the work was straight. The photographer made no advances, although Larry would not have minded. But he did introduce him to another photographer who made hardcore pornography. Larry hesitated but the money was good and the boy he would be performing with was very young and cute. A few weeks later the films were on sale in gay porno shops all over town. He bought one, although he had no projector. Still later he found prints made from the film in picture magazines on sale in the same stores, and he bought one because he remembered how cute and good in bed the other actor had been.

One night on the TV news he watched a reporter do a story about male prostitution in New York City, beginning with film clips of the Apperson murder case—a case of mistaken identity, the reporter noted, as the TV showed a body being hauled out: Pete's body. The TV report about hustlers was okay but shallow. Like the rest of the news on TV! This mention of the Apperson case was the last Larry saw or heard in the news media. That very night he went out hustling again, to a bar on Fifty-third Street. A hustler's bar, it was crowded with other hustlers, men who had picked him up in the past but shunned him now because he was no longer a new face. There were a few men he had never seen before. One finally bought him a club soda and talked with him about the theatre. An hour later they strolled up Second Avenue to Larry's apartment.

As he opened the door to let the man in, Larry Apperson had no idea he had been followed.

Larry never knew that he had been followed from the very day that he had said goodbye to Detective Lyman.

That Larry did not know he was being followed was due of two factors: first, it never occurred to him that anyone would follow him; second, the follower was an expert at it.

10.

Detective Sheldon Lyman leaned against the door. With his forehead pressed against the cool wood he listened as he had listened before to the sounds inside Larry's apartment: the small talk, the little bursts of laughter, the amiable chatting that was prelude. He heard the little click of light switches being pressed or turned. He heard the splash of water in the bathroom, the opening and slamming of the refrigerator door, the fall of a footstep on the wooden floor where carpets did not reach. He remained at the door a long time, obsessed with the sounds sifting muffled through the panels. His eyes were closed while his mind's eye pictured all that was going on in the apartment. He raised a trembling hand to brush away beads of cool sweat from his forehead.

He had begun following Larry immediately after he had walked out of the kitchen, after he had stumblingly attempted to make Larry understand how he felt, what he needed. He had gone down in another elevator, waited until Larry had left the lobby, and then walked after him. At first, he thought he would catch up to the boy and this time make it clear to him what he had failed to make clear in the kitchen of his apartment. He had not caught up. He lost him when Larry got unexpectedly onto a bus. He took a cab downtown and waited, distantly, until Larry came home. His heart sank when he saw him come home with another boy. When they went in, he followed, waiting until he was sure they were inside the apartment. Then he stood outside the door for the first time and listened to the sounds within.

He began spending all his free time watching, following. When he was off-duty or had a day off or when there was a break in the hours he had to spend with Garraty on other cases, he went back to Larry. Always at a distance, always unseen, always being careful not to be noticed, he kept communion with Larry. He knew the bars where he worked as a hustler. He knew the ones he frequented for fun. He knew the discos, the baths, the streets, the cafes, the restaurants, the supermarkets, the stores which Larry Apperson visited. He knew all and he watched and waited.

He had been slouched in his car across the street from the bar where Larry met the stranger who had walked with him up Second Avenue and into the apartment on the third floor. Lyman had left his car and walked half a block behind them, unseen, catching the pieces of conversation which floated back to him, watching the easy and tender way Larry had of reaching out and touching the stranger's arm or hand. He observed with a flash of anger how the stranger boldly circled Larry's narrow waist with his arm. From across the street, concealed by a shrub in front of a huge apartment house, Lyman peered in the glass front door to the brightly-lighted foyer of Larry's house as the stranger touched a hand to Larry's face and then clasped him at the back of the neck to draw Larry's face to his, Larry's lips to the stranger's lips.

At the kiss, Lyman sucked in breath, gasping, as if someone had suddenly punched him in the stomach. He felt the constriction of his shoulder holster and the surprisingly hard presence of his .38 special. Garraty had given him the shoulder holster as a gift. Garraty always favored shouldering a weapon over Lyman's habit of wearing his on his belt at the hip. To please Garraty, Lyman took to wearing the shoulder harness.

When Larry and the stranger went through the inner

door and up the stairs, Lyman followed, using the key he had kept from the very first day of the Apperson case, to go through the inner door with its repaired lock. He crept up the stairs to Larry's door, barely breathing, but alert to the chance that someone might find him there. "Just following up on the case," he would say if someone saw him. No one ever had.

Listening, he heard Larry and the stranger from the bar move from the living room to the bedroom. Presently, he heard the squeaking of the bed and soft, almost inaudible voices, then moans.

He touched his trembling hand to the cold hard knob of the door. He turned it, but the door was locked. From his pocket he drew the key, slipping it noiselessly into the lock and turning it. The living room was dark but light spilled onto the floor from the bedroom. He closed the door silently and paused, listening. He heard Larry moaning softly in the next room. He approached the bedroom door, being careful not to step into the light that poured through it. Flattening himself against the wall, he swallowed dryly and wiped the back of his hand across his mouth to brush away his sweat.

He heard Larry's voice, low and hoarse. "I'm going to come."

He waited through the long silence that followed until it was broken by a prolonged sigh.

The stranger said sharply, "Now, you do me."

Lyman heard the rustle of sheets, the metallic bounce of the bedspring.

Cautiously, Lyman moved, easing toward the open door until he could see into the bedroom. The naked stranger sprawled on his back, his face buried in the crook of an upraised arm. The other arm lay flung outward. Between his parted legs, naked as the glorious boy in the portrait above the bed, was Larry, his head athwart the stranger's hips, bobbing.

Lyman stepped into the doorway.

"Larry?"

His voice exploded across the room. The stranger bolted up in bed, his face ashen, his mouth agape, his eyes bulging.

Larry lifted his mouth from the stranger and looked back over his slender shoulder at the familiar figure in the doorway. He cracked a slight, sly, perplexed smile. "Sheldon? What . . . ?"

"Move away from that man, Larry."

"Hey! Listen, fella. If this is your lover, why I had no way of knowing," blurted the stranger.

"Move away from him, Larry."

Larry sat up between the stranger's shaking legs. "Sheldon, what the hell do you think you're doing?"

Lyman reached beneath his jacket. His fingers found the cold .38 special. He drew it easily from the holster and clasped it in a double-handed combat grip, his finger at the trigger. "I want you to move, Larry."

"Look, Detective Lyman, you have no right to do this."

The stranger gasped, *"Detective?"*

"I don't want to hurt you, Larry. I just want that man to get the hell out of here."

"I'm going!"

"Lyman, you can't do this."

"You shouldn't be out on the streets, Larry. You shouldn't be hustling."

"Look, man, this is what I do. I do it because I like it. It's none of your damned business. Now get the hell out of here. I'm not your concern. The case is closed, Lyman. I'm alive and I'm going to go on living the way I want to. You can't run my life. You're off my case, Lyman. Now get out. Leave me alone. I don't want you around. I don't want you messing things up for me. I don't *need* you!"

"*I* need *you.*"

Larry laughed. "You can't *have* me!"

The first bullet struck Larry in the middle of the chest and flung him backward onto the terrified, trembling body of the stranger, who was hit by the second bullet, which tore into his heart. The third bullet entered Larry Apperson's head behind the right ear. The fourth punched a hole in the middle of the painted chest of the portrait of Larry above the bed. The fifth entered the left eye of the portrait. The sixth bullet tore through the roof of Sheldon Lyman's mouth, ripped apart his brain, tore off the top of his head and lodged in the blood-spattered plaster ceiling.

William Weinstein, who had heard all six shots clearly, immediately picked up his phone and dialed 911.

Epilogue

"Garraty?"

"Yes."

"This is Danny Murphy. We were at the Academy together."

"Yeah! How the hell are you? It's been years."

"I'm up here in the Bronx. You know about the Bronx. That's where we put all the police cars in a circle and wait to be attacked by the natives."

"Still the joker, Danny."

"Listen, I was really sorry to hear about your partner, Lyman. I heard he was a great cop."

"The best."

"I was told he just sort of came apart."

"Something like that. What can I do for you, Danny?"

"Well, this may not be anything at all, but I followed that Apperson case you were on with Lyman and I think we may have something up here that might interest you. I'm working Burglary here in the Bronx, and we've been on this case for a few months—burglaries in one particular apartment house. Well, today we made an arrest of the super of that building. A guy named Da Capo."

"Antonio Da Capo?"

"The same. You know him?"

"He was the super of the building in the Apperson case."

"Well, that cinches it."

"Why?"

"When we busted Da Capo we went into his apartment to make an inventory of stolen items, and we found one of those weights that guys use when they want to build up their arms. I didn't think anything about it until we were checking up on this Da Capo guy, where he worked before, and I came across the address where you guys had that homicide. I dug out the old files which have your reports on that case, when you figured it might have been a homicide during a burglary? That's when I noticed that among the things taken was one of those weights."

"A ten pound dumbbell."

"Right."

"Jesus, Danny, do you know what you're saying?"

"That this Da Capo guy did the Apperson homicide?"

"Yes. I think so. I'm scared and hesitate to say so, but I believe you've got Peter Apperson's killer up there in the Bronx."

"Are you gonna come up and talk to this guy?"

"I'm leaving now."

There it was. As simple as that. Felony homicide during the perpetration of a burglary. Just the way Lyman figured it from the first. He didn't have to ask Antonio Da Capo how it happened. It was so obvious. Da Capo would confirm that he'd known Larry was away skiing. A good chance to get into the little faggot's place and rip him off. Grab his cameras, his stereo, anything that looked good. Just use the pass key, go in, and rip off the place. That was what Da Capo intended but he didn't know about Larry's brother, poor helpless, unlucky Peter Apperson, enjoying a nice warm bath. Da Capo didn't notice the lights in the bathroom. Probably, the kid had the door closed. Peter heard a noise in the apartment and got out of the tub to investigate. The kid made the fatal mistake, probably, of calling out. At that point, Antonio De Capo had to do something. Killing was what he did. Realizing it, he took only two things: the kid's wallet to make it look like a burglary and the murder weapon.

And all this time the jerk had hung on to that dumbbell, Garraty realized as he sped uptown.

The dumbbell kept the dumbbell!

What a joke!

Lyman would have laughed at that one.